SKYTRIBE

DEWEY M. ERLWEIN

Wasteland Press
Louisville, KY USA
www.wastelandpress.com

Skytribe
by Dewey M. Erlwein

Copyright © 2004 Dewey M. Erlwein
ALL RIGHTS RESERVED

ISBN: 1-932852-88-3
Cover art by Matthew S. Lancaster

Printed in the U.S.A.

Acknowledgement

My heartiest thanks for family and friends who encouraged
this effort, read portions and commented,
and believed in the project.

Special acknowledgement goes to my wife Marilyn, who
spent countless hours editing and proofreading, and whose
suggestions were greatly appreciated.
Thank you all.

Introduction

The setting for Skytribe is Venus, at the time a hypothetical wet planet called Baeta. A technically advanced society of Baetians developed rocket engines that carried probes out into the solar system, and men into orbit. Unmanned probes were sent to land on neighboring Earth, called Terres, where homo sapiens had evolved to the Neanderthal era. An unmanned lander spotted life on Terres, in the form of vegetation and an upright humanoid.

Fraya, a technical genius, spearheads a program for exploration of Terres. Technology on Baeta has strained the balance of carbon dioxide in the atmosphere, to the point of causing global warming. Water is being evaporated, and not returning to the surface, because of a phenomenon called Virga. The unrelenting heat has caused certain rebel forces to compete for land with water, and chaos is inevitable.

Fraya's boyfriend Rami, an environmentalist, thinks the only salvation for the Baetian species is colonization on Terres. They become involved in an independent capitalist venture, funded by an entrepreneur who wants to compete with a separate socialist government for the first manned landing.

Moonless Venus rotates so slowly, day and night are each about a half year long. The planet is now entirely surrounded by thick clouds and has a surface temperature far above the boiling point of water. Intelligent life, as we know it, probably could not exist in that environment.

Because of cloud cover on Venus, the surface cannot be visually seen. Our Magellan space craft, launched in May, 1989, went into Venusian orbit after a fifteen month trip from Earth, and with radar, mapped more than 90 per cent of the surface. It has shown that Venus has two main large continents. One is very mountainous with its Great Mons reaching up to 35,000 feet. The other lies on the equator and is shaped like a scorpian.

Here on Earth we continually dig and search for our evolutionary roots, while speculating about whether or not we are alone in the universe. Over several millions of years, we have slowly changed features and brain size until we became modern man. Many links in the evolutionary chain have been found, but one big mystery still remains. That mystery is what happened to Neanderthal, and where did modern man come from? Did we replace Neanderthal, or evolve from him? This mystery can make an active imagination flourish with speculation and ideas, and result in stories such as Skytribe.

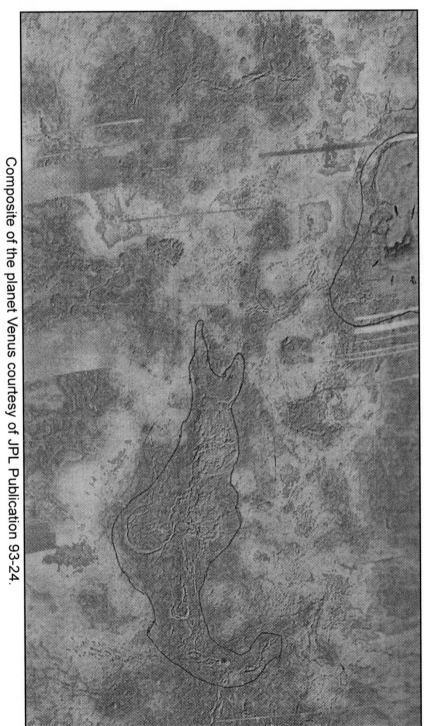

Composite of the planet Venus courtesy of JPL Publication 93-24.

1. The Celestial Research Centre

Bendal Khanwali, Centre's Senior Manager, jumped at a chance to parlay the publicity from discovering traces of water on Terres into more funding. He used the latest data from space to flag the interest of the Council, as he told about the results of the fly-by. Smiling eyes and sweeping eye contact, with pauses at just the right time, held his audience.

"Councilors, our deep-space probes are showing us things in our solar system our magnivisors never could see. Space is our new laboratory. Our manned orbiting platform is already teaching us about living in space, and now, our Terres fly-by saw water molecules on that planet. Water? You can believe we are excited! Water is the medium of life as we perceive it, and we won't be surprised if we find liquid water on the surface. And other life? If ever organisms needed a bed for carbon materials to ferment, develop and reproduce, then Terres could be that bed."

A councilor raised his hand. "Are we planning on a manned landing on Terres?" he asked.

"Definitely, councilor. Our plans call for the step-by-step investigation of Terres; first with an orbiter, then unmanned landers, and eventually a manned landing. However, our progress is constrained. At our present, plodding rate, most of us will not live to see the manned landing.

"Why is it taking so long?" The Councilor asked.

"Funding, Councilor. Our propulsion systems are archaic. We use standard, chemical systems for all our launches, and after launch, we depend on orbital free-flight to carry the crafts to their destinations. We need research and development to come up with a better engine."

"Is a new engine in your planning?"

"Yes it is Councilor, and without a new propulsion system, we couldn't think of sending travelers to Terres. The flight duration is just too long."

One councilor was particularly enthusiastic. "Well, can we leap ahead to a new propulsion system?"

"Councilor, I share your enthusiasm and I thank you for it. However, we feel the steps we have planned for interim investigation are necessary for safety and reliability. That does not mean we won't be working on a new propulsion system; just putting off development until it has priority and funding."

Khanwali's gaze swept the council. "Step one was the Terres orbiter. As you know, it is already built, launched and on its way. Step two is surface contact. Using the same, prevailing launch technology, we could get some unmanned landing probes under way fairly quickly. However, we need an accelerated program to keep up the momentum for the new engine while waiting for the landers to arrive. With adequate funding, councilors, we'll keep up that momentum. We'll start immediately on building some landers."

"Who will be your project manager for the unmanned landers, Tribune?"

Khanwali hesitated, fearing an answer might force him into an inflexible decision. Hirl Lockni had many admirers on the council.

"The probable choice will be Hirl Lockni, who manages the Terres Orbiter." Khanwali was not happy with Lockni. His attitude was flippant, and some of his decisions during the Alpha-Surveyor launch and flight had bordered on incompetence. However, Lockni did have some qualities that Khanwali used extensively to satisfy a public hungry for information about the Terres project. Lockni was glib, and a master at making presentations. His communications skills had charmed many among the councilors.

2

The members haggled about the costs and rewards, but the majority wanted to know more about space and the neighboring planets. They approved the funding requested by Khanwali.

2. Fraya Looks to the Future

Fraya Lor had an interest in the celestrium and space programs at an early age. She knew of the deep-space probes and goals through media releases, and the upcoming spacecraft planned to orbit Terres. Hirl Lockni was project manager for Alpha-Surveyor, nicknamed Alpha-Surf, and made frequent public announcements of its design and mission. He was a charming speaker, and Fraya worshipped everything he said or did.

Her home was in the western territory of Ardena, a territory with limited opportunities for advanced education and research about the celestrium. Bacamir, on the other hand, had the Celestial Research Centre, satellites, and a manned, orbiting laboratory they called the Platform. Things were happening at Centre, and Fraya was missing out. She followed the progress of Alpha-Surf on the news, and listened intently to the visi-com reports from a smiling Hirl Lockni. He seemed so assured and positive, she developed a fantasy adoration for him. When Lockni announced that Alpha-Surf was successfully launched and on its way, she couldn't restrain herself any longer. She announced to her parents she was going to move away from home, study in the eastern territory of Bacamir, and become one of those prestigious scienomies in the famous Centre.

"Are you sure you want to leave Ardena and go to Bacamir?" her mother asked, hoping her mind was not already set. "You're such a bright child, you'll easily excel in academics right here in our own

3

territory." She fussed over Fraya, brushing her shoulders and smoothing her tunic.

"I'm sure, mother, and I've known it for a long time. I've talked with my advisers, and some agree and some don't, but nobody's changed my mind. I know I'll be lonesome away from family, but going to Bacamir is what I intend to do."

Her father looked up from his reading. "You're so young and naive, Fraya, and know little about politics. I fear for your safety there. Why go to Bacamir?"

"Because they have the Celestial Research Centre, father, and I'm going to work there." Her jaw took a defiant set. "It's true, their government is different, and their old monarch had a bad reputation, but now they are changed, and the new queen has an administration with a ruling cabinet, and governing councils. I won't get into any trouble, and I'm sure I'll be treated fairly. I must try for it." She flashed a smile that spread from dimples to the crinkled corners of round, green eyes, a gesture that usually swayed her father's opinion. It worked, as usual, and he didn't argue.

3. Fraya Goes to Mizzen

Fraya was accepted in the Bacamir Graduate Institute, in Mizzen, the capitol of Bacamir and also the site of the Centre complex. Compared to the tropical heat and citron smells of home, the coastal weather of Mizzen, with its salty mist, felt good to her. Her dormitory sat next to a walkway of old brick, slippery from moss left by the wet, dark season. Dawning sunlight signaled the end of the half-year dark period, and the beginning of a half-year sunny season welcomed by most Baetians. Fraya was a star gazer and liked the dark season

4

when it was clear, but when there was an overcast, or clouds blocking the view, she found the darkness depressing.

On the front of one gazebo hung two circular carvings, one showing Baeta's two large continents, and the other the territory of Bacamir. Scorpia, shaped like an insect, straddled the equator. To the northwest was Montes, the mountainous continent with the highest point on the planet. Great Mons was actually over twelve kiloquants high.

Behind the structure, birds and small animals scurried about. She could see the bay through openings in the lattice walls, and mentally selected the gazebo's bench as her very own. She could also see launch platforms out on the end of a peninsula that jutted into the bay, and the mere sight of the launch sites excited her. One of her goals was to be in a control room during a launch. The Terres program was what she coveted most, and Hirl Lockni made the decisions as to Terres personnel. She would eventually have to convince him she would be an asset to the Terres program in order to get into a control room. Until that time, she would watch the launches from here.

Fraya was a multilingual, quick learner, and completed the academic program with ease. Her record was so impressive, the authorities awarded her a grant to stay in Mizzen and continue her studies at the Graduate Institute. To her delight, she was also awarded a part-time position at Centre as an intern. "Now," she thought, "I might get to be near Lockni. With luck, this position could lead me into the Terres program."

4. Fraya Interns at Centre

Lockni frequently gave lectures and presentations to civic groups, and Fraya attended every one she could. He was charming, and when he reported that the Terres team managed to slow Alpha-Surf into Terres orbit, she felt an empathy as if she had been a part of it. She followed Lockni to his public appearances and lectures, and always tried to think of at least one question to ask during the presentation. It was her futile attempt to draw his attention; to be noticed, but in spite of her efforts, he never appeared to distinguish her from anyone else.

Although her internship at Centre kept her busy with research, she had some freedom to visit projects and listen to the scienomies at their tasks. By choice, her spare time was mostly spent with the Alpha-Surf group, reviewing data from the orbiter. She listened and watched. Alpha-Surf confirmed that Terres did have an atmosphere, water, and land-masses, coincidentally similar to Baeta. Although heavy cloud masses frequently blocked visual observation of Terres, special radiapulsers were able to penetrate through the clouds and show the surface. When scienomies at Centre overlaid the two image types, visual and radiapulse, they produced composites revealing good surface features. Among other things, it found much of Terres actually covered with liquid water, and over the polar regions, enormous caps of ice with fissured, blue-ice fingers reaching toward the equator. Large, equatorial continents, roughly opposite each other on the sphere, were separated by enormous oceans. They were visible and ice-free around the equator, and on one hemisphere an east-west sea divided the north and south continents. Scienomies on the Terres project studied images and data being received from the orbiter, and Fraya would hear them discussing interpretations.

"Is that a volcano or an impact crater? Where is the actual shoreline? How thick would you say the ice is? Are there signs of moving crust?"

She would look over their shoulders whenever she got a chance and make her own interpretations, but soon realized her opinions were considered encroachment in a project that wasn't hers. At one time, Lockni walked in and heard her commenting on the images. He was less than civil.

"What is your name, and what are you doing here?" he asked.

"I am Fraya Lor, an intern, and I'm here by authority of the proctor. He allows us to look in on projects."

"Then look, and shut up. You are bothering the team and interfering with their tasks."

"How am I interfering? If I don't get involved, how can I learn to make judgments like they do?"

"Where are you from?"

"I was an exchange mentoree from Ardena, but now I am granted to study at the Graduate Institute."

"Ah yes, I've heard of you: A very impressive academic record. Well, keep out of the way and we might get along."

Lockni recognized her, but made it clear she was to keep her opinions to herself. She was exhilarated at finally being recognized, then crushed at the outcome. She complied, because she didn't want to make any enemies. The Terres exploration had a long way to go with unmanned landers and eventually a manned landing. Her goal to eventually become a member of the Terres team would depend upon approval from Lockni.

5. Shaman Sees a Light

Alpha-Surf, in orbit around Terres, was transmitting data back to Baeta. It's reflection was visible at times from the Terres surface, as a tiny, fast moving light, but few tribesmen noticed it. The new light in the night sky, slicing rapidly from horizon to horizon, aroused very little attention, except from the old Shaman in Arg's tribe. He was observant and curious, and he knew from many years of watching the night sky that all the points of light moved approximately the same; slowly, and together. This stray was different. It appeared every few nights, a shining dot moving much faster than the rest. After he had seen it several times, Shaman summoned the tribe's leader to come and see the light.

"What is it," Arg asked, pushing the collar of his fur tunic back away from his neck so he could lean back and look up.

Shaman shrugged ... his breath condensing in the chilly air.

"I don't know, but it worries me."

"Everything worries you Shaman. Why does this light worry you?" Arg asked, as the light disappeared over the horizon.

"I think it may be the point of a spear thrown by someone very powerful to reach so high in the sky. What if that tribe comes here and wants our caves."

"Then we will drive them away," Arg said, "like we do with Wigor and his thieves. Until then, all we can do is watch and wait. Are we not content for now, with ample game and food, ready for the cold season? Worrying about the light will do us no good."

Shaman wrinkled his brow in pensive thought, and shuffled back to the community fire in front of the cave entrance.

6. Fraya's Research

Mechanical gyros had been the mainstay of all navigation systems since early guidance development, but were subject to the frictional error and frailty of typical mechanical mechanisms. Fraya, after graduate studies, was accepted as a full scienomie at Centre and assigned to continue in the research department. The Terres Program was her goal, but she found an avenue of particle physics as exciting to her as celestial mechanics. She had theorized that the spin on subatomic particles might somehow produce a gyro effect, if the particles could be aligned. With an energetic research assistant named Karlus Maskinoff, she experimented with super-cooled metal alloys, and found that in some, the gyro effect was possible, but only if the materials were kept in the cooled condition. When the materials returned to normal temperature, a hysteresis took place and the gyro effect disappeared. They finally found one alloy that, when super-cooled and then treated in a mass-accelerator in the cold state, retained the alignment of the spinning sub-particles after they were warmed back to room temperature. This was what she was looking for, in order to make a practical application out of the phenomenon. She repeated the experiment many times to be certain the particles were uniform and consistent, and when satisfied, proceeded to adapt it to a molecular directional gyro. She confirmed the molecular gyro effect, but adapting it into a miniaturized guidance instrument proved a challenge. Karlus was enthused and worked long and hard at her side, encouraging her, and admiring her ingenuity.

"Do you think we can make it work, Tribune Fraya?"

"It looks very possible Karlus. I'm so glad you're my assistant. Your skill with these circuits is really a big help."

"I'm honored, Tribune."

9

The resulting guidance system was superior to anything Centre had available, and established her with a reputation for brilliance. The new system caught the attention of Tribune Khanwali, the Senior Technical Manager, who wanted it moved from the laboratory to field evaluations. He ordered a series of sub-orbital test flights after the gyros had been subjected to severe physical and thermal conditioning, called shake-and-bake, to determine the system's reliability. The tests showed the molecular gyros to be so much better than the analog inertial guidance units in use, Khanwali asked her to make a presentation about the results to the management council. She had never been to a council meeting before, and was flattered to be asked, but a little apprehensive and nervous.

The experience was her first chance to see Tribune Hirl Lockni try to control a meeting. Lockni expressed interest in the concept of micro-circuits integral to her guidance system, but railed about all the unknowns in this new technology, and urged more testing. Arguments ensued, and Fraya was a bit surprised and intimidated by the shouting that went on. She wondered if the council carried on so about every agenda item.

"Probably," she thought.

7. Fraya Gets Assigned

Lockni was appointed manager of the Settler-One project. Because of his popularity, some of the councilors demanded he be the manager as a condition for the funding. Some of the assigned Terres team members were not happy about Lockni continuing as manager again, especially the controllers, but there was little they could do. Lockni had interfered with the controllers during the Alpha-Surf intercept, and something went wrong. The controllers had saved

Alpha-Surf from skipping off into space, had eventually gotten the probe back into orbit, and Lockni took all the credit. The media publicized the craft's success, and Lockni's skills, but no one ever mentioned any problems.

Fraya had wanted to be a scienomie on the Terres project since she first began star-gazing back in Ardena. Now she thought she had an opportunity. After her guidance system received such favorable reception from Khanwali, she aggressively requested transfers out of research and onto the Terres program. Each time she tried, however, Lockni rejected her request, leaving her frustrated and angry. Not to be deterred, she spent her spare research time at the Settler-One design group, slipping into meetings, and listening to plans and concepts. She saw the trajectory being chosen for Settler-One was not new; it was the same as that used on Alpha-Surf, an elliptical intercept. The elliptical intercept obviously works, but it takes time and several orbits around the sun to catch up with the target planet, Something went wrong on Alpha-Surf, but nobody would talk about it. Surf had made it to the intercept point, went into a sloppy elliptical orbit around Terres, and with the help of a resourceful guidance team eventually slowed to a circular orbit. It was a clumsy, long flight.

"Why not use a hyperbolic intercept path on Settler?" She proposed. "It will cut the crossing time in half, and with the new guidance system, be more precise."

Except for a few controllers, she was generally ignored by her colleagues, and was treated as an intruder. Lockni heard about her proposal, and ordered her to keep her opinions to herself.

Feeling assertive, she decided to go directly to Khanwali, the senior manager, and ask to be assigned to the Settler-One Lander. Khanwali had early recognized that she was gifted. He was so sure her talent and her new guidance system would revolutionize the

11

technology of interplanetary navigation, he ordered Lockni to approve her transfer. At that time, she officially became a member of the Terres team over Lockni's objections, assigned to the Guidance and Control section. Then, when she tried again to get the trajectory changed from an elliptical path to a hyperbolic path, she got nowhere with Lockni nor any of his mathematicians on the project. It finally dawned on her the experts were feeling threatened by her proposals, and were not going to change their minds based on her inputs. She realized Lockni had given her a token assignment on the lander project as an atonement for irritating him. By now, Fraya's crush on Lockni sputtered and died completely as a result of his negative attitude. She was glad she hadn't foolishly pursued him, and now found it hard to even look at him. In time, she thought, I'll learn what went wrong on the Surveyor. It seemed so successful, and the data it returned is brilliant. Frustrated at having no responsibility nor authority, she decided to once again speak directly to Khanwali, but wanted to discuss it first with Rami, her friend from the Graduate Institute.

8. Enter Rami

Fraya didn't encourage a friendship with Rami, he just showed up.   She was sitting on her favorite park bench in the bright, warm sunshine, studying, and he sat down beside her.

"Hello Fraya, my name is Rami."

"I know you, Rami, we have some classes together." She had definitely noticed him in the classrooms. He had penetrating blue eyes, a high, straight forehead, light, sun-bleached hair, and a muscular build.

"I need some tutoring," he said.

"Really? Well, I'm not a tutor," she replied.

"Maybe so, but you are the smartest person I know in this Institute." He turned on a pleading look.

"Thank you, but I don't think it would work."

"Why not? I really need some help, if I'm going to graduate."

Fraya had observed him in classes, and although he seemed bright, he fumbled with concepts and questions. "Obviously," she thought, "he spends more time playing kickball than studying."

"I'm afraid it will take too much of my own study time," she told him.

"Just some guidance? Please." He turned on an engaging smile, and she was charmed. Even though she had some reservations, she agreed.

The tutoring began, and Fraya discovered some things about herself. She liked the knowledge sharing engendered by tutoring, and she liked the feeling of power from being in control. However, she cared little for fashion, and in spite of her mother's cajoling to be more fashionable, she still had little regard for clothing as a statement. She usually wore baggy trousers, heavy boots, and any type of jacket that was handy. At home, her father never criticized her outfits saying beauty was in her personality, and she radiated charisma. Whatever it was, it attracted Rami, for he, she remembered, began to get flirtatious. She felt a little flattered and womanly, and when he was close, his presence caused some unexpected fluttery sensations in her stomach. She began to have fantasy thoughts about him, and was glad they weren't youngsters in her home borough where swimming nude was a favorite activity; that is until Croak began having erections.

9. The Croaker

Croaker, so nicknamed because his voice was changing, was a neighbor that liked to star-gaze with her. Eventually, his interest shifted to her body, not the stars. She remembered having sexual curiosities, but was inexperienced on how to handle situations with boys. She asked one of her sisters for advice.

"Fraya, during the sunny, light period you spent a lot of time at the beaches with your friends, swimming nude, and nobody much cared. This past season you began developing breasts, and Croak, among others, noticed. Then when you wore coverings to keep them from sun-burning, your body became all the more interesting to the boys. You are very young for sex, but you know all about it, and you know you can get pregnant. Croak is a knot of churning hormones, so just tell him to back off. Don't encourage him, and you can tell him "no" at any time he gets too aggressive. You are in control."

So, when Rami asked her to join him in a social outing, she remembered her last encounter with Croak as frightening, and declined. She and Croak had been star-gazing with the hand-held magnivisor, and he got aroused. She felt his erection through his clothing, and feeling experimentative, let him raise her tunic and explore her beasts with his hands. To her surprise he mouthed her nipples and the areas around them. She remembered the mixed emotions she had; his actions were not unpleasant, but in his eagerness, he started to get rough and aggressive. When he exposed his stiff member; Fraya became frightened, and pushed him away.

"No Croak, that's enough. You are scaring me and I want you to stop."

"No, not now." He held her down and forced her knees apart.

With a mighty shove she pushed him aside, jumped up and ran to her home. Seeing her sobbing and distressed, her sister asked what was wrong. She told him what had happened, and her sister offered her sympathy and a hug. "I'm so sorry, Fraya, things just got out of control for you. I'm glad you are all right."

10. The Encounter

To her dismay, the emotional turmoil from being near Rami seemed to induce a few facial papules, and the thought of a social event just made them worse.

"No Rami, I don't care to socialize," she lied. "I can't spare the time from my own studies, and it would be disruptive to our tutoring progress, but thank you."

Rami became persistent, and pestered her again to socialize. She really wanted to, and analyzed her reasons for resisting. "I'm afraid of rejection," she concluded. "Normal enough reasons, but I like the feeling I have when he is near, and I want to experience some closer male friendship." On a visit back home she discussed the dilemma with her mother and talked about her frustrations.

"My daughter, of course you want some companionship. It'd be sad if you spent all your time only on academics and ignored your emotions. You've changed since you left here, you know. Other than that childish crush on that Lockni person from Centre, you left thinking only of studies, and since then have developed into a woman with many new feelings. Now you say you're afraid of being rejected and hurt by this Rami? That might happen, and if it does, remember this; your feelings are normal, and you'll survive. Life needs more than books to thrive. I'm sure you'll decide on how to handle the situation. I can't decide for you."

Inevitably, Fraya rationalized. "I'm in control of myself, have mastered several languages, and excelled in academics. Why not try a social outing with Rami, just as an experiment?" She wasn't exactly sure how to go about it, but being coy wasn't working. The next time she saw Rami she announced, rather bluntly, that she would socialize with him.

"Really," he replied. "How charitable of you. After I've asked you several times and you've refused, for whatever reasons I don't know ... now you've changed your mind? Well, so have I. Besides, I agree, it would interfere with the tutoring."

Rejection was the thing Fraya feared most. She was sure she could feel her pulse pounding in one of the more prominent papules on her face. She had taken the risk, and now was being rejected.

From her distressed expression, Rami sensed her hurt, and in a moment of compassion decided on a simple outing.

"Well, how about if we just dine together, and take in an entertainment event," he offered.

Retaliation was her first impulse. She wanted to give Rami a slap in the face, or at least a verbal slap by rejecting him... to say no ... but then she reconsidered. I'm overreacting here, she thought, her mind whirling. I'm not involved, so rejection is not an issue. It's my experiment, and I'm in control. After a reflective interlude, she agreed.

"All right then, its settled", he said.

She immediately felt self-conscious about her appearance and wanted to hurry back to her hostel and try on different outfits. She remembered her mother's attempt at controlling her appearance, and wished she had listened a little more. "Couldn't you at least strive to dress more fashionably?" she remembered.

"I will, mother," she'd replied, and wished she had.

Feeling giddy with anticipation but worried about her appearance, she stood before a mirror and fluffed her hair this way and that, until a shape seemed to compliment her round face.

"Maybe mother is right. If I spend a little time on fashion and grooming, maybe I'll feel more confident about socializing."

She made the effort, and Rami complimented her on her appearance. They dined, went to an entertainment event, and talked about things other than academics. Fraya found this new companionship stimulating, and was glad she made the decision to socialize.

11. The Romance

That one social outing didn't seem to interfere with the tutoring, except she now found her pulse would accelerate every time Rami was near. If she accidentally brushed his shoulder when seated next to him, her heart pounded. She remembered that when they next socialized, and he moved to touch her physically, she resisted very little. Parked in a secluded area in his old motor carriage, he nuzzled her hair and ears. Her breathing became rapid as he gently stroked the side of her neck, then sought and pressed his parted lips on hers. He probed with open mouth, and she responded warmly to the new, erotic sensation of tongue touching. When he groped under her tunic, she moved her arm out of the way so his hand could find her breasts. She felt him touch her hardened nipples and was surprised at the sensual shock it sent down through her body. Each time his fingers brushed a new and different area of her bared skin, she felt an exciting stimulus; a building arousal. His hand slid underneath her breasts, a subliminal act, feeling for the remnant of a third or fourth nipple occasionally found on Fenizen females from Central Scorpia. There was none. They partially disrobed while hardly parting their lips. Then he nudged her knees apart, and positioned himself so intimate contact was made. She was receptive, eager, and when the full penetration finally took place, a flood of passion overcame her. She gripped him convulsively, and left a bite mark on his shoulder.

"Some social experiment," she thought afterward, still gasping. "This is far different from the pre-puberty games I did with Croaker."

12. The Rejection

She didn't want to get pregnant, so she visited the Institute Clinic and requested a birth-control implant under her skin.

"Remember," the medico counseled, "the chemical depletes, so it must be periodically replaced."

She continued tutoring Rami through several of his more difficult classes, and the socializing continued. Their trysts became routine until she began feeling possessive. Thinking he now belonged to her, she suggested Rami move in with her, and was puzzled when he hesitated and said he would think about it. This confused her. There were no outward signs he wasn't emotionally implicated, as was she, and then she had to remind herself she started this only as an experiment. She took his lack of interest as rebuff; he seemed to be getting unresponsive.

Once again the taste of rejection welled within her, and her facial papules, which had disappeared, returned. She fell into a state of depression, and lost interest in her studies and work assignments, until she received an alarming rebuff from one of her mentorians. She sought the gazebo with her favorite park bench on the campus walkway and sat for long periods, mulling and meditating. She had let the relationship with Rami dominate her thoughts, so much so, she

18

was marginally performing her studies and intern tasks at Centre. Recognizing she had to push the infatuation with Rami aside if she was going to succeed at Centre, she charged into her academics and assignments with renewed vigor, and found new enthusiasm for her assignments. When she was ready to confront Rami again, she called him and said to meet her at the bench. He was exhilarated to hear from her, and when he sat down beside her, put an arm around her shoulders and drew her close.

"What have you been doing for yourself?" she asked.

He was quiet for awhile, studied her face, then said, "Mostly studying and gathering my thoughts. Know what I need? besides some of your close attention?"

"What?"

"I need some more tutoring if I'm going to graduate. You available?"

"What's in it for me."

"How about my word of honor to pay you later, in trade."

"I'm not sure that's a fair contract. You might deliberately procrastinate."

"I'll apply myself as I did before."

"All right, I'll consider it and let you know."

She happily continued tutoring Rami, and once again felt confident her goals were in sight and reachable. Both graduated with honors, and both received the top scholastic credential of Tribune. Rami stayed with the Institute as a Life Sciences Research Assistant. Fraya was accepted as a full Scienomie at Centre, with a starting assignment in their Research Department.

13. Views of the Planets

One of the benefits of becoming a Centre scienomie, was access to the big magnivisor in the domed facility up on the hill. During the dark, Fraya frequently invited Rami to join her, and when the weather was clear, the views of the visible planets were magnificent. The dome and the planets always impressed Rami, and it was an activity that helped break the boredom of Baeta's long, semi-annual darkness.

"Let's meet at the dome, Rami. The celestrium is very clear right now." The black atmosphere of Baeta's semi-annual darkness was especially clear, and he accepted without hesitation.

Fraya would set the target coordinates into the command unit and let the machine swing into position until it automatically locked on to a celestial point. Then she would fine-tune the focus using verniers, after which, they would watch the view together on the accompanying visiscreen. Rami loved to see the rings of planet six which were always spectacular, and they could usually see number five's red spot and many of its moons. Number four, the red planet, looked like it was crisscrossed with dark lines that some speculated were canals, but Rami felt that was a long stretch of the imagination.

Number three, the blue planet, was their main target this time. Fraya was mentally drifting, and said it was a time of special bonding to actually look at a planet, rather than a picture, regardless of how detailed the picture appeared to be. Fraya began humming, and chanted a rhyme, one of her methods of handling stress.

"Glisten, glisten, little Terres, under your cover of cloud. We'll soon be looking from your surface, instead of through your shroud."

Rami looked up at her. "How do you know that?" he asked. "You're in research, not on the Terres project."

"Not any more. That's what I wanted to tell you. I'm on the Terres program, but Lockni is not giving me any authority or responsibility."

Rami snapped her attention back to the visiscreen by asking her about the moon near Terres. She zoomed in on the moon and they briefly studied its colorless reflection.

"There don't seem to be any clouds, Fraya, it must not have an atmosphere."

"Probably not," she replied, and then re-focused on Terres. They spent a long time looking at the variations in the colors, blue and white, obviously from changing cloud patterns. Rami suddenly got quiet and thoughtful.

"I wonder what it would be like to be there?" he said. "It rotates so fast, I'll bet you can actually see the sun appear to roll from horizon to horizon. And what about that moon, so big it's almost a sister planet? It must be awesome when it's in view."

"Relative to us, it's spinning fast," she said, "three hundred and sixty-five times each circle around the sun. In contrast we only rotate once, and that's why we have the half-year each of darkness and light. The views we'll get from the landers are going to be so exciting, I can hardly contain myself. I've got to get some responsibility on that program, and that's what I want to ask you about."

"But I thought you were already assigned to the Terres program."

"I am, but being assigned and ignored is frustrating. Nobody will listen to me. If I go directly to Khanwali again, and ask for a job with meaning, I think he'll do it."

"What kind of specific job do you want?" he asked.

"I want to control the flight path of the lander."

21

Rami puckered and sucked inward. "Very ambitious, Fraya. That's a decision for the project manager, after he considers all options."

"That's just it! He won't consider my suggestions and I have a better option."

"I'd advise against going to Khanwali with this issue, Fraya."

"Why? I've talked to him before, and he knows my new guidance system. He'll listen to my proposal for a new trajectory."

"But you'll be going over Lockni's head and making him look bad."

"He doesn't need any help looking bad. He's so incompetent. You know, I've tried several times to explain how my new guidance system works, and he still doesn't understand."

Rami thought before he answered. "I can't believe that, Fraya. How did he ever become a Tribune if he's so incompetent?"

She paused, to choose her words. "He has some very talented people working for him, and his capacity to repeat facts by rote is incredible. When he does that, people think he must be some sort of genius."

"Maybe he is." Rami looked at her. "Fraya, as your friend, I'm concerned. I know how passionately you want some part of the landing program, but it's possible to be too hostile sometimes for your own good . People mysteriously disappear in Bacamir, you know........"

"You're joking," she interrupted, "about people disappearing?"

"Not really. They're sent away for mental evaluations, and just disappear."

"Without a trial or anything?" she asked.

"Its one of the government's methods for thinning the population," Rami frowned. "A person can be sent away for a mental evaluation, infirmity, or old age, and not be seen again. I wish you'd reconsider."

"I just can't see what's wrong with talking to the manager about a new trajectory when I know I'm right. I've tried to influence the guidance-lead but he won't challenge Lockni. I've made up my mind. I'm going to do it."

Rami sighed. "Somehow, I figured you would. I hope this doesn't quickly end your career here."

14. Khanwali Chooses Lockni

"No, Tribune Lor, not on this spacecraft," Khanwali told her. "Lockni has Settler-One just about ready to launch and I don't want any changes at this point. He was successful getting Surveyor into orbit, and now we hope he can repeat the success and get this one down to the surface."

"But I can get it there faster, Tribune, and more accurately. My guidance system really works."

"I know that, and I can understand your frustration, Fraya, but I also have to balance technology with politics. That's part of my job and you'll just have to accept my judgment. Furthermore, there will be many more projects besides Settler-One, and I want your talents available for them. Tell you what: We will eventually send a manned landing team to Terres, and we'll need a radically new propulsion system for that project. I'd like you to concentrate on that for now. In the meanwhile, you can gain experience by participating in the launches of supplies to the orbiting platform."

She stood, and wanting to argue, hesitated before leaving.

"Was there something else you wanted to say, Tribune Lor?"

23

She thought better of it. "No, thank you Tribune. I appreciate your listening."

15. Rami's Environmental Views

Rami had told Fraya some things about his childhood, about growing up in the mountains in a small borough of Lignus, supported by a government-owned petric mine. He told her how he had been born prematurely to an indigent young woman and not expected to live, so his birth-mother took him to a local wet-nurse in desperation. The wet-nurse, a Fenizen, came from an ethnic group in the central, equatorial lowlands of Scorpia.

"Fenizens reportedly have sharpened senses, some sort of insight, and instincts for successfully nurturing premature infants to maturity. Their healing powers defy explanation. In spite of their holistic skills, Fenizens are considered inferior by other ethnic groups. In general, Fens appear no different from others except for a sometimes rusty, ochre complexion, and occasionally an extra nipple below the others; an evolutionary throwback to when multiple births were common.

"Her name is Lethra. I thrived under her care, and lived with her and her natural son Sakeri until the government's subsistence people found out. The government doesn't allow Fens to raise a normal, so authorities took me away and placed me with foster parents who were childless. The fosters raised me until I went away to study at the Institute. They were well-meaning people, but I never deeply bonded, especially with father. His spiritual beliefs split us apart, and we argued about them ... especially creation versus evolution, and it drove a wedge between us. The pious rituals seemed so artificial - you know, the robes, the candles, the ceremonial hats, the gestures."

Fraya nodded, not in agreement, but to signify she was listening.

"The best thing I remember about those activities was chasing after girls at the retreats, with my best friend Dorvic."

Fraya nodded again and encouraged him to continue.

"Dorvic still lives in the same borough and keeps me informed about things. I visit Lethra, she's my surrogate mother, whenever I can. Did you know I thought you were a Fen when I first saw you?" Her ruddy complexion, slender body and sloppy clothes, gave him the impression she was a Fen doing janitorial labors. Fen or not, he immediately recognized she was very bright and could help him with his studies.

"No," she laughed, "but I wouldn't care. My parents operate a citrona orchard in Ardena and they employ many Fens each season to help with the harvest. I've had many good friends who were Fens."

"And so have I. As a matter of fact, Lethra's son and I were playmates until I was taken away. I lost track of him though. He may have gone to central Scorpia to join the insurgent Fens who are fighting there for more land."

"Fen insurgents? I don't know much about them."

"You know about planet warming of course, and the fact that the climate is changing? Well, the central Scorpian lowlands are suffering from droughts where the sun bakes croplands into a hardened plain and crops can't take root. When it does rain, the water can no longer soak in, and it floods. Thousands in the lowlands are dying of starvation and disease. Survivors, of course, wanting better conditions, are migrating to the higher territories seeking land and food. Naturally, those in the highlands are defending what they have. The Fens are normally peaceful people, but they are beginning offensive acts for survival. What's even worse, domestic animals are

25

overgrazing what little forage is left, then dying of starvation. Dead animals are thrown into the rivers. The carcasses of animals and starved humans are polluting the rivers making drinkable water more and more scarce. I'm afraid its only a matter of time before they start using holocaust weapons against each other."

"Holocaust weapons?" she asked.

"Yes. You know about the nuclear experiments in Ardena many annums ago resulting in thermonuclear power for electrical generators."

"Of course. It's common knowledge."

"Well, an outgrowth was the thermal holocaust weapon, which is now available on the illegal market. Many fear its only a matter of time until one is used in anger."

"How do you know all this?" she asked.

"I belong to an environmentalist group that is dedicated to preserving our environment. They research this stuff and keep us informed."

"Do you think the Fens have one?" she asked.

"What, a holocaust weapon? I doubt that, but most probably the highlanders do. There are some really radical groups in Central Scorpia that wouldn't hesitate to use one."

Fraya frowned. "What a horrible thought. Thousands could be killed."

"I know. If one is used, the worst part will be the panic, and then the retaliation. I think that's where Sakeri is."

"What is your environment group actually doing?"

"Education, mostly. It seems hopeless because nobody seems to care, and won't until they're personally affected."

"What's going to eventually happen?"

Rami paused. "Probably nothing until water becomes scarce, and it will. When the faucet is turned on and nothing but contaminated water comes out, or worse, nothing at all, then planet-wide panic will occur. Civil behavior will disappear."

"I hope you're wrong, Rami."

"So do I, Fraya. So do I."

16. Settler-One out of Control

Settler-One stayed on course and functioned normally until it was about two-thirds of the way to Terres, and then it started behaving erratically. As trackers in the control room updated the trajectory on the main visiscreen, Lockni hovered over them with commands for course corrections. The lead controller argued that he was reacting too fast, that the craft needed to stabilize after each correction to avoid compounding errors, but he wouldn't listen. No one argued with Lockni and won. When it came to communicating with satellites in local orbit, the transmission time was almost instantaneous, inasmuch as they were so close. Deep-space probes behaved differently. Because of the long distances involved, even at the speed of light each command required five milliarcs travel-time each way, and Lockni seemed to have forgotten that fact. The results of a course correction weren't known for at least forty or fifty milliarcs.

Fraya was in the control room with Karlus, her technical assistant, when the first course correction was made. She couldn't believe it when she saw Lockni order a second correction without an adequate waiting period. Settler-One was out of control.

"How often did you make course corrections on Alpha-Surf?" Fraya asked, hoping she could aid in stabilizing the erratic behavior of the Settler-One.

"I can't remember, but it's in the log books. Look them up if you want. By the way, what are you doing in here. I thought I told you to keep your opinions to yourself."

"I'm not offering any opinions; only willing to help if asked," she replied

.   "Help who? Me? Let me put this in perspective. I am the project manager and you are the novice. If any help is needed I surely wouldn't ask a novice. Would you?"

Fraya knew any further dialogue was futile, so she left and went to the files on Alpha-Surf. When she read the logs for the flight, she found that course corrections had been made by the guidance lead, not Lockni. A log entry for the retrofire command, however, said Lockni had given the order. There were two notes with the log entry; one specified the recommended time and a second recorded the actual time the button was pushed. They were different by a few milliarcs. The button was pushed late.

Fraya showed the entries to Karlus and asked him to make a copy of relevant pages for her. She didn't know what she would do with them, but maybe if Rami saw them, he might believe Lockni wasn't the genius he thinks he is.

Lockni began to get worried about the outcome of the Settler-One flight, and called a conference with the craft-controllers, the guidance lead, propulsion lead, and he also invited Fraya. He smiled at everyone around the table and with a syrupy tone, thanked everyone for coming. The erratic behavior of the spacecraft wasn't getting any better, and he was concerned its signals may be lost.

"We seem to have a temporary erratic flight path, people, and I think as a team we can straighten it out. What is the current condition of our craft?"

The guidance lead spoke first. "After that first correction a few arcs ago, we haven't been able to nail down a firm plot for the track, so we don't know where we are."

"Are the transponder signals still coming in?" Lockni asked.

The lead continued. "We're getting some signals, but when plotted they show the erratic path and don't give us time to analyze for a proper corrective burn."

Locki, still smiling, polled the group. "What would be the consensus for getting the spacecraft back on course?"

Nobody answered.

"We're all professionals here," he said, no longer smiling. "Can't anybody show some mettle and speak up? What's the matter here?" Lockni's smiling expression had changed to a look of anger.

Finally Sevik, the lead controller spoke up. "Tribune Lockni, we admire the good job you've done of getting the Settler-One built and launched, and on its way. We all want to see it continue on and make history; and the media all over the planet is watching us. None of us want to see it go astray. It would not only be a disappointment, but it would reflect badly on our project, and on the competence and reputation of each and every one of us. Right now we need to talk among ourselves and analyze the situation, privately, then get back to you with our consensus."

"Very well, I think that's a wise decision." Lockni hastily rose to leave. "I'm leaving now. Fraya, I want you to work with the group and act as coordinator. See if there is a problem and then resolve it. There's a council meeting next arc and they are expecting a favorable report on the progress. I repeat favorable. Fraya, I want you to go to that meeting in my stead, and make the report to the council. Is that clear?"

Fraya nodded. "I hope we can resolve the anomaly, Tribune, but I'll report what we find, and the resolution."

"I'm sure you'll do the right thing, Tribune Lor, to make us all look professional."

17. Fraya Fixes Settler-One

Fraya apologized to the group for being thrown into the position of coordinator. "I know many of you may have resented my hanging around your operation and making suggestions, but I did see things I wanted to change for the better."

"Some of us agreed with you, Fraya, but we were reluctant to speak up. Lockni is a difficult person to disagree with, and he had his own ideas. He must be very desperate right now to allege the Settler-One is out of control, and invite you to help resolve the problem."

"To get on with the task, I have to repeat the question Lockni asked earlier," she said. "What is the condition of the craft?"

Sevik answered. "I think it's spinning, and giving us scattered transponder readings that make the path appear erratic."

"Surely we have a roll rate input, don't we?" she asked.

"We should, based on the gyro system locking on a star, but we've lost the star."

"What did we do to lose it?" she asked.

"We made a course correction dictated by Lockni, and apparently tumbled the craft."

"Then we are in trouble," she said. "Guidance, can we backtrack and find what our position was before the tumble?"

"I don't know how to do that Fraya, but if you think you can, please take the console."

30

Fraya fumbled with the controls and watched the visiscreen. A series of dots, inputs from the transponder, appeared as the path of the craft. It was serpentine and gave her no clues as to its condition. Finally she asked the controller to repeat his last input before the course correction.

He looked at the log, then made an input to the craft. They all waited and watched the screen for thirty milliarcs before a change was noted.

"Look Fraya," the guidance lead pointed. "The serpentine path is tightening, getting more spiral. I think you're on to something."

"That means it was spinning and we just increased the spin. Controller, reverse the input you just made, then double it to see if we can stop the spin." Fifty milliarcs later the spin was stopped, and only a slow tumble remained. They worked together, and two hundred milliarcs later finally stopped the tumble and locked onto the star. They stabilized the craft, and reported to Lockni the star-nav system was re-acquired and he could make any further course corrections to keep the craft on track.

As Lockni requested, Fraya stood before the council and reported Settler-One's position and the expected date of intercept. She said Lockni had asked her to work with the controllers on a temporary basis to help resolve a minor anomaly that he was too busy to take care of, and that he asked her to make this report.

"The performance is now acceptable," she said, "and the craft is on track. The anomaly was corrected, and Lockni has control again."

Khanwali thanked Fraya. Without saying as much, he was surprised Lockni had let her come to the council alone, but his absence validated what he suspected. The favorable report was the result of

Fraya's efforts to resolve the anomaly and get Settler-One back on track.

18. Settler-One Intercepts

Settler-One flew on course after the navigation star was re-acquired, and twenty arcs later was ready for Terres orbit. Fraya walked across the campus from her lab to the control room to see the events. The control room was cool but she wasn't there for the air conditioning; she wanted to see the intercept maneuver.

The back lighted keys on the console glowed a soft amber color. Sevik, the lead controller, hunched over them while peering at the screen, with others seated around him craning for a look at the fluorescent data points. Lockni stood erect behind Sevik, his thin frame towering over the lead controller, and Fraya could see the screen if she stood on tip toes and looked between the bobbing heads. Lines depicting the path of Settler-One and the Terres orbit were visible, and about to converge.

"Check all systems on the craft," Lockni called. "We're approaching the Terres intercept point."

"We know that," Sevik replied, without looking up at Lockni. "We got the craft this far, didn't we?"

"Well, get ready to fire the retrorockets."

"It's not ready for retro," Sevik said. "Tribune Lockni, we haven't actually reached intercept, yet, and besides, the craft isn't oriented right."

"Then get it oriented, Sevik. Frankly, I'm getting tired of your insolence. It's exceeded only by your short memory about who's in charge here. You'll be relieved of your position if you don't watch your tongue.

"If you fire the retros too early, the craft will fall short, into the atmosphere, and burn up."

"Well, get it right, so it'll slow into orbit. We can't fail. We have much of the planet's media following our progress. People are waiting and listening."

"Then back off and let us do our jobs. We got it this far, and we'll get it into orbit at the right time. We want to succeed as much as you do."

"That does it you insubordinate dolt. Get away from that console and let Kassim take over."

"I don't want it." Kassim said. He had been watching the screen, and backed away. "Not now, anyway."

A loud, throat-clearing sound came from behind them and Lockni whirled to confront the source. It was Tribune Khanwali, who had quietly entered the control room.

"What is going on, may I ask?"

"I was just consulting with my technicians," Lockni said, "and they inform me we are not quite ready for intercept, the point in space where the craft crosses the path of the target planet. When we reach that point, we'll slow the travel of the craft so that it will fall into an orbit around Terres."

"I know what an intercept point is, Lockni. How soon will we be there?" Lockni looked to Sevik with a questioning shrug.

"Within a quarter-arc," Sevik replied.

"Within a quarter-arc," Lockni repeated, "but I'll have to check the calculations to be sure he's right."

"I'd like to be on hand when the command is given, Lockni." Khanwali's blazing eyes didn't appear to blink.

"Of course, Tribune. We will see that you are informed."

Sevik turned the spacecraft around so its retro-rockets faced in the direction of travel. Next, he angled the retros upward. Then he activated an on-board computer program, and waited. A timer blinked and ticked, and he signaled Lockni to press the button at zero time. With all systems in the green, a buzzer sounded, and Lockni pressed the button creating an audio beep. Even at the velocity of light the signal took a lengthy five milliarcs just to reach across the long distance to the spacecraft . After a waiting period for the round trip of signals, lights on the status-board indicated the firing went as planned, and Settler-One slowed to orbit. To be sure the new path was on course, they would have to wait thirty milliarcs or more before the corrected trajectory showed up on the console plots. Tribune Khanwali was there when the retro-fire took place, but didn't wait to see the new plot. He departed the room.

"It appears Settler-One is in orbit," he said to Lockni. "Now let's see if you can get it down, safely to the surface."

After they left, Fraya went over to Sevik and nodded toward the console. "I read the Alpha-Surf logs and know that Lockni pushed the button late for the retrofire. Wasn't it chancy to depend on a manual push for the retrofire on Settler-One?"

"Look at the screen Fraya. We got a good orbit out of it."

"You embedded a command, didn't you?"

"Are you one of Lockni's spies?"

"Are you serious? I couldn't be one of his informants if I wanted to. I have a conscience."

"All right, then push this button." Sevik pointed to the button Lockni pushed for the retrofire.

Fraya depressed the button and heard an aural beep. Sevik then reached over and pressed it several times, getting a series of beeps, and started laughing. It was infectious. Before long, both

Fraya and Sevik were alternately beeping and laughing so hard, hysterical tears were streaming from their eyes. The button was a fake, and Sevik had indeed embedded the actual retrofire command in the on-board computer.

After Lockni had resumed control, and was getting the orbiting craft ready for the landing, Settler-One disappeared. The craft had reached the point of entry into the Terres atmosphere, and then the signals stopped coming. The technicians tried vainly with every technique they could think of to get acquisition, but nothing worked.

Lockni was smooth and glib when he met with the council to report the disappearance of the craft. Without ever mentioning the earlier problem, he speculated the craft either had a power failure, or more probably, a meteorite strike damaging the power unit. He showed diagrams of the craft and pointed out the vulnerability to power loss if hit in certain places.

"An event that could not be foreseen," he said. "The odds of a strike are extremely small, but on the next one, we should have more redundancy, and more protection."

19. Arg's Tribe

The old Shaman in Arg's tribe was a master story-teller, and when the mood struck, he would sit by the community fire outside the cave relating tales passed down by the tribes' ancestors; tales of mountainous ice-rivers moving down the valleys, with nuggets of fractured ice tumbling from the frozen cliffs, pushing the nomads ahead until they came to the salty blue sea. He told how they foraged, and went hungry; how after a time the icy climate finally began to warm and the grinding, ice-masses halted.

No one in the tribe seemed to tire of his stories, especially the children, and occasionally one of them would take a turn and repeat a story they learned from the old man, imitating his arm-waving and gesturing. The Shaman encouraged the children, for they would someday be handing these stories down to their children. He told of the gradual warming, and how the fingers of ice retreated back up the valleys; and how their forefathers began picking suitable places to settle as food sources became more plentiful.

"Some of the tribes," he would say as he pointed, "went to the right along the shore of the blue sea, toward the setting sun, thinking the woolly mammoth would be more plentiful in the mountain meadows. Some tribes," he continued, "stayed near the shore, accepting what the area had to offer. Our tribe turned this way," he pointed, "toward the rising sun, away from the blue sea. Our tribal leader at the time, Arg's father, moved his family about a full moon's walk inland, and settled in a fertile valley with several inviting caves. All our tribes keep in contact, hunt together, and meet for social events. Once a year all the tribes in the area gather for games and contests, and," he waved his arms around and rolled his eyes upward, "the pairing of you unmated young people." That statement always brought out some cheers from the youngsters.

Shaman also made up stories about the stars, and the moon that changed its shape from round to crescent, and he pointed out that new little light in the night sky that moved rapidly across the horizon. When the children asked what it was, he would tell them it was a spear from another tribe, a Skytribe, but they had nothing to worry about because it was so high it wouldn't bother them.

The cave Arg's father had chosen was large enough for most of his tribe's families. Each family had an area without physical boundaries, but large enough for housekeeping, bedding, and meal preparation. The cave had a high, curved ceiling and a natural chimney that drafted the smoke from the cooking fires. The entrance was low and wide, and faced the morning sun. Chunks of rock, fallen from the overhang, formed a chest-high pile of broken boulders about half-way across, partly blocking the opening. They left the pile of rubble intact, as it provided a natural barrier against predators and weather.

With ample game in the area for most of the year, Arg and his generation remained in that same valley for most of the seasons, leaving only to follow a migrating herd of oxen or horses, or for tribal gatherings. Near the valley, a highland plateau had several briny lakes that crusted around the edges. The white, crusty deposits were highly valued for seasoning, and used to preserve meat. Life appeared good in their domain, to all but the old Shaman. He was a worrier, still concerned about that tiny, moving light in the night sky.

20. Fraya Gets Settler-Two

The council sympathized with Lockni, and shared in the disappointment. Then they approved funding for a second landing attempt, called Settler-Two, and left Lockni in the position of project manager. Khanwali, however, did not have the confidence in Lockni that he once had. After reviewing Fraya's proposals for using the new guidance system and an hyperbolic trajectory, Khanwali once again usurped Lockni's authority, and promoted Fraya directly to Lead of Guidance and Control for the new craft, a heady assignment for such a young person.

"Put your guidance system into Settler-Two, Fraya," Khanwali told her, "and use the hyperbolic path you recommended.

The crossing from Baeta to Terres was calculated to take one hundred and fifty arcs, with the arc a measure of Baetian time. Early scholars had divided Baeta's sphere into one hundred longitudinal arcs, and designated one rotation of the planet, or one hundred arcs, as an annum. The makers of calendars chose rotation rather than solar orbit as an easy, natural choice for the annum. One annum is completed in each time zone when the sun is directly overhead, regardless of the planet's position in solar orbit. Fraya was glad rotation was chosen over solar orbit because it made calculations and record keeping so much simpler.

Fraya was in charge of Settler-Two's navigation, and Lockni became very bitter. Although many of the technicians believed he had fouled the Settler-One's program for intercept, giving them all a damaged reputation, some had bought into the concept of a meteorite strike. Putting Fraya immediately in charge of Settler-Two as Guidance Lead seemed like an extreme step, even to those with whom she worked to get Settler-One straightened out. Word of her going to the boss over Lockni's head certainly got around, and caused some resentment. Some of the fickle crew's loyalties began to flip-flop back to Lockni, and Fraya, to some, was suddenly the intruder again. Most in the guidance group were cooperative with Fraya because they had jobs to carry out, but the prevailing attitude was mixed toward this newcomer.

Lockni didn't have anything positive to say about Fraya's position. "What does she know about leadership?" he quipped. "Nothing, she's a neoscion..... just an opportunist."

"She won't be able to handle the assignment," said one of Lockni's loyalists.

"And she's a foreigner," said another, "probably a Fen, if truth were known."

Karlus, her assistant in the research division and now her principal technician on the Settler-Two project, supported her without question. He was competent, energetic and knowledgeable, and she depended heavily on him, grateful he had also transferred out of research when she went to the Terres program. Settler-Two was designed and built, programmed for an hyperbolic trajectory, and moved to the pad. The launch went smoothly, and Fraya sent it on its way while uttering one of her rhymes.

"Coast across the sky, dash-two, to planet number three. I'll be here to see what you see, that's my destiny".

Fraya's team watched as it rose, and disappeared from sight. Her guidance system made small corrections to start it on the right course. The team followed its plot for the first arc, hardly ever leaving the consoles, until satisfied Settler-Two began its coasting flight on the new trajectory as planned.

This crossing from Baeta to Terres was calculated to take 122 arcs, much faster than the path of Settler-One. Even though the trajectory of Settler-Two would be electronically plotted on a screen in front of her, she fashioned a hand-made banner with one hundred and twenty-two squares, one for each arc of time to intercept, and placed it on a wall over her console. Intercept was the calculated meeting of the spacecraft with the target planet. The banner was her little reminder of the simpler things in life. Square number forty-one on the banner was the time it reached apogee, the highest point on the curving path between the two planets.

For forty arcs Fraya's team tracked the coasting trajectory of the Terres-bound craft. At this point it was now ahead of Terres and outside its orbit, but slowing to gradually turn back inward from the pull of the sun's gravity. Lockni was frequently in the control room, looming over Fraya's shoulder, checking the screen and her procedures. As

39

project manager he had a right to be in the control room, and visited quite often, but instead of feeling reassured, his company always made her feel uneasy. He watched every move, questioning her command and controlling procedures, moving even the most reserved to comment. Karlus, who seldom uttered a bad word about anybody, said, "he wished old pointy nose would point it someplace else for awhile".

Fraya planned the first major course correction at apogee, on Arc-41. When her tracking system told her it was time, she called to Karlus, and as usual, her assistant was nearby in the control room.

"Make a check of all systems on the craft. We are approaching apogee."

Shortly before, Karlus had just finished checking with each operator without being asked, but repeated the query as she requested. He keyed the intercom and alerted all the operators.

"Systems check, everybody, you know the routine. I'll make the call and you respond." He heard some grumbling, and a voice complained.

"What's she want now. We just completed a check."

"So, we'll do another one," Karlus replied. "I have to ask you know. Its my job, and yours too. We're at Arc-41 and apogee correction is coming up." Karlus looked at his checklist.

"Orientation? - he called.

"Stable, Karlus, same as the last time you asked."

"Batteries?" - "They're still in the green, Karlus."

"Gyros and guidance?" - "Check," - from another source.

"Propulsion?" - "What can I say? I know......no change."

"Tracking?" - "Updating now. Surprise - we'll need a correction."

"Come on, everyone, don't be sarcastic." Karlus made several more queries and heard from each one in turn, then reported to Fraya:

"all systems in the green".

She completed some calculations, made some keystrokes, and started a countdown. Apogee, the point at which the craft stops moving away from the sun and turns back inward, was calculated to occur on Arc-40.732. In Fraya's new flight path, the craft at apogee is actually ahead of and farther away from the sun than Terres, its target. As Settler-Two approached apogee, Fraya needed only one small correction to keep it on course. At zero-minus-transition time she pressed a button sending a command out into space, to the Settler-Two craft . The signal adjusted the craft's attitude, followed by a rocket engine burn, thrusting to alter the trajectory. The firing went as planned. Fraya turned and looked up at Tribune Lockni, who had been looming over her shoulder watching the screen. The course looked good. She seemed to sense disappointment in his expression, but quickly dismissed it as ridiculous. She reached up and crossed out square number 41 on her banner and slouched back in her chair, relaxing with her eyes half closed. The trajectory was proving to be right on track, apogee was passed, and the first major course correction was over. Lockni's voice jarred her out of her languor and she bolted upright.

21. New Engine

"Fraya, I'd like to discuss something of importance with you in my office." He whirled and led the way.

She was surprised by this summons. Usually, if he had something to say or ask her, he did it in the control room. Now, in his office, they chatted about the Settler-Two launch and he praised her on the functioning of her new guidance system. From the beginning, Fraya had little rapport with this superior. This was the first compliment she ever remembered from him, and though skeptical, she was pleased to hear it. As she sat across from him in his office, it seemed he had pushed all his resentment aside. He was smiling as he spoke.

"Now that Settler-Two is well on its way, Tribune Lor, we need to start thinking about the next step, the manned landing. We'll have a totally different set of requirements, you know, and we'll need a new type of craft. I would like to hear some of your thoughts on alternative power systems."

The subject took her by surprise. "My total preoccupation has been on Settler-Two; guiding it, and aiming it for the landing site we picked from the orbiter's imaging. I haven't given the next program any deep thought."

"Of course, I know that. But think out loud," a smiling Lockni continued. "We sometimes accomplish a great deal that way."

She nodded, paused a bit to collect her thoughts, then began.

"Well, Tribune," she continued, "the hyperbolic trajectory and the new guidance system are certainly speeding the crossing time, and I think it's working out very well."

"Yes it is," he replied, "and I must admit I was a bit hasty about objecting when you first presented it. Fortunately, better thinkers prevailed and we put your system on Settler-Two. What do think we could use for future power?" Fraya thought back on her attempts to get out of research and onto the Terres project, and of everything Lockni had done to reject her transfer requests. He had stood before the council and railed about all the unknowns in this new era of miniature silicrysts, saying they were blindly accepting it too fast.

His conservative attitude had a lot of followers on the council, except for Tribune Khanwali, the senior manager. Khanwali felt

42

Fraya's brilliance would revolutionize many aspects of space flight. After he promoted her and mandated the new guidance system be put on the Settler-Two, Lockni, who had previously rejected Fraya's request for transfer to the project, had little to say. Fraya, of course, knew the mandate was a blow to his authority, and wondered at the time if they would ever work together compatibly.

"Well," she finally spoke up, "the crossing using conventional chemical boosters takes one hundred and twenty, up to a hundred and fifty arcs or more. Keeping a crew in a small, confined area for that long doesn't seem practical. How long have we ever kept space-pilots on our orbiting platform?"

"We rotate crews every twenty arcs," Lockni replied. "We've kept some on the platform for forty arcs to see how they fared, but that's the longest. Living on the platform is far different than surviving an interplanetary crossing, you know. For the platform, we can replace supplies, take fresh stocks of food, replenish water, re-pressurize with oxygen if necessary, and remove someone in case of illness. None of that will be possible on an interplanetary flight."

"Then a faster method of crossing would reduce the problems and requirement for consumables," she replied. "We should have a power source that will give us not only boost, but a low, sustained thrust for a longer period of time."

"Like what? Do you have any ideas?" he asked.

Again she paused, gathered her thoughts and mentally sifted the alternatives she had studied after Khanwali requested she start planning for the eventual manned landing.

"I have a good friend in logistics, and have discussed this very subject with him."

"Who is it?" Lockni asked.

"Millen Cyrriz, currently coordinating the trips to the Platform."

43

"I know him. He is doing a good job."

"Millen told me carrying enough consumables for an interplanetary trip would require a very long train of supply modules, attached to the manned craft, and the same materiel would be required for the return trip. That would require an enormous amount of launches for orbital assembly here," she replied. "Not only that, keeping a crew sane and physically sound for an annum and a third, in a cubicle the size of a small motor carriage, doesn't seem possible."

"I've gotten similar feedback from some of the pilots who spend time on the orbital platform, and the platform is very roomy," Lockni said. "So what can we use? Is there anything in development that may work?"

"I know this issue is not entirely new," Fraya replied, "as Centre has been concerned about long duration crew stability for some time. The most promising I'm aware of would be nuclear thermal propulsion. I think we could get a multiple improvement in specific thrust, and do it with a reduced fuel load."

"I can see you've been doing some thinking about this," Lockni replied.

Engine alternatives hadn't been foremost in Fraya's thoughts, but nuclear propulsion was a logical avenue of interest, especially since much of the planet's electrical power was generated from reactors. "Nuclear propulsion has its risks, you know. We have no lightweight, effective radiation shield to protect the crew."

"We have to start somewhere," Lockni said, "and the engine is the first step. All the accessories and the shield will have to be designed around a feasible engine."

Her expression lightened with enthusiasm, and with Lockni being so congenial, she felt a new, but very brief bonding with her superior. To herself, she mumbled a jingle. "Be wary, be wary, he's being too merry."

Lockni didn't hear the mumbling. "I was hoping you'd come to that conclusion," he replied. "We've talked about it briefly in the steering committee." She wondered if he even understood the concept. "There are several manufacturers of stationary nuclear power plants throughout our planet. Why don't you visit a few of them, and see what they would propose for a space engine."

"But what about Settler-Two?" she voiced concern.

"It's on track, and you'll be back in plenty of time to make any further course corrections. You're becoming one of our favored new scienomies, Fraya," he spoke with emphasis on the favored, "and we wouldn't make a move on Settler-Two without your approval. For now, leave it in the hands of your capable assistants and go, my child. If you find a contractor in Ardena, take time to go to your home, and have a nice visit with your family. When you get back we'll start planning for that new engine program."

Fraya's attitude soared. So many good things seemed to be happening all at once; getting a real assignment on the Terres program, becoming Guidance Lead for the Settler-Two, the trajectory working almost perfectly, and now a chance to work on a new power system. It all seemed staggering. She was smiling broadly when Lockni broke the spell.

"Fraya, I know I disappointed you at first when you tried to transfer to the Terres program, but at the time, I thought it was premature. I apologize, and now we are mandated to work together. I feel we can accomplish many things as partners, and could make an outstanding professional team. You are a very attractive woman, and I would like to get to know you better, away from the job. Would you consider socializing with me, say, dining together after work?"

Fraya felt her skin go cold, and the thought of Lockni touching her was revolting. Her impulse was to stomp out of the office, but she reconsidered, knowing Lockni still had much influence with many members of the council. She felt protected by Khanwali but didn't want to offend Lockni.

"I might at some future time, Tribune Lockni, but at this time I'm afraid any socializing will adversely affect the professionalism we have established. Let's get Settler-Two landed, and start the planning for the manned landing mission. Thank you anyway."

She went back to the control room with her mind in a flutter. Her desire at the moment was to call Rami, talk to him, and feel his closeness once again. She sent a signal to his communicator: "Meet me!."

22. The Space-Pilot

Rami had not seen Fraya in quite some time, and wanted to share an outing with her. They picked a favorite dining place, and while waiting for their server, Rami told her about the Graduate Institute, and his position as a research assistant in the Life Sciences Mentorium. She was anxious to tell him about the Settler and the Nuper project, and interrupted him.

"I've got some news! Do you want to hear it or not?"

"News? Really," he teased. "I never would have guessed. Does it have anything to do with Khanwali?"

"Yes, among other things, but not the trajectory. That's history and Settler-Two is on its way, on my trajectory.

"Well, you went to Khanwali, over Lockni's head, and you are still around and alive. Congratulations. How's Lockni taking it?"

"Apparently very well. He obviously has much influence, so in spite of his incompetence, he's still a project manager."

"I think you're being overly sensitive and maybe misjudging him through jealousy.

Fraya's eyes snapped at Rami. "Jealousy? You misjudge me. I admire good technical talent but you haven't met him. He's belligerent, overbearing, and gets his way through bullying. People fear him."

"Maybe you should too, Fraya. Even though you are a foreigner with some consulate protection, you could still end up in a mental institution here for evaluation, and disappear."

"Now you're being ridiculous, Rami. I'm not going to get paranoid over the possibility of physical harm." She started to tell him about the problems of a future manned trip to Terres when they were interrupted. A voice new to Rami boomed out loudly over the babble of different tones and tongues from the tables around them.

"Hey Paramo", the voice called to Fraya, "where you been hiding yourself?" Rami looked at the source along with Fraya and saw an imposing figure in uniform, with dark eyes and sun-bronzed skin, swaggering over to their table. Although his hair was short-cropped, it still appeared wavy, and atop a grinning countenance, he made quite a dashing appearance.

"Well, well, it's Commander Obnoxious." Fraya acknowledged the intruder with indifference, then introduced him.

"Rami, meet Corci Kraejil, one of our space-pilots. He just returned from a tour of duty on the orbiting platform and is now going around bothering people."

She introduced Rami. They each extended a right hand and grasped wrists with a squeeze. Corci turned back to Fraya.

"Paramo, I want to congratulate you on being assigned to the new engine program."

"What engine program?" Her brow wrinkled with the question.

"That's good, Paramo, don't say anything to anyone who doesn't have a need to know."

"First of all, Commander, I've told you I don't like your bawdy nicknames. You can call me Fraya, or you can call me Tribune Lor, but I don't like Paramo. As for your engine program, I thank you must be imagining things. Where did you hear about an engine program."

"I keep my sources confidential, Paramo, but I think Khanwali picked you a long time ago for this project. You know," he picked up Fraya's drink and took a sip, "some people think you're pretty hot stuff around here and will eventually be the group manager for all propulsion and guidance. If that happens, you could end up in charge of the manned landing project, and we could work together."

Fraya frowned. "Manned project? Aren't you jumping ahead a bit?" He set her drink back down. "Good choice of wine, but I'd say a little potent for you. Off the record, I'm planning to be the one chosen to command that first Terres trip. If you do really, really good in the new assignment, I might take you out to dine sometime."

"Well, Commander Kraejil, apparently you know more about the project than I do, which is practically nothing. Go back to your fans and quit bothering me!" Fraya tried to act irritated.

He grinned at Rami. "It doesn't sound like it, but she really likes me." He looked back to Fraya. "I'll be in touch, Paramo." He grinned again, and strode off, waving to people left and right as he departed.

"He's the most egotistical person I've ever known," she said, still sounding irritated.

"He definitely leaves that impression. With so many people recognizing him, he must be famous."

"Not really, just well known among the space-pilot idolizers, and a lot of them frequent this place."

"Do you like him?" Rami asked.

"Well, he's hard not to like. He's charming and witty, and I'm a little flattered by his attention, but frankly, his ego is too big for me. He thinks Centre couldn't run without him."

"Is he technically competent?"

"Actually, he's considered one of our best space-pilots, a highly rated strato-pilot, and has a degree in celestranautics. Arrogant, yes, but people do listen to him."

"What's a Paramo?" Rami asked.

"I don't know, but he uses various nicknames on several of us at Centre. I think Paramo is some sort of word for female trophy in his native language."   "Oh?" Rami paused, and felt a jolt of jealousy. "Maybe I should be more attentive," he thought.

"The commander mentioned a manned trip. Is that in the planning stages?"

"I guess so," she replied, "but its so far in the future I don't know why he even brought it up."

"Somebody's thinking about it, Fraya. My new assignment at the Institute, the one I started telling you about, is connected with the manned Terres exploration."

"Really?" Fraya was surprised. "How so?"

"My mentorian at the Institute has a Centre contract to classify and investigate potential biological hazards just in case life is found on Terres, and I'm assigned to do some research about it."

Fraya, with palms together, pensively touched her lips in thought.

"How can you assess biological hazards on another planet without being there?"

"I don't know yet. Mainly, the first approach will be steps to prevent contamination of Terres by us, and then decontamination for the return of artifacts and pilots in case there are organisms on Terres. My mentorian says knowing all about the workings of the immune system is a start, and that's where I come in, to become the local expert on the immune system. He's going to send me to Ardena to work with a Tribune there who's a real expert. She is already a specialist on decontamination."

"Oh," she replied, trying not to show any signs of disappointment at the thought of his leaving. "Where in Ardena, and how long will you be gone?"   "I'll be staying in Solport, I guess, and don't know how long." Rami was struggling with some thoughts that Fraya might be attracted to Corci, but let them quickly pass.

"Solport, that's only a hundred kiloquants from my home. I envy you; I don't get home often enough."

They had finished their meal and were about to leave, when Rami had an impulsive idea.

"I don't know when my travel assignment will start, but after I get there, maybe you can visit me in Solport, and visit your family at the same time."

She paused, choosing her words carefully. "I'm not sure what project will occupy most of my time for awhile, but I'll see what arrangements I can come up with."

"Very well then, Fraya Lor. I hope we can get together in Solport. And, congratulations on finally getting onto the Terres project. Your dream has come true."

"One of my dreams, anyway." She wondered if he knew how deeply she really felt abut him.

"Thank you Ramizia Slade, for the well wishes. I'll keep working to accomplish all my dreams. "

23. Fraya Starts the Nuper Project

With a mandate from Lockni to survey some contractors, Fraya picked three she thought had possibilities of producing a nuclear propulsion engine, or nuper as she nicknamed it. Two, Kirken on the continent of Montes, and Prollett in Ardena, produce stationary nuclear-powered generators. A third, Stratopulse, produces large rockets used mainly by Centre. She organized trips with Karlus to visit all three, starting with Stratopulse.

Fraya was familiar with Stratopulse liquid propellant rocket engines, called boosters. The Mini-Dynamo and large Super-Dynamo engines were used for boosting flights to the platform. Stratopulse was located just south of Bacamir, and like Bacamir, was still in annurdark. As one who suffered depression during the dark season, Fraya didn't want to stay very long at Stratopulse. She steered the direction of the meeting with the technical managers right to the subject.

"If you were chosen to produce a new technology space engine, a nuper, how would you go about it?" she asked.

"Truthfully," the manager replied, "we don't know anything about reactors. But we do know an engine has to have a nozzle to make it work, and we know more about nozzles than anyone on the planet. So, if we can buy a workable reactor, we can make an engine."

"Fairly stated, and I know your nozzles are excellent," she said. "But there are so many technical problems to work out in an engine design, that you'll have a hard time competing. Perhaps you should consider subcontracting your nozzles to someone who makes reactors and can make a workable engine."

51

"We might do that, Fraya, but give us a chance to come up with a preliminary design. We may surprise you."

Fraya and Karlus immediately departed westward for their next destination, Whitecliff Villa. The flight was long and tiring, almost half way around the planet. The darkness changed to sunlight and as they flew through the terminator, Fraya's spirits brightened considerably. When the stratoliner made a refueling stop on the western end of Scorpia, she and Karlus welcomed the chance to get out and stretch before continuing a flight northward to Montes.

24. Contractor Number Two - Kirken

She had never been on the mountainous continent before and was hoping the weather would cooperate for some viewing. Montes has the highest mountains and the most volcanic activity anywhere on the planet, with a Great Mons, over twelve kiloquants high. As their stratoliner approached Whitecliff Villa, on the south end of Montes, she could see the grassy mesa above the cliffs, and the saw-tooth profile of the Scabrous Range to the northwest, but Great Mons was not visible. Clouds swirled and teased around the peak but it remained shrouded.

"I wish we could see it, Karlus, but the Mons isn't going to appear for us. Perhaps we'll get a chance some other time."

The Kirken Group, manufacturers of reactors for stationary electrical power plants, was interested in developing a smaller, lightweight unit for rail use or motorway freighters. However, they welcomed a representative from the prestigious Centre and wanted to hear about future manned flights.

"As you know," the Kirken manager told them, "we make electrical power plants, and are only just beginning to think in terms of a space engine. Rather than nuclear thermal propulsion, we'd have more interest in the concept of nuclear electric propulsion, or nulec." He spread some sketches onto a large, table.

Fraya studied the sketches. "In either case," she said, "you need accelerated mass to turn a turbine for your rail or motorway units, without discharging the mass overboard. Will nulec do this?"

The manager tapped the drawing, pointing to a loop in the piping sketch. "The nulec would use energy to ionize the propellant, and accelerate the ions through a nozzle. On the surface, the ions would be recirculated. In space, they could be dumped overboard."

"You've already put considerable effort into a possible future engine for surface movers, Fraya said. Have you considered radiation shielding?"

"Heavy lead plates are not practical for a mobile unit, we know, so one of our research projects is specifically for lightweight shielding. We have a light-weight layered blanket that shows promise as a radiation absorber. It contains beryllium and lead, alloyed with boron, gold, and a few things we can't discuss. It looks promising.

Fraya was impressed and encouraged them to keep on with the project.   "If you're successful," she said, "your lightweight shielding may become a major component of any lengthy, manned mission using nuclear power."

The manager asked: "Why is manned flight so different than that unmanned probe you already have orbiting Terres?"

Fraya explained: "A manned, interplanetary flight, has to be completely self contained. Crews can't be rotated or removed for emergencies, and all consumables and life support for an entire round trip will have to travel with the craft. Human physiology deteriorates during weightlessness, so the least time spent in the crossing, the better." A faster trip is what we're looking for."

"Would you consider our nulec concept, as an alternative to nuper?"

"I'm not sure. I'll do some calculations based on the figures you've given me, but it might not produce enough thrust," she replied.

"However, that lightweight shielding may be the big breakthrough we need to make the manned mission possible, not only as shielding from the reactor, but against radiation storms from solar flares."

Before leaving Whitecliff Villa, Fraya and Karlus briefly motored up onto the mesa, hoping for some spectacular mountain views, but again the weather wouldn't cooperate. The mesa was clear of clouds at the lower altitudes, and the chalky mesa walls above the villa appeared gleaming white, glistening as if wetted, and some were, because in places, waterfalls cascaded over the edge. As they looked toward the sea, the bright, white cliffs contrasted sharply with the wooded, green belt below, and the foaming white crests of surf. Fraya slowly panned the scene, and felt moved. "I wish Rami was here to share this beauty." she thought.

25. Contractor Number Three - Prollett

Destination number three was Solport, in Ardena, near her home. Fraya and Karlus flew from Montes south and eastward to Solport, to visit Prollet, a conglomerate in that borough. Like its competitor, Prollett produced stationary nuclear electrical generators, and was also planning a lighter, compact unit to power mobile and rail freighters.

Fraya was shown how their scienomies were actively engaged in altering a small, working model of their generator into a catalytic bed capable of breaking water into combustible hydrogen and oxygen.

They gained thrust as the superheated water was accelerated over the catalyst bed, and then gained additional thrust as the hydrogen and oxygen recombined as a chemical burner. The double-thrust concept proved even more efficient than their earlier calculations had predicted, much to Fraya's delight.

The thrust was miniature in comparison to the power that would be needed for an actual launch, but it demonstrated the feasibility. Their scienomies were already working on a larger engineering model, and designing a full-scale prototype for a nuclear rocket engine capable of actual operation.   "If the larger model produces thrust as we expect," the Prollett manager explained, "we'll build the prototype. Radiation shielding is currently a major concern, but if we can make this model work, protecting the crew from radiation can be solved in other ways."

It was there Fraya met Arin Restor, the principal owner of Prollett, and the one person who completely changed her life. She, with Karlus at her side, had spent several arcs reviewing the Prollett data and observing tests on the model, and at the end of each workshift, she and Karlus were invited to dine with some of the Prollet scienomies. On the third arc, she found Arin dining with the group. He was a bit intimidating, rotund with flushed complexion, thinning gray hair and thick, fleshy fingers. His demeanor was condescending, and he wasn't overly interested in space-junk, as he called it.

"My dear," he said while waving a corpulent hand with several gaudy rings, "we conduct business for profit here. We're developing a small engine to power rail and surface freighters. There'll be a big market for those. I know your interest is in a space-machine engine, and we'll modify our engineering model to get some thrust, but I must emphasize, we are marketeers in the business for a profit. If our prototype becomes adaptable for your missions, and we see a good potential, we will be the best in the business at producing it. If we don't quickly see ourselves as winners, we'll expend our efforts elsewhere, toward more profitable endeavors."

The profit-motive wasn't a new concept for Fraya. After all, her parents raised citrona fruits and had to make a profit, or lose their orchards and land. "Very well. I have no control over contracts, but if you are the successful bidder for a space nuper, I'm sure the profit will be there."

"True, you may only be the technical director of the engine project, (she wasn't the director but didn't bother to correct him), but when it comes to choosing a successful bidder and negotiating a contract, I know you'll be the final authority for approval. Therefore, I would like you to speak up if you see anything in our design or testing that needs direction or correction. If you think we need more expertise, I'll go buy it. That's a benefit of free enterprise, we can hire and fire as needed. If you see some way we can improve, like incorporating ideas you may have seen elsewhere, speak up."

"I appreciate your candor, but I'm sure you know I cannot morally nor legally suggest changes, if they come from my observations at a competitor." "Come, come, my dear, I know you want your space-pilots riding with the best engine available. Imagine yourself on that flight and it'll help clear your priorities."

"I think my priorities are clear enough, Presario Restor, and I've imagined myself on that space flight many times, so I understand the concept, but information from any contractor is confidential," Fraya was annoyed at Arin's prying.

"Please, just call me Arin. Why don't you become a part-time consultant for us, then you could suggest improvements as part of the consulting job. You could retain your present position with the Centre, and support us only as needed."

"We are not allowed to consult with any other agency or marketeer if it presents a conflict of interest," Fraya replied, "and that would be a conflict of interests."

"Very well. Regardless, we will have the best product for your space-pilots, and we'll win the contract on merit and superiority of design."

"And that's the way it should be won," she said.

Arin hardly changed his expression. He switched to Ardenese when he spoke next. "I apologize for what seemed like a breach of ethics, my dear. Of course such an action is out of the question. Let me make it up to you. There is a gaming casino not too far from here, with an excellent and entertaining show of performers. Let me escort you to the casino. We needn't hurry back, and we could spend the sleep period together at the Casino Inn. I would be honored." Fraya was stunned. Such a proposal was totally unexpected, and hardly believing what she'd heard, she glared, then remarked sarcastically. "I might get carried away at the gaming tables, and cost you a lot."

"Really!" Arin quipped. "Since you brought up the subject of payment, how much? "

"I was talking about the cost of the gaming. If you want a prostitute, I'm not in the market. Besides, I really think you'd be better off engaging a street-walker. Cheaper, and more in your class." She switched to Bacamirian. "Let's go, Karlus, I've had enough discussion for this arc."

Later, in the privacy of her hostel, she discussed Arin's ethics with Karlus.

"So far, his probing is not a problem because Prollet seems to be far ahead of the others, but it could become an ethics issue if we learned something at Stratopulse or Kirken, that was proprietary and let it slip here at Prollet."

"I can't imagine you telling anyone about some proprietary information you're privy to," Karlus replied. "After all, you have a very high security clearance and did develop a secret guidance system. You've never been approached or tempted to tell anyone about that, have you?"

"No, but that's different. Contractors weren't involved. Here we're overseeing the development of a new product among competing contractors. I guess I'm worrying too much, but thank you for listening. I don't know what I'd do without you, Karlus."

"It's my job, Tribune, and I'm honored to be working with you."

As a working space, Arin had offered Fraya an office to use as her own until the bid was over, and Karlus wasted no time in organizing the office and setting up a filing system. They spent several arcs reviewing the Prollett reports and observing tests on the model. When she thought they had seen enough, she sent Karlus back to Centre without her, so she could stay and spend some time visiting her family, only a hundred kiloquants away.

26. Fraya Becomes New Engine Coordinator

The control room at Centre was a buzz of normal activity when she returned,. and Fraya nudged Sevik from the console chair.

"Thank you, Sevik, I'll take over now."

Satisfied the craft was on course, she checked the hand-marked banner over her console, and crossed out all the arc-squares that had passed while she was gone. This was Arc-47. Settler-Two was more than one third of the way to the Terres intercept. She left the control-room and went to the council chamber, where she was scheduled to report on her surveys. When she walked into the meeting, the subject of the manned trip to Terres was being discussed, and Millen Cyrriz, her friend from logistics, was finishing a presentation estimating life-support consumables.

My, they're thinking ahead on this project, she thought. A list was showing on the big screen:

"The following items will be required, based on a round trip journey of eighty arcs," Millen droned, "assuming we get a nuper engine. Consumables per person, by weight in millidrums, will be needed as follows:"

He read from the list on the screen; oxygen; dried food; hydrating water; drinking water - giving weights in millidrums for each item. Tribune Khanwali, the program manager, made a few comments, thanked him for the report, and then turned to Fraya.

"Tribune Lor, we are anxious to hear what you have found regarding an advanced engine". She went to the front of the group, and noticed Lockni sitting in a front row. He avoided eye contact with her, as he usually did, and remained unsmiling as she began.

"Thank you, Tribune. I visited three marketeers; Stratopulse in Southbak, the Kirken Group in Whitecliff, and Prollet in Solport. From what I've seen, the possibility of a workable nuper will, eventually, be viable, but I don't have a timetable yet. Our first destination was Stratopulse, with whom we are all familiar. Stratopulse supplies the conventional, chemical boosters we use for most of our launches. They are interested in designing a nuper using their current rocket booster and nozzle expertise, around a reactor core from some other source. They do not make reactors, nor have any experience with them, but feel that is not a handicap if they can hire the expertise.

Kirken, makers of nuclear power generators, was our next stop, and they are proposing a nuclear-electric-pulse engine, or nulec, rather than a nuper. I don't believe the nulec will have the initial thrust we need, but Kirken does have a promising radiation-absorbing material in development that is light and flexible; a foil-like, blanket material.

Prollet, the third contractor we visited, also makes nuclear generators and are working toward a light-weight, mobile, nuper engine. They have an engineering model which should be operating very soon, and plan to modify it to produce thrust. Of the three contractors, at this time Prollet is farthest along and, I believe, the most promising."

When she completed her presentation, Tribune Lockni stood and lauded Fraya's efforts, to her surprise.

"Sustained thrust is the key to a successful round trip," he said, "and we can't start on a better engine early enough in my opinion. I recommend Tribune Lor become coordinator for development of the new engine as a high priority item, full time, even though a manned trip is still far in the future."

Fraya recognized the subtle overtness of his proposal and his motive. He wanted her out of the way.

"I agree," Khanwali said. "Fraya will be the new engine coordinator, but I want her to remain in control of Settler-Two through the landing."

Lockni looked like he had been struck. Khanwali gave his approval for additional funding on the nuclear engine development, and authorized Fraya to take a team of specialists at her discretion for additional reviews, and to spend more time with the contractors. He cautioned her on prejudging Prollet as the best until the others showed their designs.

Fraya thanked him, returned to her seat, and passed a note to Millen, asking him to meet her at the dinery. Millen, the lead logistician, had become a confidant for Fraya, and they frequently took meal breaks together, exchanging trivial news and gossip. She found him pleasant to be around, and an easier conversationalist than Rami. Also, she suspected, he really liked her. He was pledged, but his mate seemed rather shallow to Fraya. On one occasion she and Rami had dined with them and Fraya got the impression Millen's mate was totally non-technical, which she considered a failing. No wonder he likes conversation with me, she thought.

"Millen, Lockni proposed that I work on the new engine full time. Do you know what's going on around here? Does he just want me out of the way?" Millen glanced around, as if someone else might hear him.

"I know he's jealous that you are handling Settler-Two, and I happened to overhear him arguing with Khanwali awhile back. It was quite heated and the subject seemed to be personnel. I couldn't hear any of the names they were bantering about, but Khanwali finally got so angry he ordered Lockni out of his office. When Lockni came out, red-faced, he wouldn't look at any of us, just marched off. Ever since, he's been more moody than usual, and seems to be getting even less affable."

"Well, Lockni has me forced into spending more time away, visiting contractors, and I'm afraid if I leave for very long, he might do something foolish, like trying to alter the program in Settler-Two.."

"Where are you planing to land it?" Millen asked.

"Same place as Settler-One was intended, a relatively flat looking area south of the Middleterran Sea. We have it programmed to settle there."

"Well, there isn't much you can do except refuse the nuper assignment and stay here, or go on the surveys and work the nuper development. I'm sure Khanwali thinks you can do both or he wouldn't have agreed with Lockni. You and I both know you want to be involved

in that nuper development anyway. How much time before the
landing?"

"Settler-Two is a long way from intercept, so I have lots of time
for surveys. And yes, I do want to be involved in the nuper
development, so I'd better get on with the task of picking a team of
specialists. Since you know all the experts in the various disciplines,
would you help me with the selection?"

"Sure, Fraya, I'd be glad to," Millen replied. "Can I be one of
the experts?"

"I'd be in agreement, but I think we'd have trouble justifying a
logistician on a development survey." Millen looked at an
organizational chart, and began picking specialists from staff
disciplines. "You need someone from Reliability, Materials, Stress,
Quality Assurance, and Manufacturing Engineering." He circled names
on the chart. "And, you don't need a logistician yet, but keep me in
mind."

"Thank you Millen, I will."

27. Fraya's Team

Fraya marked out Arc-62 on her banner; Settler-Two was at the
half way point, and it was time to make the survey trip that Lockni
requested. This time her title was Chief Scienomie for Propulsion.
She looked at the list of technical specialists once more before
submitting it to finance for travel arrangements, and one name
suddenly caught her eye; Commander Corci Kraejil. Wondering what
was going on, she quickly contacted him on the intercom.

"Corci," she hollered, "What is your name doing on my list of
specialists? I didn't select you."

"Paramo, you've been neglecting me lately, and my feelings are hurt. I've been expecting your call and I'll be right there." Corci closed the circuit before she could object, and burst into her office.

"Hello Paramo." He slid into a chair in front of her desk.

"Why are you on my list of specialists?" she asked.

He flashed his big grin and blinked his eyes a couple of times. "I'm a specialist."

"Don't tell me you're a specialist. What kind of specialist?"

"As you wish; I'm not a specialist." He paused, leaned forward and looked unsmilingly at her, hardening his voice. "I've told you before, I plan to command the Terres manned lander. I may not be the chief space-pilot around here yet, but I'm working on it. And, if I'm going to command it, I want to see how the engine works and be in on the design. You're wrong in not having a space-pilot along on these surveys anyway."

"Why should we have a space-pilot along on a design review?" she asked. "You're just a machine driver, not a designer."

"You've heard of ergonomics, haven't you, the science of coordinating mechanical requirements with physical capabilities? Probably not, sitting here up on your pedestal as you do?"

"Don't get smart with me Corci," she replied, trying to be stern.

"Good ... spunky! I like that." He went on. " One time I was testing one of our military stratocraft when it went into an uncontrollable flat spin, and I couldn't stop it. The ergomonsters, or whatever they're called, placed the switch for ejection at the end of a pilot's reach in front of him. The spin was worse than the centrifuge we use for space-flight training. My arms were forced outward by the forces. That switch, which was an easy reach when sitting on the runway or in a simulator, might just as well have been outside. I still don't know how I ever got my hand pushed forward to activate it, but to make a long

63

story short, I did, and we redesigned the position of the switch so it could be reached in realistic conditions. In conclusion, I don't think much of the ergo designers."

"Well that is a moving story, and I'm glad you survived, but what's ergonomics got to do with engine design? A pilot doesn't sit in an engine, he sits in a crew cabin."

"Right you are. But what about throttle forces and responses. Who knows better what they should be than somebody who has to handle them? They need to be planned and perfected before they go into a crew module." Corci was persuasive.

"You do have a point, and you have technical credentials, but ... Prollett is in Ardena and I doubt if you can speak Ardenese?"

"No, I can't, but that's not an issue, Paramo. I checked and most of those Prollet guys speak Bacamirian." Corci was feeling smug about winning a point. He grinned again, and melted Fraya a little.

"All right, I'll approve the trip. When are you scheduled to go back to the platform?"

"Right after we get back from Prollet, and you and I make love," he replied.

"In your dreams, Corci, now get out of here."

Southbak was the first stop. The team, sans Corci, looked over the Stratopulse proposal then hurried on. Corci was only interested in Prollett's engineering model so skipped the first two legs of the subcontractor survey, planning to join the team in Solport.

Next was the Kirken Group at Whitecliff Villa, Montes. Kirken had very little nuper progress to show Fraya and Karlus, but obviously had spent much time on the radiation blanket . Their results were encouraging and Fraya urged them to keep up with the development work. Before leaving for Prollett, they traveled up onto the mesa, and were rewarded with a peek at the Great Mons. The swirling clouds briefly parted, and gave them a view of the mountain top. When it disappeared again in cloud, she motioned to Karlus indicating it was time to depart.

"We were fortunate, Karlus. I understand people sometimes visit here for many annums without ever seeing that peak. This time, we are among the privileged."

Corci joined the reviewing team at Prollett. The small ionizing thruster was now working and Corci hung over it like a child ogling a new toy. He worked the throttles and vectored the nozzle back and forth, enthused about its operation, and anxious for Prollet to get their large-scale model completed. After the workshift, Corci invited Fraya to join him for social companionship. Not having heard from Rami in quite some time, she felt very alone on this trip, even though she was surrounded by the people from the reviewing team. Finally concluding she could control Corci's advances, she agreed to dine with him. He was more charming than usual, reserved, and didn't display his usual arrogance. Fraya was impressed; she hadn't seen this side of him before, and was actually enjoying his company. When he ordered a very tasty wine, she drank more than she should have, and began to feel vampish. The music beckoned, and she pulled Corci by the arm, leading him out among the swaying couples on the dancing square.

"My, my," he said. "Does the genius-lady like to dance?"

"I might." she said, tilting her head coquettishly, while moving to the rhythm. Her fingers smoothed the hair on one of his temples.

"Really? Well, if you try to lead, I'll know it's just your superior attitude showing up. Actually, your usual superior attitude doesn't bother me. I'm smart enough to keep ahead of you."

She giggled for no particular reason, and snuggled closer. Her voice was slightly slurred and she felt some arousal. "You're just too smart for me." She giggled again, staggered a little and fell against his

65

chest. He had his arms around her, holding her up while they continued to move slightly to the music. The warmth and movement of his body felt good to her, stimulating, tempting, and with a flash of boldness, she reached up and touched his lips with hers.   He smiled at her, and said, "that was nice, but unexpected. Just in case you have any amorous thoughts, Paramo, keep them in your dreams, and I will too. I think the wine is clouding your judgment, but I liked the kiss."

She kissed him again, longer this time, and he responded.

"Come to my room with me, Corci." She staggered again, but he caught her.

"The wine is getting to you, Fraya. Let's go. I'll take you back to your room now."

Fraya awoke from the sleep period with a headache, found herself under the covers clad only in underwear, and couldn't remember how she got there. She called Corci and asked what happened.

"You were wonderful, Paramo. Don't you remember? I think I'm in love with you and want to move into your room immediately and be with you from now on." Corci teased.

"I remember some things, Corci, but I fell asleep. Don't tell me you took advantage of me in that condition?" she asked.

"You don't remember? Well, you can always wonder about it. I can't believe your memory doesn't recall what a great lover I am." Corci was enjoying the tormenting.

"You know, Corci, I like you a bit, but now you're getting annoying. I thought maybe there was some gentleman in you somewhere."

"All right, Paramo, here's the truth. I am a gentleman, and as such I'll never talk about this to anyone. You just keep wondering.

Fraya leaned back against the pillows and relaxed. She pulled a lock of her hair across her face, twiddling, and the scent of Corci's cologne, still lingering in her hair, reached her nostrils. A flash of arousal swept over her body, and she tingled from head to toe. She picked up the communicator, and punched Corci's code, heard it ring once, then twice, but decided against talking to him. She disconnected before he could answer, and wasn't sure why.

28. Rami Meets Clodea

Rami hadn't planned to go to Solport, but Mentorian Zeiss, his boss, had different ideas. He summoned Rami to his lab.

"I know environmental issues are your passion, Rami, but I have a priority assignment for you. We have a contract from Centre to investigate protection of space travelers from infectious antigens, in the event life-forms are found on Terres. We'll call it the "antigen" project, and Rami, you'll work that project for me. Our approach will evolve as we define the goals, but understanding the immune system is a start. Frankly, the immune system is marvelous, but it is not my current area of interest." He held up a vial containing a fuzzy liquid with some dark clusters around the edges and studied it with a swirl. Rami thought he had forgotten what he was saying, but he soon went on.

"I have a different research project right now that has me totally captivated. This undertaking, called horizontal gene transfer, involves genetic changes in offspring of fruit flies without the reproduction process. Genes are transferred by mandible fluids in insect bites. It may eventually tie in with the Centre contract but I don't have adequate time to devote to both. Centre's contract is a good one, and we can milk it for many, many annums before those people ever get ready to send a man to Terres, so I want you to learn all you can about the

67

immune system. I have a colleague in Ardena who is the real expert and we'll send you there to work with her at Centre's expense."

"Why Ardena? Aren't there other experts right here at the Institute?"

"Not as good as Polosek. She's considered the best, and I've heard she's getting some success with a uniquely new approach to broad spectrum vaccine development, stripping viruses of their protein coats, and leaving the core harmless but active. I want you to go there and work with her for awhile."

This was Rami's first trip out of Bacamir. Bacamir was moving through its half-annum of darkness, and the sunlight felt good. With Ardena being a free-market territory, he didn't really know what to expect, but found Solport not much different from his borough back home. Multitudes of pedestrians were meandering about, the streets were crowded, sidewalk vendors hawked their wares, and shopkeepers motioned for customers to come inside. Heavy mocar traffic wound around a mixture of old, rumbling trolleys, and modern transports, and just as in Mizzen, eye-stinging exhaust fumes hung heavy in the atmosphere.

Almost every head had a brimmed cap of some sort, as shade from the piercing tropical sun. Rami had previously met Tribune Polosek when she appeared as a guest mentor at the Institute, but she didn't remember him. He couldn't recall much of her lecture but did remember she was shapely, with a small waist and inviting breasts. When he introduced himself, she promptly invited him to sit and chat, and to call her Clodea.

"We're colleagues now," she said, "not tutor and mentoree."

He explained about the Terres program and Centre's concerns for the health of the crew.

68

"Rami, I understand the concerns your people have about organisms that our immune systems may not be able to handle. There are documented cases of isolated, indigenous groups being decimated by a pox relatively harmless to the majority of us. However don't underestimate the power of the basic immune defenses. They are miraculous. I've studied them for annums and am more amazed all the time." She glanced at a schedule on her desk, and looked back up at Rami.

"Why don't you get settled in your hostel, and acclimated, and come back next arc. I'll show you my experiments, and get you started on some research of your own."

Rami agreed, left Clodea's laboratories and found his way back to his hostel. With the time difference between Mizzen and Solport, and tropical heat that was new to him, he did not sleep well. when he awoke enough to move about, he found his way to Polosek's labs and joined her in her office. She sat across from him, crossed her legs as she talked, and displayed a shapely knee.

"Rami, our bodies have two basic types of immunity, natural and acquired. The natural immunity constantly wards off millions of common intruders with chemicals in the skin and mucous membranes, and it does an outstanding job. It's the acquired immunity, however, that keeps me in awe. Acquired immunity is the body's ability to recognize a specific intruder, such as a virus, and attack it with an antibody. If the intruder is new and unrecognized, and there are no existing antibodies, it makes a new one. The new antibody starts reproducing and in time usually overcomes the intruders."

"How do the antibodies ever gain control over the intruders?" Rami asked.

"Astute question. They don't always win, you know, and the host dies. It seems to be a matter of kinetics. If the antibody output is slower than the viral reproduction, the patient can die, or set off an epidemic."

Clodea ran her eyes over Rami's body while she talked.

"Were you an athlete?" she asked. "You have quite a build. I would more expect to see you on a kick-ball field than in a laboratory." She got up, moved closer to him, and squeezed the muscles in an arm.

"I do both," Rami replied. He felt his pulse quicken a bit by her closeness. "Mentorian Zeiss said you'd be easy to work with, but I had no idea he was referring to your physique", she purred.

"I'm sure he wasn't. He said you were working on a new technique which might eventually make a safer, more effective general vaccine."

"Actually we are working on several different approaches, and we'll go over them thoroughly in our next few sessions. Zeiss was probably referring to my naked DNA, in which I'm using an enzyme to strip the protein coating off viruses and render them harmless. I'm finding that when a naked DNA is injected into a host mammal, antibodies start being produced just as if the virus was still whole and virulent. Come on with me and I'll show you some of the results."

She led him to a room with bubbling beakers and flasks, and cages of rodents along one wall. Laboratory assistants were bustling about. Pointing to various cages, she explained the technique of antibody production and her hopes the same process would work in humans. Next she led him to another laboratory where they were alone. She walked over closer to him and let her hand gently brush across the front of his groin, touching, then her hand hesitated.

"You have quite a body, are you committed to a pledgemate?"

Taken a bit by surprise, he could only stammer, "no."

She touched again, lightly squeezing, and Rami felt an immediate stiffening, physical response.

70

"That's nice," Clodea said, detecting his hardness. "What say I show you some of my reproductive experiments and we take a semen sample."

Usually the aggressor in sexual encounters, he felt awkward. He gently moved her hand away and backed up a little.

"I didn't know you were involved in reproductive experiments."

"I am, and I think you are a marvelous specimen," she said.

"I'm flattered, and would love to see some of your experiments, but I'll bet you already have plenty of samples."

"One more wouldn't hurt. It's a shame to waste that big response you have there," she said, and squeezed again.

Rami was weakening; his willpower was being strained. "We're not being very professional here. Maybe I'd better go now," he mumbled, forgetting the subject they were talking about.

"Very well. Let me know if I can be of any more help....any kind of help."

"I will." Rami thanked her for the information, started to leave, then turned.

"Are you really collecting semen samples?"

"Yes I am, and freezing them for future experiments."

"Interesting," he said, then left mulling over this woman's strange behavior.

Rami purpose in coming to Solport was to see Tribune Clodea Polosek, but he wanted to talk to Fraya. When he tried to contact her at Centre, he learned she was also in Solport on business. He immediately connected her on her communicator.

"Fraya, I'm here in Solport, and I want to see you."

"Well; surprise! Have you missed me?"

"Of course."

He learned where she was staying and wasted no time in finding her.

"We have so much to talk about, but first ... " He pulled her toward her bed. She resisted.

"Wait Rami. I have to go meet with the contractor, but I won't be gone long. Why don't you stay here and relax for awhile. We can talk when I get back."

"All right," he said as he put his arms around her again. "I'll be waiting."

Fraya was thrilled at seeing Rami; she had been lonesome without him, but realized she was also enjoying Corci's flirtations and attention. When she returned, he tried to tell her how he had missed her, and although usually glib, found himself fumbling for words. Then he kissed her, but the response was not enthusiastic.

"Fraya, is something the matter?"

"Well, not really, but I am feeling a bit abandoned. I haven't seen you in a long time. To tell the truth, I went dancing with Corci and had a great time. I really enjoyed his company."

"Fraya, I'm feeling a bit jealous."

"Oh, really. You leave for long periods of time without ever contacting me, then drop in and expect me to jump into bed. I don't understand you, Rami."

"I realize I've been self-centered, not expressing an emotional commitment on my part, but I think from the start of our relationship I've always considered you as mine."

"Yours!" Her voice got louder and higher pitched. "I'll let you know when you can consider me as yours, and don't expect it to be soon."

"I'm sorry, Fraya. How about if we start all over again. I'll go out the door and come back later."

"All right, but give me enough time to shower and cool off."

When he came back in she put her arms around his neck, and mumbled something about missing him, and being sorry for the emotional outburst. She didn't understand his reply as he murmured through her smothering kiss, but his body told her his feelings for her were as strong as ever. They wiggled out of their garments, and sunk to the floor. Finally Fraya whispered, "I'm so glad you're here Rami."

Rami, exhausted and breathless gasped, "so am I."

29. The Contractor

Rami temporarily moved into Fraya's hostel with her while she was working with the Prollett project. She was much happier having Rami so close, working right here in Solport, and this time, when she invited him, he accepted her invitation to share her hostel with no thoughts of retreating or running away.

He was intimidated by Clodea, fearing she would continue to make advances, but he introduced her to Corci, who immediately took up with her. After that, Rami and Clodea continued work on a professional level.

There was still much for the Centre team to do, reviewing the nuper design and looking in on the construction of the engineering model. After each work-period, as before, many of the Centre people joined Prollet's group for dining and socializing. Fraya took Rami along to the next social so he could meet more of the nuper scienomies. He was surprised at the informality of the Ardenians. Most used first names to address each other rather than the more formal title of Presario used in Bacamir. He was also surprised at the large number of people who could converse in both Bacamirian and Ardenese.

Fraya explained that Bacamirian was becoming a multinational second language now that Bacamir was dominant in space exploration.

Rami was deeply concerned about a multinational lack of interest in the consequences of booming technology, and had made a personal study of the subtle changes in weather patterns. He was bored by the constant technical talk of the nuper, and when a lull in the conversation occurred, interjected some of his thoughts on the changing environment. Arin looked up and appeared to show some interest in what Rami had to say, so Rami spoke of the increasing green-house gases and resulting planet warming. Arin encouraged him to continue. Fraya knew Rami had strong opinions about environmental issues but had never heard him talk about potential solutions. She turned away from the others to listen to Rami.

"The symptoms are here," Rami said. "Unpolluted fresh water is getting scarce. Glaciers are melting at an alarming rate. We have gradual changes in ocean currents and the weather is changing because of them."

"How do you know we have changing ocean currents? Arin asked.

"I've read of it," Rami replied, "and they're being measured and recorded."

"Most of us take such things as ocean currents for granted," Arin said. "Just what causes these currents and why are they changing."

"I don't have all the answers, but I think of it this way. There are no gravity gradients, or hills for water to flow down in the oceans, so water movement is caused by density gradients. Densities are varied through thermal differences, or salinity concentrations. The salinity is increased in the sunny, warm areas by evaporation. Normally, the heavier brines sink, and push undercurrents northward.

74

But flooding rains are diluting the salt water, breaking the density cycle, so the driving force for the currents is weakening. How do we know this? Besides measuring; observation. Shellfish are disappearing, and those remaining are being found more northward. Tropical fishes are being seen farther north. All caused by planet-warming."

"Planet warming is chasing fish northward? That's incredulous."

"No, changing ocean currents are. And the changing currents result from changing weather patterns, caused by planet warming. We've got to stop this man-made heating cycle to survive. It can be done by controlling the output of greenhouse gases, but we'd have to get multinational cooperation in limiting atmospheric pollutants to do this."

Arin shrugged bulky shoulders. "That's an admirable goal, Rami, trying to limit pollutants, but an impossible task."

Rami was disappointed in the cynicism of Arin's answer. "Then we are eventually doomed. Life as we know it will not survive the diminishing resources of a greenhouse planet, and the proliferation of life on Baeta will come to an end."

Arin shrugged again. "That's a pretty harsh prediction, Rami. Is there no alternative?" Fraya could not tell whether Arin was serious or amused by Rami's prophecy.

Rami blurted impulsively. "The only other salvation for our species is to migrate to Terres, and colonize. Then, if this planet is left alone for a long enough time, it might eventually restore itself to normal equilibrium, and the emigrants or their descendants could return." He hadn't consciously thought of moving masses of people to Terres, but the direction of the conversation led to this alternative and it just came out, as his own opinion.

"I'm afraid I don't share your pessimism Rami, and the idea of moving masses of people to a different planet is technically and economically unfeasible. One might even go as far as saying it is absurd. But the prospect of a colony is stirring my imagination. What do you suppose a colony on Terres might find of value for me?"

Rami thought for awhile before answering. "I don't understand your question. The purpose of a colony would be to survive and multiply on Terres, not bring something back here. This planet will be lifeless.

Fraya felt obliged to intervene on Rami's behalf. "We have no idea what might be found. I guess it will be like our planet before life blossomed."

"But," Arin countered, "suppose we could fly back and forth and bring a payload each time? Do you suppose mineral deposits are similar?" he asked. The thought of a colony for profit was obviously stimulating Arin's appetite for a new business.

"We have no idea," Rami said. "Terres is a planet that hasn't been tapped and may be like Baeta in geology. We'll know more when Settler-Two lands and sends back some surface images and samples,"

"We'll definitely know in a few annums," Fraya added, "when space-pilots land there. That manned voyage is counting on a nuper engine from one of you three contractors, you know."

Arin smiled. "We'll make our engine work, and we expect to make it financially rewarding. Prollet is just one of my many investments, and I don't very often invest without getting a profit. If it doesn't make me any profits, I'll lose my interest in it very fast."

"That's certainly to the point," she replied. "The Prollet Group stands to make profits by superior performance of its engine, developed by your dedicated engineers and scienomies. I think your specialists here have a vast expertise, a fascination for this space thing, as you put it, and want to be a part of it."

"My dear naive lady. I bought this technology. I bought the designers and the talent. People are just commodities available on the market, to the highest bidder. This nuper project is a big financial gamble, and I took a chance on buying the right people. Now it had better pay off or I'll have to return these people-commodities back onto the market to fend for themselves. To be competitive, we've already replaced some of the older people with younger ones for a cheaper price. Experience is very valuable, of course, but many older people don't really have many annums of experience like they claim, they just have a few annums of experience, repeated over and over. They are dedicated, all right, dedicated to the concept they are somehow irreplaceable."

Fraya wanted to argue but maintained her composure. Subconsciously, she knew some of the things he said were true about older professionals not contributing anything new. Certainly some of the scienomies at Centre were the same way; tenure kept them in their jobs. She wondered about working in the Ardenese free market system, compared to the collectivist system, and which might be more challenging to her. Salaries paid by the Bacamirian government were not very rewarding, but the technical aspect of her work at the Centre was everything she had hoped for, and she had been given awesome responsibilities. Her thoughts were interrupted by Arin.

"You are originally from Ardena, aren't you. How did you end up working for the government in Bacamir?"

Fraya explained her interest in rocketry and stellar science, and her goal to work for the Celestial Research Centre because they were the leaders in space exploration.

"It appears the technology of propulsion is fortunate to have gotten you. Our intelligence people learned that your position and influence are partly responsible for Centre's decision to fund development of the nuclear propulsion engine. Our directors here anticipated that decision, and we poured a lot of our own funds into the nuper. We hope to recoup it, of course."

Fraya was innocently surprised to hear the word intelligence; that he had early knowledge of the nuper development, and apparently some background information about her. The thought startled her a little. Intelligence, she knew, was a fancy word for spying and it meant he must have contacts within Centre. An image impulsively flashed through her mind wondering "who," and if she knew any of the contacts. That thought frightened her even more.

"I have no control over contract terms," Fraya replied. "My staff and I will do the technical evaluations, and contracts people will decide who is the most appropriate supplier based on performance, competitive price, and viability."

"My dear." Fraya was getting annoyed at his calling her my dear. "You, as technical evaluator wouldn't want to ride on a launcher built by the lowest bidder, would you?" Fraya drifted with a fleeting thought about riding in a space craft.

"Going into space is a fantasy of most children, and as a child I was no exception. I would leap at the chance for a space flight, and, you're right, I wouldn't approve a design I didn't have complete confidence in, regardless of how inexpensive it might appear."

"Good. Now then, my dear, instead of being a consultant which you seem to think is unethical, how would you like to leave Centre and come to work for Prollet, full time, on our nuper project. You could share top responsibility with our chief scienomie. What ever your salary is now, we'll increase it. In addition, we'll furnish you a moc, and a hospice. I have been in your Centre labs and offices, and I know they are very austere. Here, your working conditions would be much more comfortable."

"And just how might I add to the progress and profits of Prollet?" she asked.

"You would have a very responsible position on the engine project, and with your connections, and genius for propulsion, could make us the certain winner of the contract," Arin replied.

"And after the contract was awarded, what would I do?" she probed. "Well, we would find something for you, I'm sure."

"But just a short time ago you said the commodity is flung back onto the market when you are through with it. I'm a commodity, and that doesn't sound like a very challenging or secure future to me," Fraya countered.

Arin was unruffled by her reply. "Security? There is no certain security anywhere in life, unless," he philosophized, "you are a slave or an indigent on subsistence." Then he returned to the point. "As an alternative, think again about being a consultant. You could receive an equitable fee, and show up here periodically, at your discretion."

"I may appear very young and naive, but we both know you are trying to influence a contract decision. Such an arrangement will not work for several reasons. First, it would be a conflict of interest and I would have to quit the Terres project, which I'm not about to do. Second, Centre doesn't allow us to consult for a fee while employed by the government, and third, I don't like your ethics."

Karlus chuckled at her reply, and Rami listened with interest. As a biologist at the Institute, he had never dealt with a marketeer or contractor, and this interaction was new to him. He had very little knowledge of how a design concept evolved into a manufacturing project.

Arin hardly changed his expression. "Again I must apologize for what seemed like a breach of ethics, my dear. Of course such an action is out of the question. Forget my suggestion about becoming a consultant. I can readily see your standards for professional conduct would be in conflict with such an arrangement. We have a performing arts theater new to the borough. Let my chauffeur escort you and Rami there, for some entertainment at my expense, as a token of my appreciation for the fine work you are doing. I would be honored to have you two go as my guests."

Fraya again recognized Arin was slyly attempting to put her in a position of obligation. Expensive entertainment was not in the realm of reasonable subcontractor hospitality, but theater tickets seemed innocuous.

"Really! That's very generous of you. That is an offer I will accept."

With that, she turned to Rami. "Are you in agreement with some entertainment?" Rami's ears were ringing from technical talk and he was more than ready for a diversion.

"Let's go," he said.

30. Arin's Proposal

Next arc, after Fraya departed for work and Rami was about to leave for Polosek's lab, he received a call from one of Arin's staff members. The caller said Presario Restor was interested in learning more about greenhouse gases, and asked if Rami would be willing to meet briefly with him. Rami responded affirmatively, and a chauffeur picked him up at the hostel. The meeting, carried out in Arin's office, was politely conversational. Arin began.

"I want you to know I respect your ideas of controlling atmospheric pollutants, and want to help. With your concurrence, I'll send a letter to your Minister of Industry and Commerce, and suggest we mutually initiate some action concerning industrial pollutants. If he agrees, it'll be a start, and that may spur other territorial governments to become involved. You understand we can't be shutting down factories, don't you? That would stop production of consumer products, including chemical fertilizers and herbicides. The result would put millions out of work, with planet-scale starvation and total chaos."

Rami was well-versed on the chemistry of pollutants. The environment had been his alternate technical passion since graduation, and he felt he could discuss most aspects of the subject with Arin.

"I understand factories can't be indiscriminately shut down, but the majority of the heat entrapment is caused by just a few major gases, and efforts should be made to control the outputs of those gases, or find alternatives."

"You're very passionate about this subject, I can see. Like what gases?" asked Arin.

"The major offender is petron-dioxide. It's a fact that the level in the stratosphere remained relatively constant for thousands of annums. We know this, because gases trapped in ancient glacial ice are being sampled and analyzed. The level of petron-dioxide in the atmosphere is suddenly going up, very rapidly, and just in our lifetime."

"All right, where is it all coming from?"

"The excess is coming from burning fossil fuels; from carriage motors, factory exhaust stacks, and the like. The cycle is getting out of balance."

"Interesting," Arin mused. "Tell me about the cycle."

"As a biologist, I can tell you petron-dioxide is produced naturally from decaying vegetation, fires, and from volcanoes, and is consumed by forests in the photosynthesis process, scrubbed by rain, and absorbed by the oceans. Nature has maintained a balance. Now, the forests are going away, falling to developers, and we are overwhelming the cycle by burning fossil fuels."

"What can we do?" Arin asked.

Rami had one answer. "The common propellant in an aerosol spray is a bi-halo-petron, a strong greenhouse gas, and thousands of kilodrums are pumped into the atmosphere every arc. They aren't absorbed, and don't break down. Let's consider an alternative to those propellants, for a start, just to get everyone's attention."

"Well," Arin replied, "I have one chemical factory producing nothing but bi-halo-petrons for aerosol sprays. It employs three hundred people. Should I shut that down, and throw those people out of work?"

"A chemist friend of mine told me that a light-weight tri-hydro-petron will act just as well as bi-halo-petron for a propellant, and it's non-polluting. Why don't you have your factory change from manufacturing bi-halos to tri-petrane. It could be made from petrifoss." Rami thought he sounded convincing at the moment. "That would be a start."

"We might be able to do that," Arin replied. " I'll have a committee look into it and try to correspond with your ministers about a mutual effort."

Rami felt very pleased thinking that somehow, five thousand kiloquants from home, an inroad had been made to start the reduction of stratospheric pollutants. He didn't realize Arin really invited him here to discuss an entirely different subject.

"Rami, I am intrigued by your idea of a colony on Terres. Apparently you have given this survival of the species augury a lot of thought."

Rami had often thought about greenhouse-gas consequences, but always assumed the solution lay in controlling the atmosphere by limiting the output of greenhouse gasses, not abandoning the planet. The idea of moving colonies of people to Terres was spontaneous - something he impulsively blurted only as meal-time conversation. He decided to play along to see what Arin had in mind.

"Yes, Presario Restor, if we fail in our efforts to stem the buildup of greenhouse gases, the warming trend will continue heating the atmosphere, and the surface, and our species may not be able to survive the consequences.

Arin leaned forward. "Call me Arin. Do you really think a little heat is a serious problem, and not just a swing in a natural cycle?"

"Yes I do." Rami was emphatic. "The most serious problem will be loss of fresh, potable water. Then water will become scarce for irrigation. Battles will follow for diverted river water, even if it's polluted. If we continue to indiscriminately pump overdoses of petron-dioxide into our atmosphere, the scenario will get ugly.

"Go on. How so?"

"Climate change. Rising temperatures will cause alternating flooding, and then drought. Once fresh water becomes scarce, and it will, competition for water will turn us into barbarians.

"The idea of sending a colony to another planet won't help us, but it is a way to preserve our species until this planet can return to normal conditions. It's a very serious problem," Rami replied.

"I'm afraid I'm more optimistic than you are about the ability of our planet to counter anything we pitiful little creatures can throw at it. However, I am interested in one of your ideas. I'd like to pursue the possibility of a manned trip to Terres to look for minerals and gems." He paused, looking for a reaction from Rami, who was astonished. "Even worthless rocks, or a grain of sand, auctioned off here would bring in a fortune from collectors."

"What?" Rami, surprised by Arin's proposal, was groping for words. "Are you talking about a manned, round trip expedition? Competing with Centre? You know of course that Centre has a plan for an eventual manned landing."

"Of course, and Prollet's engine will be involved on that project. I'm thinking of a separate, commercial venture, using existing hardware and systems that are available on the market. I would like you to privately discuss this with your lady-friend. No other ears are to hear it. She is a genius in her field, and has the contacts for all the right specialists that would be involved. If the concept is possible, see what sort of plan you would devise, just as if you were the project managers, for a series of expeditions. Then, lets have an informal meeting, just the three of us, to see if it's even feasible."

Rami went on to his work at Polosek's labs, but he could hardly concentrate. He went back to the Fraya's hostel, where he flopped on the bed, stared up at the ceiling and tried to digest what he had just heard from Arin. His mind danced with illusions of a trip to Terres, and his mood was euphoric. Up to this point, all space flights were done by competitive, highly trained space-pilots, and a commoner could never think of breaking into that clique. A colony, however, could include a variety of non-pilot specialists from many different fields. He could hardly wait for Fraya, to hear her enthusiastic response.

When she returned, he told her about Arin's proposal, and flinched at her outburst.

"He can't be serious! The idea is ludicrous." Fraya leaned back on the bed, resting on her elbows.

84

"Centre has spent many annums and millions already, planning and working toward an eventual manned landing. The engineering and testing alone will take many more annums. Then there's the training and more testing, followed by actual construction of the flight hardware. It will take time, and thousands of people working to get it done."

"Well," Rami replied, slightly vanquished, not expecting such negativity, "he only wanted to discuss it. He did say that the project would use his nuper in off-the-shelf available designs and equipment, and he is a successful capitalist, not prone to high risk investments."

"And you think he was serious?" she asked. "The costs would be celestranomical."

"He only wants to talk about it, to see if it's possible. Couldn't we spend a little time making a rough idea of the feasibility?" Rami was hoping she would agree. He had never been involved in such a planning session and thought the experience would be educational, even if nothing ever materialized.

Fraya briefly thought Arin might be finessing again, manipulating to sway her into a consulting agreement. She couldn't help but be intrigued that anyone would consider a commercial venture to another planet. "Did he say what kind of venture he had in mind?" she asked.

"He said he was primarily interested in discussing the subject, and to find out what might be involved in putting together such a project. His motive is profit, even to bringing back worthless rocks for a start, which he says will sell for millions. He knows you have the knowledge and contacts to make it possible, and he thinks I have the colonizing concept all thought out."

Rami was getting more enthused as he talked.

"Planning an interplanetary journey, putting together all the equipment, and maybe personally going along is an exciting thought.

85

The very idea of traveling in space is probably a desire in most everyone, and admit it, you're no exception." As he talked, he couldn't hide his excitement. "Just think ... if we became managers of the project, we could assign ourselves as part of the crew and make the trip," he said. "How does that sound to you?"

She pushed her hair back from her face. "Like a fantasy. Like someone should appear and wave a magic wand over your head and bring you back to reality."

"Is it even feasible? I mean, with off-the-shelf equipment?"

"Rami, I don't think any individual could accomplish such a feat."

"But you're tempted, right?"

"Of course I am. I'm just being practical and realistic, and I don't want my Centre position threatened. You do understand, don't you?"

"Yes, I understand, but it's certainly easy to get enthused about such an idea."

Fraya's long-held interest in working on space projects never seriously included traveling in space. She had to admit the idea was alluring.

"Well, to get real for a moment, the problems are overwhelming but not insurmountable. If it would satisfy your curiosity, lets set up an appointment with the old windbag to see what he has in mind."

"Oh, one other thing, he doesn't want anyone else to know about this."

"Not even Karlus? He handles all my files and is my confidant."

"He never mentioned specific names, but was pretty emphatic when he said no one is to hear about, or learn of this idea."

Fraya arranged a private meeting with Arin at the end of the next work period, coinciding with a time Rami could get away from

Polosek and join them. They huddled around Arin's desk in his ornate office.

"Before I say anything about my plans," Arin began, "I would like your word that whatever we discuss will remain confidential between us three. That means no discussion with your friends, co-workers, management or even your pets if you have any."

"Why the secrecy?" Rami asked.

"Competitive advantage," he replied. "All I want is your word. You really have nothing to fear, and a verbal agreement doesn't obligate you to anything except keeping this discussion to yourselves. Furthermore, I couldn't enforce the agreement anyway...it is strictly honorary."

Rami and Fraya conferred quietly with each other, and finally decided they had nothing to risk, so agreed to Arin's terms.

"Very well, then. I'm interested in funding a commercial, manned, round trip expedition to Terres. From my cursory research, I know the costs would be enormous and I'd undertake such a project only if there was high probability of achievement. If this project is to be financially prosperous, then my crew must be the first to make a manned landing on Terres. I repeat - the <u>First.</u> Tremendous profits and prestige will be there for the first to land and return. Centre would have no inkling there is competition, and that, my friends, will be my main advantage."

"Centre's doing this for science, not profit," Fraya ventured.

Arin snorted. "Centre needs funding to keep operating, and your government doesn't have an unlimited supply of funds just to keep Centre functional," he explained. "It may surprise you, but Centre is concerned about profit...getting some return for their consortium investors, usually in proprietary rights to new technology. There has to be some economic return, or the agency wouldn't last very long. The commercial satellites they launch and monitor are for profit."

Fraya briefly pondered Arin's example, mulling the idea that Centre had some economic motives. It was not something she had considered before, but sounded reasonable the way he explained it.

"Then you really are serious about this project?" Fraya asked.

"Let me put it in perspective. I start new ventures quite often, and build consumer products to make a profit. Some ventures work out, and some don't, but all take a lot of analysis and planning before the investment is made. The concept of a Terres trip excites me like nothing ever has before, not only from a profit angle, but for the challenge of a great accomplishment. I don't know what the technical risks will be, and that's why I need you two. To pursue this venture I'd need both of you on my team to manage it." He paused and waited for an answer.

Fraya wiggled uneasily in her chair, absorbed in the enormity of Arin's proposal. "I'm sure you realize Centre has been planning this for annums," she finally muttered. "They'd have a huge head start over your project. Even with all the experience they have in manned flight, there are still many annums of design, test, and construction needed before a manned trip to Terres can be accomplished. What makes you think you could compete with them?"

"By having you on my team, using their experience, and using off-the-shelf equipment. I've heard estimates that Centre will take from six to ten annums, but I don't really care. I've built dams, bridges, rail systems, and huge buildings so I have a pretty good idea of how to work a project. Whatever the time-table is for Centre, our crew would have to beat it."

"What further do you want from us?" Rami asked.

"I want you to think about the possibility of being a part of this venture as managers of the project. Without you two I wouldn't even know what technical specialists to hire, so if you choose not to be a part of this, the concept dies in secrecy and the project doesn't even start. Make an outline of what the project might look like so we can all think about it, and get back to me when you can ... the sooner the better. Meanwhile, we all have separate and individual responsibilities. You have your current jobs which occupy a good share of your thoughts, and I ... I mean Prollet, has a nuper engine to build for Centre."

Recognizing Arin had his reasons for secrecy, Rami and Fraya said they understood, agreed to be discreet, and went back to her office. Both of them sat in deep thought, digesting what they heard, and without saying as much, a little excited about the possibility of being a part of such a venture.

"I have no more idea than Arin on how this could be accomplished, but if you'll begin educating me I'll make notes as you talk; and this time I'll really pay attention." Rami got out a notepad and began writing. The project, they conjectured, could be divided into categories. Phase one, the first and simplest approach, could be a short round trip with a small crew, able to quickly gather enough rocks and artifacts to pay for the trip and make Restor a profit. They continued planning and making notes until quite late.

"That's enough for starters," she finally said. "Next arc, let's corner Arin and give him our ideas."

Karlus poked his head into her office. "You two are working pretty late. Is their anything I can do to help before I leave?"

"No Karlus, thank you. I appreciate your offer, but Rami and I are just going over some personal plans for the two of us. See you next arc."

Karlus grinned, nodded, and disappeared. Fraya closed some files and they left.

31. The Intrusion

By the end of the next work period, Rami found it hard it to concentrate on anything but the venture. He didn't accomplish much with Tribune Polosek and hurried off to be with Fraya. In her hostel, he was looking out a window, watching the crowds of mocs and pedestrians in the street below, and she was changing out of her work clothes.

"I'm overwhelmed," he said. "This has such exciting possibilities. Do you know of any specialists who might be interested in joining this project?"

"I know of some. If we decided to accept, the question is how and when would I actually contact them. I guess that part of it can wait until the nuper design is complete and the contract is awarded."

Tired of watching the activities in the street below them, Rami began wandering around the room. He usually watched Fraya getting dressed. He loved the way she gracefully moved about, coyly, in scant underwear, pretending he wasn't watching. This time his mind was elsewhere, and he began looking blankly at pictures on the walls, not looking for anything in particular. A thin wire showing at the edge of one picture caught his attention and he signaled Fraya, while holding a finger to his lips, to come closer for a look. They quietly raised the picture and found a small minitran taped to the back of it. He went over to the transcom and unscrewed the cap from the mouthpiece. A device had been planted in the instrument. A cold fear came over them both as they realized that everything they had discussed in the room or over the com-instrument was being monitored by someone. Who and why?

"I'm hungry," Fraya feigned and signaled to Rami. "Let's go out for something to eat."

Rami mumbled agreement, and they left the hostel. Once outside, Rami slapped his leg, cursed, and said they had been duped. "Arin is monitoring us. If we had laid out the complete program, he'd know all about it and have no need for us. He'd hire his own managers and crew, and we'd be out."

Fraya was pensive. "I'm not sure that's the case. Since we first talked about the adventure when you came back from Arin's office, we haven't had time to discuss enough details to do him any good. Also, he doesn't have any space experts here in Ardena ... most have gravitated toward Bacamir, like I did. Of course there's a lot of excellent technical talent in this territory, but not enough to put together a manned space journey in a reasonable time."

They shuffled along the street, rather aimlessly. Finally Fraya broke the silence. "If the minitrans were planted by Arin, the object must have been to see if we're honoring our secrecy agreement. The only thing he may have learned so far, if the room was bugged at the time, is that I think he's a windbag, and he knows that already."

Rami nodded. "You're probably right, but we may be looking for any excuse to believe he's sincere, like two eager children. He may just be checking our fidelity and enthusiasm for the project. Let's confront him, and not discuss it anymore in our hostel until we do."

"Good idea," Fraya replied. "Suspicion and mistrust are not a way to start, in case we were to go along with this project."

Rami and Fraya met with Arin in his office the following arc. "Before we tell you anything technical regarding your project, we have a question." Fraya had an icy tone in her voice as she told him about their findings and asked him what he hoped to learn.

Arin was expressionless. "Are you sure these were listening devices you found?"

"No mistake," Rami replied. "Of course I don't have a trained eye, but the minitran behind the picture has a small wire antenna attached to it. The bug in the transcom was obvious once the mouthpiece was removed."

"I didn't bug your room." Arin still didn't change his expression. "I'm not above bugging for information if the need arises, either for security or for a competitive edge, but in this case, I can assure you there was no point in my monitoring your hostel. So, who did, and why? Let's try to figure this out. I'm really concerned. Fraya, how many other agencies on this planet might want to pick your brains, and why?"

Rami and Fraya were so sure the devices were placed by Arin's security people they hadn't even considered any other possibility. "I don't know." She paused, thinking. "I'm not involved with any weapons development. Rebel factions throughout the planet already have the thermal holocaust weapons. Propulsion systems are available commercially. Only super guidance systems are still secret and may be sought after, because they could be used in offensive orbiting weapons ... but we never discuss those when we're out of secure areas."

"Rami, how about you?" Arin asked.

"I'm still in shock by your statement that you're not responsible for the bugs, and I can't think of any knowledge I have at this time that would be of interest to anyone. Why, I can't even convince others to get concerned about planet-warming."

"It wasn't me," repeated Arin. "If you join my team, we'll have no secrets from each other, and I'll be in on every aspect of the project anyway. In fact, I'll want to approve every phase before I release financing."

Arin locked his fingers behind his head, and continued, thinking out loud. "Short range missiles and their clumsy guidance systems are available on the open market.... common knowledge. You're knowledgeable about the bigger systems, Fraya, big boosters with sophisticated guidance for orbit and re-entry. Perhaps some territory or group is interested in what you know about long range rockets, or guidance." He buzzed his receptionist. "Get the head of security up here right away, please," Arin commanded.

Rami and Fraya were at a loss to understand what was happening, and were very frightened by this unanticipated event. The group manager for security entered Arin's chamber with two assistants, and Arin told them of the bugs that were found. The security manager said he would like to see the devices to be sure, but most likely they were planted by agents from the government of Bacamir.

"Our own government?" Rami was bewildered.

"Your government is notorious for checking on its citizens, especially those in responsible positions. My first guess would be Fraya is being monitored by your own agency to check on her loyalty. Any time anyone visits a capitalist territory on business, they worry about that person accepting bribes or selling information. We even get inquiries from your agents from time to time to buy information for your government. Sometimes we swap information. The game is multinational and played quite often between opposing security agencies." Rami and Fraya were in shock.

"We are so ignorant of these things," Fraya said. "Technical people don't think much about such activities."

"Max and Hunter," the security manager ordered the two agents, " I would like you two to check on the devices and see if you can identify them." The two got up to leave.

"Will you need a key?" Fraya asked.

With a snort, one of the agents tossed his head without answering, and they both left.

"If you discussed the commercial venture, or leaving your government and joining our organization after the bugs were planted, our competitive edge through secrecy is gone," Arin said. "Not only that, but you are probably in danger of losing your position or maybe even going to prison. We had better have our agents do some quick investigating to find out whatever they can before you return to Bacamir. You have an asylum here if you need it."

Fraya was gripped with fear. The idea of her privacy being invaded, and being monitored, suddenly made her feel violated and unclean. Reprisal wasn't something she anticipated in the event she ever changed employers. She tried to remember if she had said anything damaging or compromising about split loyalties between the Centre and the commercial project? She couldn't remember for sure, but they hadn't had time for much of anything. They had talked about the complexities of a commercial venture, but she didn't think she said anything about resigning or actually joining the commercial group.

"Last arc, when Rami told me about your proposal, we discussed it a little. We hardly said anything technical ... only how ridiculous your proposal sounded."

"What actually did you talk about just before you discovered the wire?" Arin, generally expressionless, raised his eyebrows.

"Very little," Rami replied. "I remember asking Fraya if she knew any individuals who might be interested in the project, but didn't say for what."

"I'll have security try to find out what they know. We don't know how long the bugs have been there, or whether your office is bugged. If the office is monitored, you are definitely in trouble."

Rami and Fraya left Arin's office in disbelief. "I've never been in real trouble before, Rami, what should we do?"

"What can we do? If the office was monitored by our government, we are definitely stuck here. If your hostel was bugged before we talked about the venture, they'll construe our plans to switch loyalties as treasonous. If the office wasn't bugged, we do business as usual, I guess. You'll continue with your nuper review as professionally as you can, and I'll go back to my studies with Polosek. We'll see what happens after that."

"Are we treasonous, Rami?"

"I don't think so, but I'm biased. We're not acting to overthrow the government, we are not giving away information, and we haven't agreed to support Arin. I suppose one might say you are betraying a loyalty to Centre."

"Me? But I never contracted to stay in Centre forever."

"I know, but the Government may think you owe them an allegiance. I'm just guessing ... thinking out loud. Let's see what Arin's security comes up with."

They slept fitfully. When they awoke they made trite conversation about how well the nuper project was going at Prollett, and that Fraya still had two other marketeers to visit and evaluate. Rami talked about his newest interest, genetics, and Polosek's vaccine experiments. He complained some about the causes of planet-warming and the fact that no one will listen to him. He also mentioned that Arin Restor planned to send a letter to one of the Bacamirian ministers, and might convert a factory producing bi-halo-petrons to making tri-petrane.

When they next met with Arin, he told them security found no listening devices in the office she used at Prollet, much to their relief, and that his security was still checking to find out where the bugs came from. A cursory report from Arin's contact within the Bacamirian government indicated they had no disparaging information in Fraya's file. With that news in mind, they proceeded with their normal activities under somewhat fewer anxieties.

Rami completed some tests with Polosek, then left Fraya and returned to Mizzen. Fraya had to finish the nuper review at Prollet, so she and her crew spent the next few arcs watching tests on the modified propulsion engine model. They also observed the assembly of the full-scale engineering model taking place in the remote facility. The full-scale nuper engine would be ungainly and too heavy to fly but would prove the concept of nuper thrust on a large scale. A separate, three sided gantry-structure, about a kiloquant from the main factory, had been built to serve as the housing for the test facility. When completed, the engine would be tethered in the vertical position, and exhaust the thrust gases out the open side of the gantry during the tests. The remote location was necessary for safety, in case the engine ruptured, or overheated and melted. The live reactor core, housed in a lead-lined closet, was ready for installation into the engine when power-up time arrived.

None of Fraya's colleagues appeared to act differently, leading her to believe none were involved in the wiretap. As usual she relied heavily on Karlus, her assistant, who frequently bustled in and out of her office, being helpful. He seemed especially concerned and considerate, asking her at one point if she was feeling all right. She replied that she was just tired, and then, in spite of her anxieties about the invasion of privacy, made an effort to act as normally as she could.

She left the bugs in her room intact, and called no one except her family during the remainder of her stay.

Fraya was anxious to leave Solport, and the unknown covert activities that were going on. When she arrived back in Mizzen, there was no question Rami was glad to see her. It was comforting to be back in her own hostel in Rami's arms, and their lovemaking was more an emotional catharsis than an act of intimacy. Settler-Two was two-thirds of the way to Terres and she anticipated her involvement with the intercept and landing would keep her mind so occupied she wouldn't be able to dwell on the invasion of her quarters in Solport. Rami told her he had already gone over the rooms in detail looking for planted devices, but didn't find any. He was no expert, but none were obvious to his untrained eye. Just in case, they agreed to never mention the commercial venture in their hostel or their mocs, just to be safe.

Fraya returned to her work at the Centre with apprehension, but everything seemed normal. She reported on the reviews and Prollet nuper tests to Tribune Khanwali, and for the next several arcs participated in the steering committee meetings, as she usually did. The council authorized funds for functional testing of the Prollet engine, and gave her a go-ahead for another review.

She couldn't help feeling insecure and uneasy in her surroundings at Centre. After all, she still didn't know who monitored her or why, or whether it was still going on. If it were any of her colleagues, they certainly weren't acting any differently than usual, as far as she could tell. Paranoia crept into her relationships and she began to suspect everybody, even Millen. Tribune Lockni, appearing unusually pleasant, summoned her to his office and asked her for a personal account of the activities at Prollet. She described the construction going on and the forthcoming full scale test of the nuper engineering model. Then, when she left, Lockni followed her back to the control room. He queried her once again on the step-by-step programming for the landing, after Settler-Two was established into orbit. She explained the process, step-by-step again, as she had done before.

Sitting at her Centre console and concentrating on the Settler-Two trajectory kept Fraya focused, and fortunately the path was near to that predicted. Rami was concerned she was not getting enough rest, but she claimed it was therapeutic for her to be at her work station. At one point he insisted she take some time for a walk with him.

They went toward the waterfront and entered the brick walkway around Fraya's old tutorium. Trees overhanging the walkway gave it a canopy appearance and ambiance of tranquillity. They were beginning to relax in their stroll, when a voice from behind suddenly startled them.

"Don't turn around or look back. Keep walking and pretend you are talking the same way you were a moment ago. Use hand gestures. There are two of us here, from the Prollet security force. We met you in Restor's office, and we said we would try to find out if your government is investigating you and if you are in any danger. Our contact within your government tells us they have nothing on you so far, and no indications they are investigating you. At this point we still don't know where the minitrans came from, but we will continue to investigate until we find out. It is possible your hostel and mocs are bugged, and you are probably being tailed. Be careful what you say ... that is all. Don't mention this to any colleague nor your management just yet, until we find out who did the bugging. If you want to see us, sit down on the next park bench and let us wander by. Glance but don't stare. Use "bench" as the code-word for future contact."

Rami and Fraya sat down in shock. Neither had any knowledge of clandestine activities other than what they had read in fiction and seen on the visicom. The individuals who spoke behind them walked on by, then disappeared from sight. Rami said he recognized one of them from Arin's office, but Fraya was so shaken she said she couldn't remember.

"Rami, this is not fun any more. I came here to work on my technical dream, and apparently am involved in something sinister. Now I'm not sure if this is a good position. Maybe I should quit."

"You have two choices, which are to run, or to stay. For the moment I can't see any reason to run. I think we should do our jobs as best possible, and act like we have nothing to hide, and we really don't."

"Well, I'm frightened. Not knowing who is responsible or what's going on is the worst part. It reminds me of the time I broke one of mother's favorite dishes, and hid the pieces. The pieces mysteriously disappeared from the hiding place, and she never said a word. Waiting for some repercussion was the worst part, and nearly drove me crazy. I finally confessed, just to get the issue resolved." Fraya got up from the bench and started walking. "I really feel like discussing this with Khanwali. Then we'd know one way or the other. He'd tell me if I'm in trouble."

"Don't do it yet, Fraya. You know what the agents said; wait until they get the source identified. Be patient. We'd better get back. Our crockery has probably overcooked the meal by now."

Fraya was depressed. "I don't really care. I don't have much of an appetite anyway."

32. Full Scale Nuper Test

Back at work, Fraya looked up at the banner above her console, reached up, and marked out Arc-80 for Settler-Two. She was tired - she and Rami had hardly slept. They had lain awake half the sleep-period talking. Questions - who? why? kept running through her mind. She was very glad to be back at the console, and for a short time, was able to forget the intrigue that had most recently entered her life. Settler-Two was more than two-thirds of the way to Terres, right on course, and floating in a powered-down condition to conserve thruster fuel. All systems were operating normally, but she felt like exercising the thrusters anyway. She awakened the sleeping systems on board the craft and changed its orientation so the solar panels faced the sun. This position allowed the batteries to recharge, and made her feel like she was accomplishing something. She was staring upward, trying to visualize the craft in deep space, when Tribune Lockni made one of his surprise appearances. At the sound of his voice, Fraya jumped, and looked over her shoulder. Lockni was peering at the lines on her screen, and nodded approval.

"Things are going so well here," he said," I'd like you to go back to Prollett again and review the nuper engine progress. Don't worry about Settler-Two, there's plenty of time for another visit before the intercept." Without another word, Lockni spun around and left.

Fraya seethed. He didn't ask for her opinion of the nuper progress, nor whether a trip was warranted, he just departed. She briefly thought of complaining to Khanwali, but decided not to challenge Lockni again. She checked all the systems, left the console to Sevik, her selected alternate, stomped off to her office and slammed the door. She sat down, picked up her communicator, and called Rami. Rami tried to reassure her.

"I know you're not happy about leaving again, Fraya, but try to be amenable.   Your Settler-Two isn't going anywhere. You say all systems are normal, and you have plenty of time. I think you are worrying too much about it. Besides, we have a future to talk about when you get through with this survey. "

"You're right, Rami, I know, but I'm still worried Lockni will change something on the program and cause a failure."

"There is nothing you can do, Fraya. The craft is in Lockni's control while you are away. Just go, and do your survey. I'll continue with my work here, and meet you again in Solport."

The survey team once again assembled for the journey. Fraya reversed the order of visits, going to Prollet first, so Corci could see the engineering model. He had argued that he should be on the evaluation team, and this time Fraya didn't protest. On the stratoliner journey to Solport, Corci used his celebrity status and wit to keep some of the passengers amused, and no one within hearing distance seemed to object. Cabin attendants clucked around him, and the pilots invited him to come up to the flight deck, which he did. When meal service was brought out for the passengers, an attendant asked Corci which type meat he would like ... red or white?

"Is there a difference?" he asked.

"Not much," she replied.

He chuckled at her honesty." What does the red meat taste like?"

"Pretty much just like the white," she replied, smiling broadly, then asked, "what are your meals like on the space platform?"

He grinned. "Everything tastes the same. Sometimes we play "guess the meat"."

At Prollet, the full-scale nuper model was ready for its first startup. Prollett Scienomies and Fraya's crew all gathered in the rockcrete observation and control building a half kiloquant away, and waited. Fraya watched the reactor temperature slowly rise as pumps circulated the water-variant around the catalytic core. Ionizing temperature was reached, and the water began breaking apart into molecular hydrogen and oxygen. A throttling valve was opened and masses of the superheated liquid shot into the combustion chamber, ignited, then exited into the nozzle throat. The engine shuddered loudly in the test stand as roaring, high pressure gasses gushed from its exhaust nozzle with such force the observation building shook. The fiery plumes hit the diverter and fanned into the sky. It was a very impressive first test, but revealed a major flaw. While the team members watched, an attempt was made to throttle back the thrust. A stubborn valve stuck in the open position threatening to cause a runaway engine, but the chief operator initiated an emergency shutdown. The engine stopped quickly and without further incident.

Corci complained loudly about the anomaly, so Fraya put a hold on any further demonstrations until the valve was fixed. The embarrassed Prollet scienomies assured Fraya and Corci a simple redesign would correct the problem, and it would operate smoothly when they came for the next review. Fraya understood the problem and proposed fix, so she released her team, except Karlus, to go home . She planned on visiting both Kirken and Stratopulse before returning, and wanted Karlus with her.

Arin was away from Solport on other business, but he contacted Fraya by communicator. After she briefed him on the status of the nuper test, he brought up the commercial enterprise.

"Fraya, until now, I was only investigating the feasibility of such a venture. I believe the endeavor is financially and logistically feasible, and I have already begun to get commitments for financing. I haven't made a decision for go-ahead yet, but when I do, I really want you managing this project. I am serious."

"I couldn't, nor wouldn't leave my current assignment until my obligation to Centre for the nuper development is complete," she replied.

"I think it's admirable that you have such loyalty to complete an assignment. As a matter of fact, if you didn't, I probably wouldn't trust you," Arin replied. But, since you didn't say no, I will assume you are in until I hear otherwise."

Fraya and Karlus went on to Kirken and Stratopulse, and found them lagging in design efforts. She returned to work at Centre still feeling a persistent aura of uneasiness, but everything again seemed normal. She called Rami to let him know she was back and at work. Because her report on the Prollet nuper was so positive, the consortium authorized funds for building a flight test version, and gave her approval to proceed with the upcoming final review at Prollet, contingent upon the valve problem being fixed.

Arin's agents obviously still didn't know who monitored her or why, and whether it was still going on, but she did have an idea who it might have been. Something she saw at Stratopulse made her think that contractor was worth further overt investigation. She called Arin from her work station at Centre, and when he came on the circuit said she was just coordinating, that nothing had changed and she would return to Prollet soon for the final review. Then she said she felt confined in the office and was going for a walk after work and relax on a park bench for awhile. He said he understood and closed the circuit. She then called Rami and asked him to meet her.

Rami and Fraya strolled down the brick walkway as they had done so many times, chatting and gesturing until they came to the bench they sat on before, when they were contacted by the Prollet security agents. They sat there for awhile, people- watching, and waiting for some sort of contact. They saw men in suits, vagrants, tourists, street cleaners, children playing games, and military personnel. An older looking lady dressed in ragged clothes, with a cloth head-cover tied around her chin, was feeding friendly little furry animals on the grass behind them. She wandered over closer and asked if they were enjoying the bench. They said yes, and Fraya asked if they could help with the feeding, as they had brought nothing for the little animals. The lady gave them some of her nuts to throw out, and asked, "do you like this particular bench?"

"Oh yes," Fraya volunteered, wishing the lady would leave. "We come here quite often."

"Yes, it is a nice bench, don't you think?"

Getting a little impatient, Fraya threw out the rest of the nuts the lady had given her, and then said, "yes, thank you, but we can't talk right now. We're waiting for someone."

"If you understand bench, you can talk to me," she said.

"Bench?" It slowly sunk in. Startled, this was not what Fraya expected. She was looking for two intelligent looking men in neat suits to listen to her concerns, and wondered if this woman was competent. She had no choice.

"Are you a friend of our friend?" Fraya asked.

"Yes, and you two seem a little dense. My name is Maggie."

"What is the code word," Fraya asked.

"Well, you do have enough intelligence to ask the right question. I said it four times already. Bench." Then she began to speak more forcefully and gave Fraya the confidence she needed.

"I am part of the Prollet security force, and I know of the bugs that were put in your hostel in Solport. We've been trying to figure out who put them there because it concerns us greatly. Our contact in

104

your agency tells us there is no file on you that leads us to believe you are being investigated by your own security forces. If that is true, that leaves one of our competitors, or somebody who wants to pick your brains. You called and gave the code word to Restor. Do you have something new to tell us?"

"This is only a suspicion, but I've just returned from Stratopulse in Grace, Southbak. On a previous visit our team found a design which is similar to Prollet's, and a model well enough along to surprise us. We didn't expect that. On this last visit they hadn't made any progress. My immediate thought was some earlier industrial espionage had taken place, and now the contact is gone, so their progress has stopped."

"Those people have the scruples of roadside carrion. Sorry to blast a competitor of ours, but it's true. We do have a mutual back scratching arrangement with their security people, however, so we'll flat-out ask them what is going on. You'll be hearing from us. Anything else?" Maggie asked.

"No, that's it. I sure would like to get to the bottom of this. I vacillated about going to my management; was going to; then I changed my mind, then I ... I'm getting paranoid," Fraya said.

"Hopefully we'll get it solved soon. Don't discuss this with your management yet, nor even mention the subject to any of your friends. We will see you next in Solport. By the way, we scoured your hostel and office every arc while you were there, so you can rest assured it was free of bugs."

Maggie slowly strolled off, feeding the animals again as she left. Hearing there was no chronicle in the government files which censured or indicted either of them was good news. It gave them both a sense of relief. Now they could go back to their respective jobs feeling less threatened, at least until the actual perpetrators were identified.

33. The Sticking Throttle

The Settler-Two flight was going well, and the craft was curving back inward toward the sun, to intercept the track of Terres. Fraya anticipated no problem with the braking maneuver to slow it into orbit, but after that, she reminded herself, the timing for the landing was critical. After all, the Settler-one craft didn't survive, and how it perished was still a mystery.

She reviewed the landing program again for Lockni, who seemed overly interested in details and calculations she had previously explained. The entry into the Terres stratosphere would start at a pinpoint in space millions of kiloquants from the control Centre on Baeta, all managed with signals that travel across space at the velocity of light, but still, because of the distance, take over five milliarcs to reach the receivers on the spacecraft. Accounting for the time lag was very critical. Any miscalculation could cause a water landing, or a sloppy orbit that could take many arcs and much fuel just to straighten it out. Getting it into orbit was not a concern, but settling onto a rotating land mass where the surface was two thirds water was a challenge.

Settler-Two still had forty-two arcs to go, to intercept, giving Fraya enough time to make another trip to Prollet before the braking maneuver would take place. She felt more confidence this time about leaving the control room to Lockni. So far he hadn't changed anything, nor planned to as far as she could tell. She was also anxious to get back to Prollet and talk some more with Arin about the commercial venture. She was getting enthused about the possibility of a new project where she would be in complete control, and the prospect was titillating. She didn't know how she would handle the change from

Centre to the new project, but wasn't concerned for now. That would happen in time. She left with her team for Prollet and another review.

The Prollett people went through presentations prior to leading Fraya's team to the operation site. Corci yawned a few times, obviously bored, but if it offended anyone, they didn't let on. He did surprise Fraya by occasionally asking some very astute questions regarding details. Fraya was glad she let him be a part of the team. During the review, the specialists would ask questions about design and operation, record keeping, and test results, and assign action items if anything was inclusive. If possible, the action items were resolved and closed during the review. At the conclusion, there was only one open item left. The Reliability specialist said there were not enough data nor experience to be certain the new valving arrangement would be reliable in space, and asked that Prollett cycle it ten more times in the stratosphere and then ten times in a vacuum, simulating space.

For the throttle-up test of the big engineering model, the Centre team gathered in the observation building along with the Prollet scienomies as they had done before. They watched as the engine temperature was brought up to thrust temperature, and the power in the ionized water released. The engine shuddered and flamed in the test stand as expected, and as before, in the first test, the awesome power vibrated the observation building. Corci manipulated the controls and throttled the engine up and down several times. It appeared to operate smoothly. The engine's nozzle was vectored from side to side in simulated steering maneuvers, and side thrusts were recorded as satisfactory. The last step in the demonstration was a stop-start exercise, performed several times, to test the reliability. The demonstration was mostly successful but when they analyzed the graphs showing thrust during the throttle-down tests, perturbations in the data-lines indicated an intermittent erratic thrust, probably caused by the redesigned valve, sporadically sticking. That marred an otherwise smooth performance, and a discouraged Fraya told the Prollet people there would be no final approval of design until the valves and actuators demonstrated full reliability. After some conferring, their scienomies assured Fraya and Corci it was a minor problem, easily solvable. The team members, except for Fraya left Solport and went back to Centre. Fraya requested a separate meeting with Arin, and gave him a briefing on the results of the review. He was disturbed an anomaly in the valving had reoccurred, but said he hoped the technical people would resolve it quickly.

Abruptly switching subjects, he asked her about the commercial venture.

34. Arin Commits

"Have you made your decision about joining my project?"

"Not yet, Arin. Rami and I need to talk more and haven't had a chance to do that. We will set aside time for that when I get back to Mizzen."

"But Rami is right here in Solport, working at the Polosek labs. Why don't you two make the decision right away, before you leave this time."

"That would be all right with me," she replied, "but I can't speak for Rami."

"In anticipation of a meeting with the three of us again, one of my agents has contacted Rami at his hostel here in Solport, and he will come here next arc."

"And what if I had disagreed with your pushing for a decision?" she raised her eyebrows.

"In that case, we simply would have un-invited Rami."

After work Fraya was relaxing in her room when she heard a knock on the door. Eagerly thinking it was Rami, she leapt up, opened the door and found a lady in a well-tailored suit who asked if she could come in. Fraya saw she had reddish hair done in a very neat, short, upsweep.

"May I ask what you want?" Fraya asked.

"My name is Maggie. I need to talk to you."

"Maggie? Do I know you?" The name was familiar, but it took Fraya a milliarc to connect the ragged lady in the park with this person, and when she did her mouth fell open in surprise.

"Ah yes. You looked much older when we met before. I never would have recognized you. Please come in."

"Thank you, I'll take that as a compliment to my work. We can talk freely. We've checked and there are no listening devices in the room."

"Have you found out who did the bugging?" Fraya asked.

"Maybe. We think it was the Stratopulse people, as you suspected. For such a big marketeer, they were a bit careless. We know they've gotten to some others in our organization and copied some of our nuper design, and that's why theirs looked similar to ours. We also know some of their security people and have an agreement for occasional information exchange. You know, like the vice-detective who has a street contact that trades information for protection."

"Do you have any idea what they hoped to learn from me?" Fraya asked.

"We can only guess," Maggie went on. "Stratopulse would love to know more about guidance systems. They know you're one of the global specialists on the subject. It probably won't be too long before the necessary combination of mikrontas and gyros is well known, and even appearing in textbooks. Hell, you can learn how to build a holocaust weapon at the public libra. We believe Stratopulse wants the guidance system, and just wanted to see if they could get a little jump on the rest.....bunch of amateurs."

"Is Prollet after the system?" Fraya asked.

"Sure. Arin would love to have it, and he knows he'll eventually get it from you. He's hooked you solid as a fish for this commercial venture."

"You're rather presumptuous, aren't you."

"Maybe. Nothing personal you know. I believe in telling it like it is, that's my nature. I'm always blunt and to the point. Beating around the bush doesn't work well in my job. You in on the project?"

"Well, we haven't decided yet. We don't know about working with Arin, or if he's sincere about this project."

"Don't be alarmed by Arin. He's a slob, but he's sincere about this commercial venture and his word has always been straight and good. He proposition you yet?"

A little startled by the question, Fraya replied honestly. "As a matter of fact, he did the first time I was here. I cut him off smartly."

"Don't worry about it. He propositions every young thing. He's mostly impotent, and thinks a beauty like you might rejuvenate him. The prostitutes tell me they don't even like him to call because he's too much work. They take turns and he pays them well, but he's a lousy job. His mate left him years ago because of neglect. He devotes so much time and energy to making money that his health is very poor. He eats antacids by the handsful and is on high doses of blood-pressure depressants. In spite of it all, I kinda like the old slob. His word is good, he's not hypocritical, does have some ethics, and is a brilliant businessman."

"What happens now?" Fraya asked

"You and Rami make your decision. Even if you decide against our organization, we'll keep looking out for you until this surveillance issue is resolved. We'll also keep checking on your office and hostel to see that they are not bugged again. And we'll keep checking with our contacts at Centre and other places until we get answers. Meanwhile, it would appear you have divulged nothing, and are in no danger. I'll leave now. If you want another contact, use the code word with Arin."

Fraya felt herself being drawn into a vortex with no retreating. The technical challenges of the commercial project, she rationalized, might be more compelling than she would find if she stayed at Centre. And, she further concluded, I wouldn't be abandoning my goal of working on celestial projects. Then she thought of the first conversation with Restor, when he said that technology and people could be bought very easily, and he had tried blatantly to bribe her into influencing the contract for Prollet. Now she wondered if she was being manipulated, and blinded by thinking about the remote possibility of riding a rocket to Terres. Then the probability of Restor's real motive began to enter her mind. Was he still trying to bribe her for the contract in another way? She was wrestling with the possibility when she heard a knock on the door. I hope its Rami this time, she thought.

Rami stood in the open door. She was so happy to see him, she pulled him into the room and threw her arms around him. "Well, it's about time you showed up. We have much to talk about, and Arin is pushing for us to make a decision. Make yourself comfortable and I'll go fix us a beverage."

When she got back and sat down beside Rami, she said "where shall I begin?"

"How about, what has gone on while I was back in Mizzen."

Fraya sipped the beverage, then told him about Maggie, and her reassurances that Arin was sincere. "I hardly recognized her; she seems very professional."

He put his arms around her.

"This is so nice, Rami, I don't want it to end." They cuddled in silence, and after some time, Fraya broke the serenity and told him about her concern that Arin may be finessing them, to win the contract.

"How many other marketeers are competing for the contract?" Rami asked.

"There are only two others on the planet with the technology and capability right now."

"Is Prollet ahead in the field?"

"Unless we find some major technical flaws during these design reviews, or their pricing is totally outrageous, they practically have the contract in hand. We will end up selecting one of the other two contractors to develop a backup design, and the backup contractor could come up with a better and cheaper engine for future contracts, but Prollet is the front runner right now."

"What's the purpose of a backup?" Rami was still mystified by the procedures for design and production of a major project, and in awe that Fraya was so knowledgeable.

"With so much turmoil, like rebels taking control of unstable governments, people encroaching on borders, and sectdoms fighting over their principles, it's not very wise for any major contractor to depend solely on one marketeer for delivery of a component. A subcontracting marketeer can be unexpectedly crushed by bankruptcy or civil war, and leave the major contractor with a huge schedule delay while waiting for another marketeer to develop and manufacture the component. That's why we have a backup."

"Is Prollet on shaky grounds, from the stability standpoint I mean?" Rami asked.

"As far as we know, Prollet is stable and the government of Ardena is stable," Fraya replied.

"Then, I would say Arin is not too worried about losing the engine contract to a competitor. Let's assume he is sincere, and wants to finance an interplanetary voyage to Terres for profit. And let's be real about our feelings here, we both want to believe the commercial venture is going to take place, and that Arin has no other motive. As a matter of fact, the enticement is so appealing, the mighty Zhu probably couldn't talk us out of going along with Arin right now. The problem is ... it sounds too good to be true. Anything that sounds too good to be true, usually is."

"That was a wonderful jumble of thinking out loud, but what should we do?" Fraya ventured.

"Well, summing it up, if Arin Restor knows the contract for the nuclear propulsion engine is fairly certain for Prollet, he can gain very little by bribing you."

"I tend to agree with you," said Fraya. "But he might use his advantage to pad the price when he negotiates with our contracts people. Fortunately, I don't have anything to do with the negotiations."

"Then let's agree to manage the colony project for him," Rami said.

"I hope I'm not buying into being a commodity that is going to be thrown out when the project gets started," Fraya fretted.

"I hope you're wrong, but we both know what we are going to do. Let's have a toast and then say it together. They touched glasses. "On the count of three......"

"Yes!" They both yelled.

Next arc, when Fraya entered her Prollet office to finish some documents before meeting with the team, Karlus was in her office as usual, shuffling papers and straightening files. The file folder with the notes and requirements she and Rami had made for the commercial venture had been removed from its drawer slot, and was lying on her desk.

"What's this doing out, Karlus?" she asked.

"When I was sorting things in file drawers, to put them in proper order, I noticed it seemed to be out of place. I left it out, to ask you where it should go."

"It doesn't fit in with the rest of the files....that's why it seemed out of place, Karlus. It's for a project different from anything Centre is involved with. I may be asking you to help with it in the near future, but not now."

"What's it all about?" Karlus looked surprised.

"There's no need to discuss it at this time, but rest assured, you will be one of the first in Centre that I inform when the time is appropriate."

Karlus nodded with his usual attitude of servitude, and backed out of the room. Fraya wondered if he had looked into the folders, but had little concern about the faithful Karlus seeing anything in any of the files. She picked up the folder and left.

With Rami, she met with Arin and told him they would join the project. Then she opened the file folder with the proposal outlines, and began.

"For starters, the first round trip should be a quick trip with a crew of six people. This spacecraft will be an assembly, put together in orbit here, and will travel to Terres using the nuper engine for power. When reaching Terres, the assembly will separate into two sections, one to remain in orbit, and the other to descend to the surface. Two

114

space-pilots will remain in the orbiting section, and the other four will land and collect cargo. The landing assembly will have a descent module, with an inflatable shelter for living quarters, and an ascent module . The people on the surface will never leave the shelter without isolation suits to protect against biological contamination. The payload and crew will return to Baeta and rendezvous with a landing craft we'll place in orbit here while they are gone. The landing craft will bring the crew and payload back to the Baetian surface." Arin nodded, in thought. Fraya continued.

"If successful, and if you wanted to expand the project, we could move on to a second operation. This could be more ambitious, a larger craft with more participants, and a supply barge sent ahead to circle Terres and remain in orbit. Scienomies and space-pilots would descend from the barge to explore and gather more selective cargo. Again, all exposure outside the landing hospice would still be in isolation suits. Cargo would be gathered, sorted, and selected, and sent to the barge on robotic cargo packs. When the weight quota was achieved, the space-pilots on the surface would take the crew back into orbit, then all would leave the barge and make the space journey back to Baeta.

The third stage, if it ever got this far, would be a permanent colony, assuming no biological hazards were present. Colony members would return home to Baeta with cargo on a rotating basis, or remain on Terres indefinitely if that was their choice, shipping cargo back here remotely."

Arin said he was very impressed. "From what you say, the project sounds technically feasible. I know I can do it from the materiel and logistics standpoints, at least for what you call the first trip. With your contacts and ingenuity, I'm ready to make a go-ahead commitment. When can I count on you to start here full time?"

"Both Rami and I are enthused, and have agreed to accept your offer. When the nuper contract is completely settled, and I consider my obligation to Centre complete, I will resign and come here."

"I'm pleased you have the integrity to complete an assignment," said Arin. Fraya tilted her head up in pride "The thought of not fulfilling my obligation hadn't crossed my mind. I know of no other way to operate."

Arin, who hardly ever changed expression, smiled in appreciation. "We'll get along. Meanwhile, do you have a list of specialists I can be hiring for you ?" he asked.

"Only one so far, if you can get him. He's the radiation specialist from the Kirken Group in Whitecliff. He has an innovation on lightweight shielding and if it works, we'll definitely need his expertise. "

"We'll hire him if we can, but I may decide just to buy the material we need from them. What else?" Arin asked. "How about a mission planner?"

"I have a friend in Centre who is good. His name is Millen Cyrriz, and I'll talk to him about joining the group," said Fraya.

"Good, as long as I don't have to pronounce his name. I'll have security check him out. If that's it, have a good trip back and we'll see you soon."

35. The Trial

Fraya was excited to be returning to Centre. Settler-Two was about to reach the intercept point, and the nuper project was going well. Arin and his security people had put her fears to rest about Centre being responsible for the wiretaps. She felt giddy as she entered the building, and went straight to Khanwali's office. She

116

looked in and Khanwali was gone; Lockni was sitting at Khanwali's desk. She turned and ran to the control room. A different controller was at her console. Apparently Lockni had replaced Sevik.

"Now what's going on?" she asked him. "What are you doing here?"

"You had better go talk to Lockni," he said. "He can explain better than I."

Fraya went back to Khanwali's office and confronted Lockni. "Would you mind telling me what's going on around here?"

Lockni smirked, no longer exhibiting the smiling composure he displayed in the recent past.

"In due time, Tribune Lor, but for now, suffice it to say, Khanwali has had a mental breakdown and has been removed from Centre for rest and rehabilitation. I am now in charge."

Fraya nearly lost her balance. A dizziness weakened her knees as she suddenly realized Khanwali was in a shelter, never to be seen again, and her fate was now in Lockni's hands.

"And what is your controller doing at my console?"

"It's his console now. I've replaced you. He is very competent and takes orders better than you. You will assist him when requested."

"And what about the nuper engine?"

"You've done a good job so far, but we think you are getting too familiar with the contractor's people. That can lead to sympathies not in the best interest of Centre. Someone else will take charge of the project."

"I won't stand for this," Fraya bellowed. "I'll take this to the council: I'll tell the legal staff what is going on here."

"Tribune Lor!" Lockni yelled, "you had better control yourself, and understand this. I am in charge here now. I am also in charge of the council."

"We'll see about that!" She stormed out of the building and returned to her hostel in a daze. As she was sitting alone contemplating her future, a knock sounded at the door. She answered the knock and was confronted by two men she didn't recognize.

"Fraya Lor, we are from the Government Investigational Service. Will you please come with us."

"What for?" she asked.

"You have violated security agreements with the Centre and are under arrest by the government of Bacamir."

"You people have no right to arrest me. I am an Ardenian citizen. I haven't violated any security agreements. Why are you doing this?"

"Tribune Lockni's orders. Agent Maskinof has found that you were plotting to defect, and use the knowledge you gained in Centre to your advantage against the government of Bacamir."

"Karlus?" an astonished Fraya shouted. "Karlus is an agent? He has been my closest confidant and loyal assistant since I've been here."

"If you will be rational for a moment, do you think the Government would let any individual, let alone one from another territory, work in the most secret of operations without constant surveillance? Not hardly."

After the Prollet security people told her Stratopulse was probably the culprit who placed the bugs in her room, she had practically forgotten the incident. Now all her fears and concerns about the government's agents suddenly leaped back into her mind. She could only think of her father and his warning;

You're so young and naive, Fraya, and know nothing about politics. I fear for your safety there. Why go to Bacamir?

Fraya turned frosty. "I protest, and want a hearing with counsel!"

"And you shall get a hearing. For now, you are to come with us.

Without giving her a chance to gather any of her personal items or leave a message for Rami, they forcefully led her away. She was taken to a government building where she was confined, and told she would be provided counsel. She shivered with fright, and could hardly believe she had been under surveillance by Karlus, a friend and confidant. All those times he took care of her files, he was examining them, checking on her. Had he learned about the commercial venture? Her notes may have given parts of it away. It must have been him who planted the bugs. Who else might be an agent, she wondered. What about Millen? And where is Rami? Is he in danger? Only an indifferent individual who brought her meals interrupted her isolation. Time went by very slowly with no communications, and no reading materials, fueling her thoughts of impending misfortune. She felt totally helpless, and her immediate fear was being sent to a shelter and disappearing without anyone knowing. By the second arc, her imagination was running wild.

"What if I just disappeared?" She visualized her father saying to himself; "I knew it. I told her not to go there." Rami would have to break the news to them ... poor Rami, carrying the message that their daughter had been a victim of the system, and he had no way of finding out what happened. She even visualized the memorial and mourning back home.

Rami had remained in Solport to finish some work with Tribune Polosek. When he arrived back in Mizzen and found Fraya's hostel empty, he wasn't surprised. It wasn't unusual for her to be away, and sometimes she never left her job until way past time her shift ended.

He was expecting her to be there, however, having left a message telling her his arrival time. When he saw some of the personal items she usually carried still on the entry table, he became alarmed. A call to her control room was answered by Karlus who told Rami he didn't know where she was. A call to Tribune Khanwali's office left him in shock. Lockni answered and told him Khanwali was ill and had been taken to a shelter. He also said he had no knowledge of Fraya's whereabouts. Rami's mind raced to the improbable. Something sinister was happening. Khanwali was taken to a shelter which meant he was literally dead. Had Fraya also been taken to a shelter? Rami called the control room again and tried to get more information from Karlus, but he claimed to have no further knowledge. He needed a plan of action, but his mind was not functioning very well. In near panic, all he could think of was calling Arin Restor for help. He left his hostel and made contact from a public transcom to tell Arin about his frantic concern.

"Believe it or not Rami, I am already aware of the situation. Agents of your government have incarcerated her, but I don't know any of the details. My security people are digging. Apparently your government planted the recording devices after all, and our security missed finding that out. Try not to worry, I will use my influence to see that a competent counselor is assigned to her. As far as I know, there are no charges filed against you. I don't know when you'll be able to contact her, but it shouldn't be long."

Arin also said he didn't want to elaborate, but his agents had some very strong bargaining positions against very responsible individuals in the Bacamirian government, people who had events in their lives they wished to keep secret, events which if known would cause the person to lose his position, or worse.

Fraya was kept in isolation for several arcs before being allowed to contact anyone. Finally a counselor appeared and said he was assigned to defend her. He first had to calm her fears, seeing her in near hysteria.

"How do I know you're not on their side?" she asked.

"Does the name Restor mean anything to you?"

"Arin? His enterprise is working on a contract for Centre. Why?"

"He has influenced the chambers to appoint me as your defense. You'll have to trust me, and that's about all the assurance I can give you."

"All right, what happens next?"

"Let's take this a step at a time, Fraya, and see where we stand. I have a list of the charges and maybe some are false, but lets talk about them one at a time. The first is embezzlement of information proprietary to Centre. Any basis for that?"

"Of course not," she replied. "I have a very high clearance; I invented a superior guidance system, and am privy to Centre's complex designs, but I haven't had any notion of using any information illegally."

"Secondly, were you encouraging anyone to leave Centre for any reason?"

"No. It's true I planned to eventually resign from Centre and move back to Ardena, my home territory, and work on another project, but not before I satisfactorily finished my current assignments . After I left, I would have tried to hire certain specialists to join me in the new project."

"I see. The third was violation of trust. I suppose that means someone is worried you know too much about the guidance system."

"I should!" she exclaimed. "I invented it. But Centre has all the records and technology."

"Tell me," he said, "what do you think is going on here ... why the charges?"

Fraya took a deep breath. "I couldn't see it at the time, and find it hard to accept now, but I think the project manager had this planned for a long time. I must have been in his way, and now he's done it - taken over the entire program."

The counselor made some notes, told her he would be back next arc, and left.

Rami had been in near panic after his conversation with Tribune Lockni, but Arin's reassurances helped ease his fears. When Fraya was finally allowed to communicate, she naturally called Rami.

"Rami, I'm so frightened, I don't know what's going on. Karlus did this to me, and I trusted him implicitly. He's also the one who planted the bugs. He's one of their agents, and had access to all my files."

"We don't know whom to trust," Rami tried to be composed. "Arin says not to worry, that he has contacts and will see that you get good counsel. He also said this call will be monitored so we should say as little as possible, ... to just trust him."

"Whatever you say Rami. I've been talking to a new counselor and he seems very competent. I just hope he is not one of them."

The initial hearing took place five arcs later. Karlus Maskinof was there, and had copies of Fraya's files showing some sort of commercial venture in the planning stages, and some transcripts of conversations he claimed were recorded from listening devices he had planted in her hostel. The prosecutor arrogantly stepped up to the lectern and began his presentation.

"There are three charges against this defendant, Presario Overseer, stemming from the fact that Tribune Fraya Lor planned to forfeit her position at Centre, leave, and work for another government. One...she is charged with embezzlement of proprietary information for use against the government of Bacamir: Two...seditious solicitation of key personnel in government positions, and three... perfidious actions against Centre's trust." He went on to elaborate, saying they had copies of files proving these charges, and recordings of conversations in her hostel backing up the files.

"We have incontestable evidence, Presario Overseer."

Fraya's appointed defense counsel countered by saying the evidence gathered by Karlus was forged to further his own cause, to gain promotions within Centre, and therefore, being false, the evidence was meaningless. He stated that Fraya may have been considering returning to her native territory to live and work, but she considered that a right, not a crime. He further stated they would prove she had neither stolen nor embezzled anything, nor ever intended to, and asked that she be released on her own recognizance until a proper defense could be prepared. The Overseer agreed with the defense counselor, and released Fraya with the stipulation she must remain in Mizzen until the trial, which was set for ten arcs later.

Being released from confinement helped Fraya's attitude but she hated confrontation, and hoped the trial would end quickly and favorably. She was escorted from the confinement building and taken to Centre's administration complex for an exit interview, to be conducted by a panel of Centre's legals. She didn't want to face them alone, and requested her counselor be present during the interview. The head panelist, who said he could see no harm in granting her request, overrode objections from the panel members and let her counselor join them.

The administrative lead wasted no words in addressing Fraya.

"Your career at Centre is over, Tribune Lor. You are hereby advised that anything you have seen here, learned here, or developed here is proprietary and is Centre's property. Any violations will result in your incarceration whether you remain in this territory, or move to another territory. We can, and will, hunt you down if necessary."

Fraya's counselor raised his hand, and interrupted the panelist.

"Before you go any further, Presario, I believe you're overstepping your authority here. My client warned me you might make such demands, and has assured me nothing is leaving here except her mind and memories. All reports, notebooks, documents, procedures and specifications are in the file cabinets in the control room. You cannot mandate she forget her technical knowledge, nor restrict the use of her mind."

"Counselor, you forget whom you are working for, and under what government. We can and we will enforce our policies if necessary."

"Contrare, Presario, I am fully aware of my obligations to the Bacamirian government, for whom I work. I am also aware that we have a new regime with more civilized policies than in the past. You, Presario, are obviously from the old regime and haven't kept up with the progress. My client is from Ardena. Do you want to cause an international conflict?"

"I'm not concerned about Ardena; I'm concerned about doing my job. Tribune Lor, here is a paper for you to sign saying that you have left all records of your work, and in addition, agree to refrain from using any proprietary knowledge."

"I can't do that." Fraya objected, and looked to her counselor for guidance. The counselor grabbed the paper, and with his pen crossed out the provision against using proprietary knowledge, and in

124

its place wrote, "I have been notified of the Bacamirian policy regarding termination from The Celestial Research Centre." Then told her it was clarified and reasonable to sign, which she did.

While waiting for the trial, Fraya mostly confined herself to their hostel, keeping busy by helping Rami with his reports on the immunity vaccine development. Rami was shattered by this turn of events, and wondered how something as exhilarating as the commercial venture could have suddenly caused so much distress in their lives. Things got worse. Shortly thereafter, the managers of the hostel complex ordered them to move from their upper-level sea-view rooms to a smaller, first-level hostel of inferior quality. They moved, reluctantly, and assumed the new place was wired with enough listening devices to record their every breath.

Rami went to a public transcom, called Arin, and told him what had transpired. "We're staying close to our hostel now, biding our time until the trial," he said. "Fraya has an appointed defense counsel, but we are naturally worried."

Arin tried to reassure Rami. "The counselor is Bacamirian, Rami, but I know him and he is trustworthy. I also know about the charges, and although there are no guarantees, I do have contacts and some influences all over this planet. I'm reasonably sure Fraya has little to be worried about concerning the charges. Tell her to stay put until the trial, and work with her counselor. Both of you be careful what you say, anywhere."

Even though presuming they would be watched, Rami took Fraya for a stroll along the stone walkway and repeated the news from Arin. They even sat on the bench and watched the little animals scurrying about. The outing helped to cheer her some, but left them both wondering how Arin could influence a trial in another territory. They had no recourse but to hope his contacts were influential.

"If Arin pulls this off, Rami, I want to get out of here, back to Ardena to stay. I dread confronting my father who warned me I was too naive for the politics here, but I hope he won't brand me a failure."

"At this point, I wouldn't worry about what your father thinks. Let's just hope you are painlessly acquitted, and released so you can get away."

"To think otherwise makes me physically ill, Rami. I'm still having a hard time accepting the fact I'm in trouble."

When the time came for the trial, Fraya entered the chamber with her counselor, and took her place beside him. Rami stayed in the observation section. Charges were repeated, and a smug prosecutor entered the recording discs and copies of the files from Karlus as evidence. Karlus would seldom look in Fraya's direction, and when he did, he blushed and would not make eye contact.

The defense counselor read a passage from the "Declaration of Peoples Rights", even though rights in a collectivist government are extremely nebulous. The passage stated that, "no individual shall be persecuted for personal beliefs that are not detrimental to government operation or organization." He further went on to state the charges were contrived, the recordings were obvious fakes with poorly done voice-overs, and the evidence was forged to further the career and benefit of one, Karlus Maskinof, who was promised a promotion for his efforts. He requested the charges be dropped on the grounds they have no basis.

A startled prosecutor heard the Overseer say he agreed, ordered the charges be dropped, and declared the case closed. The prosecutors were shocked at the Overseer's statement. The head prosecutor leaped up and shook his fist in the air, and demanded an explanation.

"First of all Presario Prosecutor, I don't have to explain anything to you, but in the interest of finality, I made the decision as soon as I heard the phony recordings."

Amid some shouting and rapping of his gavel, the Overseer convinced the lead prosecutor that he was out of control and had better drop the subject, before he found himself confined to a shelter for mental evaluation. Few who went to a shelter for a mental cause were ever seen again, so the prosecutor wisely stopped his tirade.

Security forces throughout the different territories frequently traded information and favors. Unknown to the prosecutors, the Overseer had been recruiting sexual encounters with several young males in the cadre of cabinet scribes and interns. Exposure would have surely brought him disgrace, and cost him his position in the government, and maybe a trip to a shelter. Arin's security people had obtained a discreet, diplomatic agreement, in cooperation with the Centre security force, for the Overseer to drop the case. In return, they would keep the information they had on his errant sexual behavior hidden.

After the trial was over, Fraya promptly packed her belongings with the intention of leaving Bacamir forever.

"I'm going back home, Rami, to stay. I still dread facing my father.

"I think your father will be very happy you're alive and home, Fraya. You did some very good work here, and no one can say you were a failure. I'm happy the trial is over. Before you take leave, we should contact Arin and see if you are still in any danger, and how we should get you out of Bacamir. Lockni may still want you under his control, and may try to block your leaving."

"Why would he do that, Rami? He certainly doesn't want me at the console any more, even though I would jump at a chance to land

Settler-Two."   "You might be his excuse for another failure. Should anything go wrong with the lander, he could blame it on you."

"How about you, Rami. What are you going to do?"

"I'm required to stay and finish some work with Mentorian Zeiss on Centre's contract, and then coordinate again with Tribune Polosek. I, too, plan to make a permanent move to Ardena. Before you leave, I really would like you to travel to Lignus with me, and meet my friends and family. I have to go there soon, before much more time passes, as Dorvic left me a message that Lethra is ill and her time may be short."

"I really planned on leaving Bacamir as quickly as I could, Rami, but I've always wanted to see your home. If there is a chance I'm still in danger, maybe we can combine a way to get me out of Bacamir with a visit to Lignus.

They called Arin and he affirmed Rami's suspicion; that any appearances of permanently departing Bacamir might be risky.

"Fraya, you are still very much in danger, and Lockni has no intention of letting you vacate Bacamir. I am going to smuggle you out. Here is the plan. Leave most of your belongings in Mizzen, and forget them. Go with Rami to Lignus, and make it look like you are going on a short visit. Don't delay. I have some agents overtly looking out for you, and they'll contact you with instructions. I'll see you soon."

36. Fraya Departs Bacamir

Rami and Fraya made plans to make it appear as if they were going on a short trip, as Arin suggested. Rami left word with Tribune Zeiss that he had business in Lignus and would be gone for a few arcs, but would come straight back to Mizzen and finish his work. With that done, they packed small bags and left. As they stepped out of the building and Rami breathed in the acrid, pewter-brown air, his nostrils flinched. The pollution seemed a little worse than usual and even the aroma of the nearby sea didn't mask the scent.

"Can you believe this Fraya? Fossil fuels cause this pollution, and nobody seems to care." He inhaled and coughed.

Fraya put her hand over her mouth. "I'll actually be glad to get out of this borough for good," she said.

"I sometimes think I'm conditioned to it," Rami replied, "but when the fumes get ugly, I'm reminded it is not going to get better."

He piled Fraya's bag in the moc, and they left. From the parking area, Rami maneuvered south and eastward onto the open paveways. The sun was full above the western horizon, brightening the sky and ending the half annum of darkness, but it was dimmed by the brownish cloud they were motoring through.

By the time they left the suburbs toward the large valley to the southeast, they were out of the haze. Except for a band of clouds further south, visibly dropping a curtain of evaporating rain, it was dry and fair, so he stopped and removed the top from his moc.

"I love this Rami, and this clearer atmosphere does make breathing more pleasant."

They continued on southward, on the way to Lignus, away from the coast and the big borough, and as he accelerated, he began to relax. He felt the exhilaration, and looked over at Fraya, obviously enjoying the ride. She had leaned back with face to the sky, and let the breeze flip her hair.

"Smell the aromas, Fraya," he said, "fresh dirt. The fields are awakening from the long darkness, and field workers are milling around the equipment? They're preparing for planting."

"I know a little something about farming, Rami. My parents have a citrona orchard you know. But I love this scenery - I've never seen it before."

He crossed the valley and began climbing into the foothills, out of the fields and into fruit trees budding new leaves, then into a coniferous forest. Just beyond a narrow opening between two, long, rugged, steep ridges, he entered Lignus.

Slowly motoring through the borough, he waved occasionally at a familiar face, and near the end of the main motorway turned up a side lane toward the hillside dwelling of Urza-Slade, his foster parents. He planned to visit briefly with them before seeing Dorvic, and then going to Lethra.

When they arrived, Jerod and Milda came out to meet them, greeting Rami with a hug.

"Rami, we haven't seen you in so long. What a nice surprise," chirped Milda. "And this must be Fraya."

"Yes," Fraya said. "I'm very glad to meet you."

Jerod grasped Rami's wrist, shook it, then turned to Fraya. Rami introduced her, after which Jerod gently shook Fraya's hand, then turned back to Rami.

"Welcome son, come in and bring us up to date."

Milda embraced Fraya like she was her own child. She fussed around her saying she was finally glad to meet her, and Jerod, after looking her over to see whether or not she had the build of a Fen, seemed to accept her.

"Rami has told us so much about you it's as if we know you already. I love your accent," Milda told her.

Fraya was not aware Rami had even mentioned her to them and was a bit surprised. "Thank you. It doesn't sound to me that I have an accent, but I guess I do."

Jerod brightly agreed. "You make this old language of ours sound rather good. I hope talking with that son of ours doesn't cause you to lose it."

"I'll try not to let him influence me too much," she replied, wondering why Rami had not told her more about his parents.

Milda put her arm through Rami's and motioned for Fraya to follow.

"Come on in and tell us all about your work. People ask about you all the time, and we don't even know what you are working on any more. We want to hear all about it..... and, before I forget, Dorvic called. He wants to see you." "Thank you, mother, I'll see Dorvic before I leave. Things haven't changed much for me. You know I stayed on at the Institute after graduation, and I am now working as a research assistant for a biology mentor."

"Biology," Jerod exclaimed. "That sounds impressive."

"Really," Milda added. "Well, if you'd rather be doing that than be a Dominary, we can only wish you well. I hope you have enough time to join us for a meal and we'll have a good chat."

When the meal was ready, Milda seated everyone around the table.

"Rami, would you like to say a blessing before we eat?"

"No, mother, you know I don't do that. But you and father please go ahead."

"Well, I thought maybe....."

Jerod cut her off in mid sentence, said a blessing with bowed head, and then he and Milda waved the customary sign of the sect with their hands. As they ate, Rami and Jerod made light talk about the weather and crops, their activities, and the usual dismal news on the visicom. Central Scorpia, mostly inhabited with Fens, had severe flooding in one lowland area, and a drought with forest fires occurring in another area not too distant from the floods.

"Strange twists of nature," Rami said. "Drought and floods in the same general area. That's just a start on what planet-warming can do to us."

Jerod heard about a civil uprising taking place, with people battling each other for food and resources made scarce by the drought.

"They're worse than animals," Jerod glowered. "Overpopulated and breeding like rodents. At least the animals don't use weapons." Jerod was referring to the thermal holocaust explosives.

"That technology sure went astray." Rami knew what Jerod was talking about.

"What started as a physics experiment developed into an energy source for power generators. Then somebody made an explosive out of it. Fortunately, none has ever been used."

Jerod pushed his empty plate aside and leaned back.

"But it's no secret the weapons are being made in a lot of different territories, with strong rumors rebel groups are illegally buying them. It's only a matter of time, Rami."

"I hope you're wrong, father, but why else would rebels buy them if not to use them."

Fraya entered her opinion. "It could be the bully mentality, don't you think? You know...I have a big stick so you'd better let me have my way."

They completed the meal and made more small talk. "Do you miss working in the mine, father?"

"Not a bit. My limp from the accident has never gone away, and I'm still bitter about working side-by-side with Fens and never getting a promotion, but I'm gradually getting over it."

Rami sympathized, and brought Fraya into the conversation, explaining that she was a Centre scienomie. "Rami tells us you work on space programs, like that exploration of Terres that's going on. That so?" asked Jerod.

"Yes, and I have been so fortunate. I originally came to this territory on an exchange program, and ended up getting all my credentials here. When I was offered a position at the Celestial Centre, I couldn't believe it. I had dreamed of doing stellar research since I was a child."

"Why, if I may ask?" said Milda.

"Curiosity. They say you learn your own language better by studying another language. I think we'll learn more about our own planet if we continue to study other planets. I'm curious about so many things, like why a seed grows into a plant, what forces hold a rock together, and what happens when it breaks. We all have curiosities. My curiosity just happens to reach out into our stellar system."

Jerod leaned forward in his chair. "I agree we all have curiosities, but some of us just accept things, without being rebels." Rami felt the little jab at his rebellious youth.

"We all accept some things," Fraya replied, "including scienomies. We don't know what makes a seed grow, but we know it does. We plant it, give it water and light, and it works. Take gravity for instance; a fruit that falls out of a tree is pulled down by gravity. We don't know what gravity is but we all use its forces every arc."

"Do I use it?" asked Milda.

"I believe so." She groped for a simple example." When you run water into the sink, gravity drains the water away." Milda could readily visualize the example, and Fraya got a nod of approval from her.

"And you are curious about other planets." Jerod interjected. "What sectdom are you, if I may ask?"

133

"My family are mostly Believers, and I was raised that way. I don't practice the rituals, however."

"The news media says you plan to look for life on Terres," said Jerod. "Well, you won't find any. Zhu put life only on this planet."

Rami cringed, embarrassed that Fraya was being forced to defend her work, but she gently responded. "You may be right, Presario Slade, but I personally give Zhu much more credit than that."

"What do you mean by that?" Jerod asked. "And please, call me Jerod."

"If a farmer threw out one seed into a field, he wouldn't get much of a crop. If Zhu populated only one planet, his crop of children might not survive. You've looked up at the stars many times and wondered about them, I'm sure. There are millions and millions of them that we can see. Our sun is just one of those stars. I can see no reason why a creator would bet on only one little planet near one little star, when he has all those billions out there to use and take care of. Around those billions of stars, he must have placed millions of planets in the right temperate zones, like a farmer preparing his fields.
Zhu has probably planted seeds all over and every single one would get his constant attention." Fraya had obviously thought this concept out ahead of time, and Rami found himself listening as intently as Milda and Jerod.

"In our sect we have those who claim to have lineage clear back to Zhu. In your concept, could there be such lineage on another planet?" Jerod asked.

"Why not? If there is a Zhu, and he felt the need to place a lineage on this planet for some reason, then he could do that on any of his planets."

Rami noticed that Fraya gave Jerod and Milda a reason to bolster faith in their own belief if they so wanted, and also to accept life

134

throughout the celestrium. She did so without being forced to defend her own faith. Very tactful, he thought.

Fraya went on. "Personally, I think Zhu is as smart as any farmer, and planted seeds of life all over the celestrium, like a farmer planting a field. Not all seeds survive, so planting many seeds is assurance that at least some will grow."

Rami found himself intrigued by Fraya's explanation. She was obviously charming Jerod.

"I've never thought about it that way," Jerod replied. "It does sort of make sense when you put it that way. Do you think if there is life on other planets, they would look just like us?"

Rami started to form an answer based on evolution, then backed off, deciding not to rekindle an old argument.

"They could," Fraya replied. "Why ... Rami was just telling me about a theory that a common DNA molecule, that's Zhu's seeds of life, has been sprinkled over all the planets in our solar system by an outside source, such as a comet. It's such an interesting theory that my curiosity wants to find out."

After some more small talk, Rami and Fraya said good-bye, then left to visit his friends. Dorvic and Rachek lived in the forest outside the limits of Lignus with their two children, a girl at pre-tutelary age, and a boy one annum older. When they arrived, Rachek screamed joyously and threw her arms around Rami's neck in a greeting, while Dorvic grasped his wrist and vigorously pumped his hand.

"Is this creature treating you with the royal respect you deserve?" Rami asked Rachek in jest.

"Remember, I'm still crazy about you and will rescue you from here any time." She giggled and squeezed him again. He bent down

135

and hugged Rubel, and gave her a doll he had brought from Mizzen. Then he hugged Dory, and gave him a small slingshot.

"Here you are, Dory. Practice with this and you will be as good as your father some day."

Rami introduced Fraya, and Rachek asked her about her work and travels. She commented on her accent, and Fraya blushed a little. "I try to hide it," she said, "but it just slips out."

"Oh, don't hide it, Fraya, it sounds so soft and pleasing, I wish I could talk that way," Rachek replied. After some talk of work, and families, Rami asked about Lethra.

"How is she, Dorvic?"

"Not so ill as she is old and weak. I've visited her every few arcs lately, and I think she is fading fast. They'll put her in a protective shelter soon, and I knew you wanted to see her before they took her away."

Both knew what the shelter meant, and Rami explained to Fraya. "Our Government provides food and care for the elderly and leaves them in a personal domicile until they become feeble or unable to tend themselves. Then they put the individual in the shelter. After a short time in the shelter, the person disappears."

Fraya frowned. She realized what Rami had meant when he tried to tell her about people disappearing. Euthanasia!

"They should put elderlies in a shelter much earlier while they still have good use of their faculties," she said. "That way they could enjoy some companionship for awhile before their time came."

"That would make more sense, but I suppose it would be more costly," Dorvic replied. "I'm sure some government efficiency experts have it all figured out."

Rami paused, and nodded toward Fraya. "And now we must go." Rami thanked Dorvic for keeping him informed about Lethra.

136

They said good-byes and then motored to another section of the villa, into a group of dwellings where Fens had ghettoized. Rami parked near the small, old building where he spent his youth. They went into Lethra's domicile, and found her very weak, but alert. Rami felt a warmth to the leathery-skinned old woman that was stronger than the closeness he felt for Milda. She leaned forward in her chair, resting on her elbows and greeted Rami with a warm smile. She always seemed grateful for his company, and obviously had some pride in having contributed to his life. "Lethra, I want you to meet my lady. Her name is Fraya."

Lethra nodded and gripped Fraya's hands. Rami gave her a hug and chatted with her for awhile. She gripped his hands, and she didn't want to let go. "It gets lonesome here, Rami.

"I know, Lethra. I wish I could help more." Rami had brought her a visicom several annums ago, and found it was not working anymore.

"I'll get you a new one, Lethra." Then he asked, "Your son, Sakeri, where is he now?"

She told him her son migrated to central Scorpia, and couldn't get back very often.

Rami asked if he could hire a caretaker for her, but she declined, saying she was getting along just fine, and the gummint people looked in on her quite often. She blinked several times, and formed a tear in the corner of each eye.

"Rami, I want you to do something for me. Here is an envelope with some documents. I want you to get it to Sakeri somehow. Not right away....but...later, after I'm gone."

"Gone?" Then he checked himself before he said more. He knew what she meant. He was puzzled about the request, but gave her the answer she wanted.

"Of course I will honor your request, and try to get it to Sakeri." The closeness they had over the annums and the realization the end was near was very painful to Rami.

"Lethra, I'll come visit you again as soon as I can, and bring you that new visicom."

"I know you will Rami." She smiled. Sadly, he kissed her on the forehead and then they left. Once outside, Fraya burst into tears. Knowledge of the government's procedures created more pathos than she could hold in check.

Rami stopped at a retail store and bought a new visicom; and made arrangements that it to be delivered to Lethra.

37. Fraya Escapes, Back to Ardena

As Arin instructed, Fraya and Rami sequestered themselves in a remote inn. Then, Fraya made a call to Arin telling him she was ready to leave, and asked what happens next.

"Arin, I thought all I had to do was get to a stratoport and depart. Are there complications?"

"Maybe, and we're taking no chances. Even though you were acquitted of the charges, we are dealing with an unpredictable individual, wielding a lot of power. He might trump up new charges, or just make some attempt to keep you in Bacamir."

"Other than to place blame if Settler-Two fails, why would Lockni want to keep me in Bacamir?" She asked.

"After he heard from that assistant of yours about some notes he may have seen, regarding some commercial space venture, he may be guessing you are involved in competing with him and his projects, and want to keep you confined. Let's hope he thinks the plans are merely for launching a commercial satellite, rather than the project we really have planned. I may be over-reacting, but I'm going to secretly get you out of there. I have two agents in Lignus right now. They will move you; first to a hidden mocar which will take you to a verticraft, and then the verticraft will take you to a remote stratoport in the mountains, where a smaller commuter-craft awaits. The small craft will lift you over the border, out of Bacamir where you will then transfer to a stratoliner for a flight to Solport. My agents will have the appropriate papers for border-crossing, and will stay with you for the entire trip."

"How did I get into such a mess?" she wondered out loud, and Arin, hearing her, gave her an answer.

"By being so smart, Fraya, and ambitious. If you had more aggressiveness, I'd be afraid of you myself. Stick with me and let me handle the political rough stuff."

"At least you're not trying to hide the fact you're using me. Actually, in a way I'm using you too, to accomplish some of my own technical goals."

"I know that, and as I said before, we'll get along. Now, let's get you out of Bacamir and over to Solport so you can work for me."

Rami and Fraya were cuddling in bed, far too perturbed for anything but fitful sleep, when they heard a light tap on the door. Rami went to the door and asked who it was.

"We're the bench people, two of us, and we're here to get Fraya."

"Show some identification," Rami asked, and opened the door a crack.

Two men pushed their way into the room, knocking Rami aside, and then headed for Fraya. She let out an hysterical scream and pulled the covers up to her neck, in a futile, defensive act. One of the two intruders grabbed her by the wrist, while the other stood threateningly in front of Rami.

"What do you want? Rami hollered.

"To take you back to Mizzen. Lockni wants you back."

As the first intruder started to pull Fraya out of the bed, a third, different voice hollered: "Stop!" Two more men entered the room.

The intruder let go of Fraya. In the dim light, it looked as if he was reaching into his jacket for a weapon, and a muffled shot collapsed him over the end of the bed. The other intruder threw his hands above his head.

"Don't shoot," he said. "I'm unarmed."

"And I'm the queen of Bacamir," replied the individual who fired the shot. "Search him! Hunter, see if he's really unarmed."

Rami backed against a wall to avoid getting into a line of fire.

"Surprise, Max," Hunter called out. "Here's a weapon in his unarmed jacket. He must have forgotten about this one."

Hunter moved the intruder to a chair and secured him with wrist manacles. Max stood there watching over them with his weapon pointed.

"I'll check out the body," Hunter said, as he walked over to the prone figure at the end of the bed. He checked him for breathing and pulse, found him alive - beginning to stir.

"You're losing your touch, Max, he's still alive."

"Oh well, maybe he'll die of an infection or a heart attack." Hunter looked over the body and dabbed at the wound with some of the bed sheet. Then, shining a light in the wounded man's face, recognized the intruder.

"Breezy Shagun? You? You could get yourself killed being so careless. What are trying to do here, Breez. We've been protecting these two for several arcs against people like you."

"Some protectors," Breezy replied, "letting us walk right in through the door." He looked toward Max. "I'm lucky you're such a

140

lousy shot, Max. Bristol should have shot you as you came through the door."

Max shined his light in the direction of the manacled intruder. "Well, what do you know. It's Herron Bristol. If I know Herron, he was probably afraid if he shot and missed he would get himself killed. Right Herron?"

"Big words with my weapon in your hand, you loser." Herron spat at Max.

A bewildered Rami, in an angry voice, stepped forward and hollered at the strangers in the room.

"What's going on here?"

"Well Rami," said the man who fired the shot, "I'm Max Burro, and my partner is Hunter Kronk. We're Arin Restor's boys. You saw us in his office once, when we started investigating the minitrans you found." He looked over at Fraya and told her to get dressed. She jumped out of the bed and began donning her clothes, as Rami stood near her.

Rami, still confused, directed a question to Max. "You all seem to know each other. Is that true?"

"Oh, sort of," Max replied. He went to a wall switch and turned on the light. "Herron, the one with the manacles, used to work with us in Arin's corps, but nobody liked him so he left and joined with Centre. His partner, the corpse over there, is Breezy Shagun."

"I'm not a corpse yet, Max Burro. You'll be one before I am." Shagun pressed some of the bed sheet against his wound.

Max moved to the center of the room. "Hunter, my partner, used to work for Centre with Shagun. Hunter's a good agent and fortunately is now on our side."

Rami was confused. "How do we know where your current loyalties stand?"

"You don't," Max replied, "but you'll have to trust us. Arin has ordered Hunter and I take you two out of here."

Max turned to the intruders. "We'll call authorities after we leave and have them set you free and patch up the hole in Shagun."

Shagun was sitting up now, holding his side.

"I wish you were on our side, Max. We could work well together."

"We probably could, Breez. And you are good, one of the best. I can hardly believe you let us take you so easily."

"It's an embarrassment, Max. So, in respect for our profession, why don't you just leave, and let us tend ourselves. The local authorities don't have to know about this."

"All right, Breez, but give me your word. You won't trail us for an arc?"

"You have my word, Max. By the way, where were you aiming. I always thought you could shoot better than that."

"You know better, Breez. I hit where I aimed, but next time I'll aim higher." Max turned to the now-dressed Rami and Fraya, told them to grab their bags, and go out the door.

"Get in our moc, Fraya. Rami, you're on your own. Get in your own moc, and if I were you, I'd head right back to Mizzen. You're not implicated in any of this intrigue, and nobody need know about it. We'll take Fraya back to Solport. As soon as you're out of sight, I'll release Herron."

"This is all crazy," Rami complained.

"Yes it is, but just do it - get in the mocs."

Rami put Fraya's bag in Max's moc, grabbed his own bag, gave Fraya a hug and left. Max went back inside.

"I have your word, Breezy, remember? I'm releasing Herron now, and leaving. Breezy, you can get yourself some medical attention if you want, and you can start trailing us next arc if you feel up to it. Your word, right?"

"My word, Max."

Max and Hunter, with Fraya as a passenger, sped off. The three motored westward toward the narrow entrance to the valley, where the canyon walls converged. As they neared the point called the Gateway, they pulled off onto a side branch and stopped out of sight, near an empty vehicle. Max moved Fraya quickly into the empty parked moc, and then, as planned, waved Hunter off toward the gateway to act as a decoy. He figured Breez would ignore the agreement and be close behind them. Allowing a short time to pass, Max then drove Fraya in a reverse direction, back up through Lignus, to a waiting verticraft. The verticraft flew them up and out of the canyon, to a pick-up spot in the valley beyond the Gateway. They landed near Hunter, took him aboard, and flew the verticraft to a small stratoport on the north side of the valley's farmland, almost in sight of Mizzen. The three of them then boarded a small commuter-craft that took them to a main stratoport beyond the border of Bacamir. Mizzen was visible in the distance from the air, and as they passed by, Fraya could see the clay-colored, mushroom-shaped cloud of haze that hung over the borough. She shuddered and wondered how she survived, breathing such an atmosphere.

At the large stratoport, they mingled and blended with a myriad of other passengers. An agent known to Max and Hunter gave them new credentials and documents, which they presented to border officials. Shortly thereafter, they departed for Solport on a stratoliner.

When she reached Solport, Fraya let out a sigh of relief, and thanked Max and Hunter for looking after her.

"You haven't seen the last of us, Fraya. Arin wants continuous protection for you, at least for awhile. We'll be checking for bugs, and watching your hostel. Here is a small necklace with an alarm-transmitter on it. Wear it, and if you press the button, one of us will come to your aid. Someone will always be nearby."

"I wonder, is this really necessary?" she asked. "After all, we're half-way around the planet from Bacamir."

"Probably not, but Arin is taking no chances. He wants you protected until we're reasonably certain nobody wants you returned to Bacamir."

38. The Settler-Two Approach

Fraya immediately visited her parents, and had to confront her father.

"Fraya, what have you gotten yourself into? International notoriety, technical acclamation for achievements, then accused of crimes in Bacamir, smuggled out under guard, and now, back to Ardena."

"Father, I know you told me ...." He stopped her with a raised hand.

"You are still my little girl and I am so glad to see you safely here, I am going to withhold the "I told you so." With tears wetting her cheeks, she hugged her father for a long time.

Fraya even settled into her old room, temporarily. The room seemed small and confining compared to the upper-level hostel she enjoyed as a rising star at Centre, but getting reacquainted with her sisters, and renewing the family bonding she had forsaken when she left home for Bacamir, kept her mind from dwelling on the recent trauma. Croak, her childhood friend came to visit and talk about old times, and reminisce about star gazing with her. He glanced at her chest.

"Your figure has certainly filled out since those times, Fraya. You look very nice." Fraya blushed a little at his comment.

Croak was a musician, and had remained friends with the family while pursuing his career. He was considered a family member when it came to entertainment. Most in Fraya's family were musical, except her. Fraya had no talent for playing an instrument, but loved the musical gatherings that were commonplace at the Lor household. She looked forward to Rami participating in a family party.

After a few commutes between her home and Solport, Fraya decided on a more permanent move, and settled into a hostel near Prollet. Agents always seemed to be nearby, so she resigned herself to the limited privacy she was going to have. She tried to keep Centre and the ordeal of the confinement and trial from dominating her thoughts, but it wasn't easy. She worried about Rami and his whereabouts, and the fate of Khanwali, no doubt sent on to his next life by the euthanists. She wondered how Lockni carried out the coup, but figured Khanwali was too trusting and let himself become vulnerable. She seethed when she thought of Lockni. He had gained control, as he had planned all along, letting nothing stand in his way. And Karlus; she still could hardly believe he had been spying on her.

Arin was anxious to get Fraya started on the commercial design, but knew the fate of Settler-Two was the most prevalent on her mind. He asked if she would like to set up a small tracking station in the Prollet offices, and she eagerly accepted.

"This is Arc-118 of Settler-Two's journey," she said. "Intercept is Arc-122 so I don't have much time."

She was given a cubicle, and access to stores of electronic equipment in Arin's inventory, and before long had put together enough receiving hardware to tune in signals, not only from the Settler-Two on its way to Terres, but also from Alpha-Surf, still circling Terres. None of her equipment would give her any control over Settler-Two, but at least she could track it.

On Arc-122, orbital intercept time, she listened, for possible sounds from Centre, of the countdown when Lockni would send the command for retrofire and enter the orbit. She wanted it to succeed, for the satisfaction of seeing her design work as planned, as well as for the thrill of discovery, of actually seeing the surface of another planet close up. She knew if the landing went as planned, Lockni would take the credit. If it failed, he would blame her in absentia and point out how astute he was in getting rid of her.

Sitting on a stool with an elbow on one knee and her chin cupped in her hand, she pointed to the little screen, and explained what was occurring to Arin, who had stopped in to see her.

"I've tuned the receivers to get the signals I want, Arin. The convergence of the two lines is the intercept point.

"Let me know when Settler-Two get close." He left, and patted a nearby security guard on the shoulder as he went by.

As she sat there staring at the monitor, she was interrupted by a signal on her communicator. It was Rami. back from Mizzen and here in Solport. She had the guard usher him in and greeted him with a hug and a kiss.

"What a greeting?" he breathed

.   "I'm glad you're here, Rami. I need the moral support. I should really be there, at Centre, you know. Settler-Two was my project, and it's my program in the craft's system. I wanted to be there when the lens opened and gave us that first look at the surface of another planet."

"I know, Fraya, but you're alive and well, away from Lockni, and have a great new project coming up. And, we'll see the view on your little screen right here, won't we?"

146

"I hope so. Even if we do, It's not quite the same," she replied.

"It's the best we can do and we have to accept it. Remember, good things are coming out of all this after all," Rami reassured her.

They sat together, looking at the monitor. Rami told her of his events the last few arcs, how he had returned to the Institute and made a progress report to Tribune Zeiss, his mentor, and then resigned. Wasting no time, he came here to Solport and visited Tribune Polosek. She asked him to continue working on the immune-system project for her. He agreed, and was now an associate of the Polosek Labs. He told Fraya, "it's the best of all lots for me. I'm here with you, still working on my project, free to travel back to Bacamir if I need to, and we have the commercial venture to look forward to."

Three arcs later the signal finally came; Lockni had sent the electronic command for retrofire. Fraya's equipment had picked up the transmission. The tracking beam, pulsing from a transponder on the craft, was quickly lost as Settler-Two swung around the backside into the shadow of Terres, called the blackout zone. Fifteen milliarcs later, the beam reappeared. She watched it for several circuits into and out of the blackout zone and concluded Settler-Two had settled into a large, elliptical orbit.

"So far - so good," she said.

Lockni and the technomies would have to initiate a series of small burns over a period of several arcs to circularize the orbit, and move it into the correct orbital plane. Fraya had stored a program into the craft's intelligencer for the landing sequence, but the initial timing and the proper orbital plane were very critical for the landing. Settler-Two would be descending soon.

39. Arg's Outing

The cave faced east, and by chance was oriented so the entrance received the beams of early sun. As usual, Zema had gotten out of their bedding earlier, before Arg, and stoked their little cooking fire. Thin fog sometimes spread the pale sunlight into a fan that felt good to Zema, and on this day Arg arose into the pallid, warming rays as they flooded over the entrance rocks. The rays fleetingly poked into the back reaches of the cave, then changed to shadows as the sun moved higher.

Arg went outside and looked up at the fast moving clouds. The morning's chilly breeze urged him to move a little closer toward the glowing community fire, and nudge into the circle of men.

"What we hunt today, Arg?" Asked one of the tribesmen, warming his hands. Arg didn't answer right away. Zema had walked up behind him and placed a hand on his shoulder.

"There won't be roots and seeds much longer, Arg. The growing time is near the end and the cold will be here before long."

"We have plenty of roots and seeds, Zema. Why we need more?"

"We never have enough. The ocotee seeds we grind are still plentiful but not for long. Nuts are falling from the trees. The onions are drying in the ground, and the tubers will soon be gone. The birds and small animals are beating us to the fruits. We should go and gather more while they last. Today I will take the children out. Will you come along?"

"That is woman's work," he replied loudly, raising his head and glancing around the circle, making sure all the men heard him. "Woman's work," he repeated, "but if we not hunt today, I will come."

"Woman's work," chortled several of the men. "Woman's work ... Arg will do woman's work."

Shaman, who had been quietly listening, raised a hand. "Silence," he commanded. "You will do well to follow your leader's example. He has taken good care of this tribe, and the nuts and seeds will soon be no more. So when you go and hunt today.... hunt seeds." The chattering group fell silent.

Zema went back inside the cave and busied herself around the cooking fire. The children, now up and about, went outside to find Arg.

"Papa, we go, we go," shouted the children as they began pulling at him. He had hinted they would go on an outing if the weather was good, and they were eager.

Arg and Zema, with their two children, left the cave and went out into the fields to gather what was left of pods and seeds. Brisk air was tugging at the yellowing leaves, and knocking nuts to the ground. Although the gathering of tubers and fruits was traditionally that of women and children, Arg enjoyed the outings and frequently broke convention to be with his family.

The weather was good and they made the outing a time of play, to watch the small animals scurry with cheeks full, and birds arguing over a morsel. Suddenly Arg hushed them. A growl had gotten his attention, and he motioned for them to crouch down while he investigated. He moved downwind from the sound and crept to a knoll for a better view. When he peered through the bushes, he saw a big feline in the distance playing with her two kittens.

What are they doing here, he wondered? There must be game nearby. The kittens were half as big as her, indicating they had been born early in the season, about the time the trees formed new leaves. As big as they were, they still acted like babies. One was nosing under her belly looking to nurse, and she playfully cuffed it away. Arg

149

motioned for Zema and the children to quietly come and watch, and they silently enjoyed the drama of felines frolicking in the sun. One of the kittens backed off for a distance, and charged the mother cat. He hit her broadside with his head, and she rolled over as if stunned. Both kittens leaped on top of her biting into the loose skin around her neck. She boxed them away, jumped up and chased them around, nipping at their flanks. When they stopped, both sat on their haunches while she began licking their faces, washing them. The purring from the kittens could be heard clear over where Arg and his family were hiding, and the children began to giggle and laugh. The noise startled the cats. They stood up and disappeared into bushes in the opposite direction.

Arg scolded them. "Now see what you done. You scared them and they ran away. Now you better run away." The children giggled some more and took off in separate directions with Arg and Zema chasing after them.

Life was good. Except for the occasional thieving carnivores, and impulsive raids by the bandits from Wigor's tribe, their existence was simple and contented. They returned to the cave with baskets full of bounty for the winter.

40. Settler-Two Lands

Fraya intermittently watched the screen and tracked the path of Settler-Two for three more arcs, while wondering if Lockni was adequately compensating for the Terres rotation. She certainly had explained it to him enough times, she thought. A slight miscalculation and it could land in the water, resulting in loss of the craft and another complete mission failure. Not only was Settler-Two traveling at orbital velocity around a spinning planet, it was in the blackout zone for half of its 30 milliarc orbit; all factors that complicate the landing maneuvers.

After tracking the craft for several circuits around the planet, Fraya feared the orbital plane was slightly off for the landing entry she had planned, but there was nothing she could do to correct it. Whether Lockni considered the error significant or not, she couldn't guess.

"What's going to happen next?" It was Arin's voice. He had arrived at her cubicle and squeezed in with Fraya and Rami to view the screen.

Fraya pointed at the curving lines on the screen.

"When Lockni's satisfied with the orbit, he'll start the landing sequence, which I programmed into the craft."

"Will there be anything to watch?" Arin asked.

"Not until it lands and the imager begins to operate," she replied. "And that may take a while."

"Keep me informed." As Arin started to leave, a faint voice came from the speaker and Arin stopped, turned around to listen. It was Lockni, making a verbal countdown. Rami leaned closer to Fraya, as if he could see the voice on the screen. Lockni's voice, coming through the speaker, had a chorus of others in Centre's control room joining in the count. This event, sending a command millions of kiloquants across the solar system, caused a ripple of sensation on the back of Fraya's neck. He was transmitting voice but she didn't know why. The thought occurred to her he knew she would be listening, and wanted to taunt her.

".......... three, two, one, activate!" came over the speaker.

"What's he doing now?" Arin asked.

"Starting the landing. First the solar arrays are jettisoned, and then the main antennas are stowed," she replied. "When the time was at hand, he pushed the button to start the sequence. All further control is pre-programmed, so events will happen automatically. If he started it at the correct time, the landing will come off as I scripted it."

"What's the craft going through now?" Arin asked.

"Settler-Two was already turned around backwards so its retrorockets were pointed in the direction of travel." She held a pencil horizontally, with the bulbous, eraser-end simulating the retrorockets. "By now, thrusters should be tilting the end of the craft upward so its retros are angled to slow the craft and push it down into the atmosphere." She demonstrated the tilt with the pencil, then paused, watching a timepiece on the wall.

"Automatic sequencers should be firing the retros .... and now it's slowing below orbital velocity, starting down out of space and into the stratosphere." She again showed the tilt-angle with the pencil, then moved it in a downward arc illustrating the entry into the stratosphere.

"The retro package should be jettisoned by now (she pulled the eraser off) leaving only a shell of insulation around the craft, to protect it during entry."

Five milliarcs passed before she began talking again, holding the pencil vertical this time. "Now its entering the frictional heat zone, flaming, and slowing until it gets to a lower, cooler altitude." She waited for another five milliarcs. "If it survived the descent through the hot zone, the fabric canopies should be deployed by now, and floating the craft down near the surface." She watched the timepiece some more, in silence.

"It should be within five hundred quants of the surface now, blowing away its shields of insulation, and igniting the landing rocket .... canopies should be disconnected and floating away. I hope they don't follow the craft down and accidentally collapse over it." More time passed. "If all went well, the craft is down. We should be seeing a contact signal within another five milliarcs."

The three of them were all waiting now, to hear the signal that Settler-Two had landed, on dry land, upright, and functional. When the

152

contact signal arrived, Fraya collapsed against the back of her chair. She had been holding her neck and shoulder muscles in tension without realizing it, and the strain had left her shaking and perspiring. Her navigation and program had accomplished the first known interplanetary landing, and all her dreams, desires, goals and studies seemed epitomized in that one signal, but she felt depressed. No one would know she had a part in it. Lockni would get all the credit.

"Where do you suppose it landed, Fraya?" Rami asked.

She managed a shaky reply. "I couldn't even guess. The orbital plane was off, so it could be north or south of my planned touchdown point, but apparently it missed the water and descended on a land mass somewhere. The fact that it sent a contact signal means the craft is down on a hard surface and in an upright position."

"Upright? You mean it could have toppled or fallen over?"

"Yes, but it has roll bars. Within limits, if it wasn't damaged, or hit a rock and flipped upside down, the legs would flex around and roll it upright."

Arin, who was still in the cubicle, asked about the images.

"What kind of images will it send? Still? Moving? Color?"

"Still, and gray-tone at first. There are two image processors, a main and a backup that can pivot vertically and horizontally on servo drivers. An image is absorbed into an intelligencer, transmitted on a carrier signal, stored, and then enhanced. With the equipment we have in this cubicle, we should be able to see the image as soon as they see it at Centre."

"When will that be?" Arin asked.

"It takes a while to get the power systems and batteries set for surface operation, the roll bars out of the way, antennas and imagers deployed, and all systems calibrated and working. Also, Terres is rotating and the craft has to be pointed toward Baeta in order for the

153

signal to be received here. So ... ", she began calculating, "Terres rotates about two and a half times for each of our arcs. That means, the lander is pointed at us about five times every two arcs, for a short open period of about 70 milliarcs each time. Not much time, but hopefully we'll see something within the next quarter-arc. It's really exciting, isn't it. Too bad Lockni will get the credit for all this, when Khanwali was the real mastermind of the overall project."

Arin looked absorbed. "I'm thinking of a ploy to thwart Lockni's gloating, and maybe help us get financing for the commercial venture. I'm going to call a media conference, Fraya, and let them know about your involvement. The fact that you were formerly with Centre, that it was your program on that lander, and that you now work for us will promote the Prollet image. After your role in the lander is made public, and the commercial project is announced, it will help me get backers. We need to strike now for the publicity. Also, if we can give the media a copy of that first image, it will be all the better. Is that all right with you?"

Fraya brightened. "I'll be glad to help. I wish I could see Lockni's expression when he hears about it."

41. Arg Sees the Lander

When Arg saw the big cats, he knew there must be large game in the area to attract them. He decided to take a hunting party and search for spoor. The next morning, as the smoke from Zema's cooking fire curled upward, Arg was sitting on his bedding, watching flickering shadows from the fire playing on the walls. He had selected about half the males in the tribe to go on a hunt this morning to search for signs of curlyhorns, a small, agile antlerpod that was a delicacy to the tribe-people, and was also fair game for the big, feline carnivores.

"Arg, we go, we go!" the men called.

He jumped up, pulled on his coverings, and joined them around the fire. When communicating, they used many words and sounds in combination, with vigorous gestures and hand movements. One of the experienced hunters was telling the younger ones about seeing curlyhorns in action.

"Jump this high," he exclaimed, and jumped into the air while raising his arm in a high arc. "Curlyhorns are fast, and hard to kill; not herd over a cliff like mammoth, or wild horse. They just turn around and jump away. We try to spear, but sometimes miss." The hunter demonstrated jabbing a spear at a phantom curlyhorn as it leaped over his head. "Not easy, so we hide in a pit and jump out at them."

The attempt was seldom successful on the first try, but when it finally happened and a curlyhorn was bagged, it was a great accomplishment. The hunters would brag about a kill for a long time. The goal today was hunting for spoor, and hopefully to see some animals. They gathered their spears and some dried food, and left for the fields.

This day was productive for the hunting party. They found a field where curlyhorns had frequented, and even found the remains of an animal the cats had downed. They whooped and hollered, and danced in a ritual circle, feinting toward imaginary animals with their spears until the participants were sweating and wild-eyed. After they had cooled down, they marked the field, and then went back to the cave for supplies. The fields were about a half day's walk from the cave so the leisurely round trip took most of the day. The sun was low on the horizon when they reached the cave, tired and ready to rest. Tomorrow they wouldn't walk; they would trot, as they usually did when in a hurry or trying to cover a great distance.

Now, on a new day, they gathered tools and supplies, and began the hike through the morning fog back to the fields for the actual hunt. The rising sun soon melted away the mist, and the weather was clear. The thrill of the hunt was theirs, and they were in a heightened state. The sun was nearly mid-morning when they reached the grassy field. They looked again for the curlyhorn signs and not only found the old marks, but many new ones, meaning more curlyhorns had been in the area since yesterday. The excitement of the hunters intensified.

Arg and his hunters walked around the field, noting prevailing winds and bushy cover, to find a suitable location for the pits. Unexpectedly, their concentration was broken by a loud, crackling roar from above, and all the heads pivoted upward, searching for the source of the strange sound. One of the hunters shouted and pointed to a strange object floating downward. The others near him peered into the bright sky in the direction he was pointing, and saw the object. It had three large, circular wind catchers billowing above it, like inverted baskets, and fire shooting downward from the object's bottom. The object made a roaring noise louder than a waterfall. A single loud pop, like the snapping of a dry limb, added to the noise. The wind catchers broke loose, then floated away with an undulating flutter, leaving the fire-spouting object standing still in the air.

Instead of falling, the object hovered for a moment like a stubby, wingless bird, then slowly descended on the pillar of flame looking like a mushroom on a big, sun-colored stem. The object disappeared below the tree line in a distant field, then the noise suddenly ceased. The group of hunters, excitedly talking and pointing, ran to Arg for counsel and reassurance. Confused and frightened himself, he had no explanation. Together, the group hurried back to the cave to discuss the event with the Shaman and the elders of the pack. They arrived as the sun was approaching the mid-afternoon

156

horizon. Several small cooking fires were smoldering in the cave, with a few women fussing with meat over the coals. Zema, Arg's mate, and several other women were outside the cave working with some of the children, weaving fibers into baskets. When she saw the look on Arg's face, she asked him what was wrong, fearing one of them had come to some harm. He motioned her away.

"I will tell later," he said, and went inside the cave. He stood with arms upraised and uttered a bellow. All in the pack knew this was their leader's call to order, and hushed. Arg waved to the elders and motioned them to join him for a meeting. The Shaman and the family leaders followed him outside the cave, where they sat in a circle. With much gesturing of hands and arms, Arg described the sight they had seen; a huge, flaming object in the sky floating downward on wind catchers, wind catchers that let go and flew away, and a fire underneath as it sank out of sight. He asked each to search his memory and speak, in turn, but amid much animated speculation, he heard nothing that might identify what they had seen. Most agreed it must be one of the fiery rocks that sometimes fall from the sky, leaving a quick glow in the air, and what looked like wind catchers must have been flocks of huge birds flying around it. Their Shaman was not so sure. He had seen the tiny light time and again, and had a strong premonition about the strange event.

"Arg, we must find it," he said, "and look closely before deciding what it is. Maybe not a fiery rock. Maybe something alive and dangerous. Or, maybe made by a tribe with special skills, may come back to get it. And, they may be hostile."

Arg agreed, and declared that tomorrow all the hunters except for the cave guards would go. Most tribes in the area maintained a code of possession, with mutual sharing if and when necessary. Arg's neighboring tribe led by Wigor, however, had some culprits who preferred to steal rather than hunt. Wigor himself was a nefarious miscreant, and ignored the acts of his wayward hunters - sometimes even glorifying the bandits and their stolen loot. Arg had little choice except to post cave-guards to ward off stray outlaws from Wigor's tribe.

The next morning the tribe's hunters left at dawn to look for the object. Circling about in the direction it disappeared below the tree line, it didn't take long to find it. One of them had spotted it in an adjacent field, and reported back to Arg. From a safe range, much pointing and chattering took place. Arg had them surround it at a distance, staying hidden from view, then furtively approach from different directions, darting from bush to rock as if stalking an animal. They presumed it would be aggressive, and each readied for defense as they watched it from hiding. After a while, when it didn't appear to move, Arg motioned the others to stay out of sight while he got closer. He taunted it by exposing his head, then his shoulders, and then he walked out into plain view, closer, but still distant. He briefly paraded back and forth a few times as if to test the object for aggressiveness, but still it didn't move. A whirring noise in the "thing" startled him and he ran for cover, retreating out of sight. He and the others peeked from hiding and watched, not knowing what to expect. Finally, some became bored with watching and wanted to get closer, but Arg waved them back. It was getting late and he wanted to return to the cave before dark.

****

Back on Baeta, the technomies in Centre's control room were powering up the systems on Settler-Two, one-by-one, step-by-step, waiting for each auto-test light to show green. Just after Arg disappeared out of view of the lander, the technomies activated the imagers, which deployed out of their compartments by noisy electrical servo motors. They unfurled the antenna and it snapped open like an inverted umbrella. Imager and transmitter indications were in the green so they attempted the first pictures. Images started to take shape, but by then, darkness had covered the area on Terres and nothing was discernible.

"Our timing is off," Lockni declared. "It's sitting in darkside on the planet, but the imager appears to have opened its lenses and is working. We'll have to wait for sunlight to get an image. We'll know if all is well in a quarter arc."

Half-way around the planet from Centre, Fraya sat anxiously looking at her screen at the Prollet site, while the Settler-Two imager transmitted the first, dark, fuzzy picture.

"Not enough light there for detail," she said.

"The Settler-Two must be in the dark part of Terres's revolution."

"How long before it will be light there," asked Arin who was watching the screen.

"Terres rotates about twice for every one of our arcs, so the terminator will pass over the Settler-Two in about two hundred milliarcs. It'll be light enough then."

"We'll just have to wait. Let's take some time away from this cubicle for a meal break." Arin squeezed out of the room. Rami gave Fraya a helping hand to get up, and both followed Arin to the dinery.

42. The Images

The morning sunlight on Terres washed over the landing site of Settler-Two. Fraya and Rami were sitting in the little cubicle when the first daylight image began arriving from the craft on the surface of

Terres. The picture was forming from transmissions of individual, overlapping strips as the secondary imager panned up and down, then moved to the side for more sweeps, creating a black and white mosaic on a small screen. The small, secondary imager had been brought up to power first. They would have to wait for activation of the primary imager to see larger pictures in color.

"If we were back at Centre," she explained to Rami, "we would see the mosaic projected onto a large screen, but we'll have to settle for our small, visiscreen picture for now." Fraya called Arin to witness the first image with them, and he poked his head into the cubicle to see the screen. As the image began to take shape, it had the three onlookers riveted. The image showed vegetation that looked like grasses, bushes and trees. Arin whistled.

"It appears the existence of living matter is not unique to this planet. Are we recording this?"

"Of course," Fraya replied. A silence fell over the three of them, each momentarily absorbed in private thoughts. Fraya expected to see rocks and bare, erosion patterns. Rami thought life on Terres might exist as organic scum in stagnant ponds. Arin was immediately thinking ahead to his commercial venture.

Fraya finally broke the silence.

"Cell structure is either very advanced on Terres, or we're getting a false image from some source on our Scorpian high plains."

Rami was deep in thought.

"One of my mentorians predicted a similarity if life is seen on Terres. He theorized that a source outside the solar system, such as meteorites or comets, could have spread petric dust or other molecules of organic matter throughout all the planets in our solar system. Maybe some common nucleotides or DNA has been sprinkled on both Baeta and Terres."

"Or, maybe a meteorite blasted some rock with organic cells off Baeta and it eventually landed on Terres," Fraya added.

"Regardless of how they started," said Rami, "grass and trees that look similar on two different planets supports the concept of evolution and adaptation."

"This is really good," said Arin. "Make us a copy of that image. I'd like to beat Centre at releasing it to the media and see if I can't use the publicity to some advantage."

"Now that living matter has been seen on Terres, I would think Centre will put a very high priority on funding a manned expedition," Rami said.

"For sure," Arin replied, "which means our program has to start immediately if we're going to be first." He looked at Fraya. "Centre probably suspects Prollet has some ambitious ideas, based on that snoop you had working for you, looking at your files, but I doubt if they believe any organization could be serious about competing with them for a manned trip." He turned back toward Rami so he could address both of them. "So ... as of now, the commercial venture will be separated from Prollet. Prollet will honor the contract with Centre and produce nuper engines for them, but the commercial venture will be a new, secret organization. We'll call it Restor Enterprises."

****

Lockni team was trying to figure out where Settler-Two landed, combining a coordinating cross-fix from the orbiter, and signals from Settler-Two. The Lead pointed to the trees near Settler-Two.

"We apparently had some good luck in the landing site. If we had landed in a clump of those unanticipated trees, we might have toppled and crashed." "Our surface sensors picked out a flat spot and

161

kept us out of the trees, Tribune Lockni," Karlus told him, parroting what he had just heard from the guidance lead.

"Otherwise it might have been catastrophic."

"Without reflective image-guidance," the lead added, "we couldn't tell what we were landing on."

"How close to our coordinates did we hit?" Lockni asked.

"We missed by quite a distance. Instead of that relatively flat looking area south of the Middleterren Sea, we landed north of it near the east end. The magnetic field is stronger than we thought and distorted a gyro. Also the rotational forces of the planet threw us off. Excellent job, Tribune Lockni. You proved we didn't need Tribune Lor."

Lockni bristled at the mention of Fraya's name, then nodded in approval at the compliment from his subordinate. Karlus however, cringed. He still felt some loyalty to Fraya and hadn't been able to shake the guilt he felt about teaming with Lockni to frame her.

"We can dispense with the mechanical scoop and the search for petron compounds," ordered Lockni.

"We obviously don't need to look for living matter if we can see it in a picture. Let's get right on with activating the large imager so we can get some color, and zoom to a larger focus."

"Right," said one of the scienomies, already reaching for knobs on the controller.

****

Fraya looked up at Arin. "A media conference? Not that I wouldn't like to embarrass my ex-boss, but wouldn't a media conference defeat the concept of secrecy, I mean, if your motive was funding for a commercial venture?"

"Remember Fraya, I said I was going to come up with a way of vindicating you and beating Lockni to the punch. We won't leak anything about the commercial venture. I just want to get you some multinational credit for the accomplishment, and keep ahead of your old counterparts at Centre. Showing the first image is just one way to accomplish that. For now, the details of our plans and progress must remain secret from them. I want you both on the program full time, right away. Any reason you can't join us Rami?"

"I'm working with a very smart geneticist here in Solport, with technology that may help our people stay healthy if they get exposed to infectious organisms on Terres. It would be to our advantage if I continue working with her at least on a part-time basis. Other than that, I don't see why not. I've already resigned my position at the Institute."

"That's good." Arin, who seldom displayed emotion or changed expression, smiled, shook Rami's hand, then patted Fraya on the head.

"Don't worry the details, Fraya, I'll handle everything."

On the subsequent arc, Arin released an image of the Terres vegetation to the news media, and scheduled a conference to highlight Fraya and her accomplishments. He wanted to beat Centre and did. The auditorium was packed with the curious, bubbling with questions, and Arin basked in the spotlight. He introduced Fraya and explained how she had developed many of the systems that navigated the spacecraft to Terres; and, that it was her program that resulted in the successful landing.

"And," he added, "prior to the landing, she was released from her position at Centre, but her systems worked automatically. We are happy she was released, because now," he said, "she's here, working for Restor Enterprises, a new company that will develop commercial space projects and compete with Centre for satellite business."

"What kind of satellite business will you compete for?" One in the audience asked.

"Communications, mostly," Arin replied. "We won't be doing any research nor deep-probe launches. We'll leave that to Centre. After all, they have the expertise and the resources. We'll have to sell our satellites and make profits if we're going to stay in business very long."

"How can you possibly compete with an organization that has been involved in space research as long as The Celestial Research Centre? Another asked.

"Because we have Tribune Fraya Lor on our side." Arin raised his chin in a smug pose as he replied.

"You see, they've lost a brilliant innovator and will remain technically stagnant, while we leap ahead in new technology.

"Why was Tribune Lor released from Centre?"

Arin glanced at Fraya and gave her a reassuring smile. He knew this question would come up and he was prepared. He planned to be forthright. Fraya just stared at Arin, wondering how he would answer. Rami grabbed her hand and gave it a squeeze.

"Along with her responsibility of navigating the lander and getting it successfully to the Terres surface, Tribune Lor was handling a very sensitive new program for Centre. You might remember, the first attempt at a landing was a failure. Tribune Lor was not involved with the Settler-One and that landing attempt, but was determined that Settler-Two would not fail in its mission. She was handling both the new project and the Settler-Two assignments quite admirably. Certain people at Centre misinterpreted some of her dedication to the new project, and saw it as an opportunity to wrest the lander program away from her. She was charged with treason and sent to trial, but was acquitted. I repeat, she was found innocent. In spite of being found innocent, she felt she could no longer function effectively at Centre, and left. She had to watch her lander, with her programs and equipment, make the first successful landing on Terres on a small screen here at Restor Enterprises."

Fraya was impressed with his reply, and relieved.

"Who took over the landing program after she left?"

"The same individual that failed with the Settler-One. His name is Hirl Lockni. Fortunately he didn't change any of Tribune Lor's on-board guidance programs."

Another hand in the audience shot up. "Let's get to the subject of life on Terres. How do you explain that and what does it all mean?"

Arin introduced Rami, explained that he was a biologist, and would handle the queries about the foliage seen in the picture.

Rami began. "There are so many unknowns about our beginnings and our existence that the curious will never get enough answers. One of the most prevalent questions in the minds of scientists, and theologians, and of course the philosopher in most all of us, has been about the scope of life. Are we, on this planet for example, the only living things in the entire celestrium? In our solar system? That question has now been partially answered. We have now seen vegetation on Terres. Whether animal life exists on Terres, we don't know at this point, but we can assume photosynthesis works there as it does here, and the cycle includes animals." Rami went on to explain as best he could about the common DNA theory, and the possibility that if it came from outside the solar system, there could be life not only on Baeta and Terres, but all throughout the celestrium.

"Does this change all the theologies that believe in only one Zhu?" Another asked.

"Like so many other theological questions, I can only give you my opinion. No, it needn't change beliefs about Zhu." Rami told the audience about the comparison of Zhu with a farmer sprinkling seeds, a story he heard Fraya tell his mother and father. It seemed to be accepted by many in the audience.

The conference ended. Rami heard a page asking him to come to the main reception area for a call. He excused himself wondering who would be calling him here. Taking the instrument from the receptionist, he was surprised to hear his father's voice.

"I've just seen the image on the visinews, Rami. The image is pretty clear. That vegetation looks somewhat like we would see on the high plains of Scorpia, with grass, bushes, and trees - clumps of them. You didn't attempt to explain the similarity during the news conference, Rami."

Similar? Rami thought he was going to get into another confrontation with Jerod over creation versus evolution.

"I don't have an explanation, Jerod, I don't know what it all means?"

Jerod surprised him. "Well, if Zhu did create a second living world, why would it be any different from the first?"

Rami was surprised at Jerod's acceptance and explanation. "Thank you father. I appreciate your opinion. Arin disappeared to take care of other business. Rami departed for his work at the labs of Tribune Polosek, and Fraya went back to her cubicle, waiting and watching for other images.

43. The Humanoid

On Terres, the whirring noise from the object had frightened Arg. He and his party left the field and the thing for the night, and mingled around the fire at the entrance to the cave. The thing was the talk of everyone. Arg was so sure the thing must be alive and dangerous, he wanted a vigil to stand guard at the cave entrance throughout the night. At a meeting of the elders around the fire he spoke his fears, but Shaman was more philosophical than most. He said noises do not mean it is alive.

"A rock rolling down a cliff causes noise. The wind can make a tree fall and make noise. Even ice on a lake, shifting so slowly you can't see it move, makes loud noises." Arg felt less anxiety about the object after listening to the Shaman, but the object was strange and different, and strange and different meant danger.

Everyone wanted to see the sky-object, so the next morning Arg picked half the members in the tribe go to the field. Some had to stay and keep coals glowing in the main fire, and guard the cave. Arg invited Shaman to go along, and allowed Zema and some of the other women and children to join them. They approached the object carefully, with the hunters creeping up first, into positions of advantage for seeing the object without being seen. It was still there in the same place, apparently stationary, so they moved closer and closer. Finally, Arg stepped out of the hiding places and motioned for Shaman to follow, but with some range between them. The women and children all came out into the open but Arg wanted them to remain off to the side, for safety. Some of the hunters, pressed together, peered around each other, and viewed it from a distance, but fear kept them from getting too close. The strange object stayed very still, except for slight movement of something near the top, that seemed to sway slightly from side to side, as if in the wind. Arg decided to test the object up close for aggressiveness. He told Shaman to remain back until he signaled, then boldly walked right up to the thing, within arm's reach. The thing was quiet, and he wondered if he really heard noises when he was here yesterday. It just sat there, never moving. Two hard half-shells, like large turtles clinging to its sides made it look like a

167

huge bug. It was about the same height as he, and twice as wide as it was tall. It had a large, slanted, loosely woven shallow basket sitting on top that looked like it was open to the sky. Its fat body had spindly legs that never moved, and he could see no head or tail. The grass was scorched and burned all around where it sat. Arg got very close, standing there in the stillness, examining and ready to fight if necessary. As the imagers started pivoting, the drive motors made a sudden whirring noise, startling him and he instinctively lashed out with his club, striking it several times. The blows dislodged both the primary and the secondary imagers from their mounts. They fell sideways, amid a myriad of wires splayed in all directions. Arg listened for the whirring sound after he struck the object, but it had stopped. "If it was alive," he thought, "I must have killed it."

After a while, as he stood there watching the dead object, some of the others came up next to him for a closer look. He reached out and touched the thing. It was harder than a turtle's shell, but smoother, more like the tusk on a mammoth. He pulled on the dangling parts that he had smashed, and a piece came loose. It was light in weight and had a sharp edge. He passed it around and each curiously looked at it, feeling its smooth hardness, and grunting opinions. Arg decided to carry it back to the cave for others to see. He thought it might even make a good hide scraper.

When the party arrived back at the cave, they were immediately surrounded by curious members of the pack who had stayed behind. The piece from the thing was passed around from person to person, with each one sniffing and scratching, trying to identify it. Stories from their ancient lore included descriptions of large sky rocks that had flamed above with a roaring noise before impact. They concluded this hard material must be similar to a sky rock, which explained the flame and noise but no one offered an explanation for the wind catchers and the whirring noises, or the shell and legs on the object.

On Baeta, the Centre scienomies had shut down the primary imager and were in the process of converting it to motion mode when their screens went blank. For some unexplained reason, the lander quit transmitting images. When it happened, some of the technomies tapped on their gauges as a natural reaction, like tapping the quantity indicator when a moc runs out fuel. They tweaked on knobs and levers, but still stared at blank screens.

Less than four arcs had gone by since Settler-Two had successfully landed. It had worked almost perfectly since going on line, and was transmitting with normal signal acquisition, and then suddenly went dead. No interruptions, sputtering, or weak signals, it just abruptly quit. The systems specialists labored diligently to restore life to the machine, but to no avail. Trying to diagnose and work around the signal loss, they checked the power unit, the imagers, the transmitters, any of which might have short circuited or burned out a component, but nothing worked. The lander had redundant systems even to an auxiliary antenna, but none were effective. It wasn't battery failure because a carrier signal was still being received. However, the carrier signal was blank. They tried to activate the backup imager, which was housed with the main imager for simplicity, but it, too, was dead. The specialist in charge of imaging told Lockni nothing seems to help, and it looked like imaging was lost. Lockni cursed and banged his fist down repeatedly.

"Keep trying to reactivate it," he shouted. "Fraya must have put something in the program to shut it down in case she wasn't here."

He threw a clipboard at the main console, but the specialist standing nearby deflected it with his hand. Lockni stomped off. The specialist then made an announcement over the laboratory speakers so all would be appraised that the Settler-Two's imagers had quit transmitting. Mumbles of disappointment passed from person to person throughout the Centre labs.

Arg had confronted the object while the main imager was inactive, and the Centre crew missed seeing him because their screen was blank during the transition. They had captured an image of Arg from the secondary unit, which operated until it was smashed, but didn't know it. The image was stored in the receiver's memory without appearing on their screen.

In Ardena, Fraya's receiver in her little cubicle was tuned to both imagers. Her split screen, rather than going blank, showed a brief glimpse of the humanoid from the secondary imager before Arg smashed them. The signals stopped coming in from Settler-Two for some reason, but she had captured an image of a humanoid on Terres, without knowing that the control room techs at Centre hadn't seen it. The screen was now blank but she recovered the image from the memory bank, and brought the picture back onto the screen. She stared at the picture and gulped. The realization a humanoid exists on Terres was startling. Fraya immediately called Rami at Polosek's lab.

"Rami, get over here right away if you can. We've got an image that looks like a man, or at least an upright animal on two legs. The signals from Settler-Two have stopped coming and I don't know why, but we did get this one image."

Rami put an experiment on hold, and told Polosek that Fraya had an exciting new image from Terres to look at. Clodea had followed the news of the vegetation image with as much enthusiasm as anyone on the planet, already thinking of the genetic comparison and compatibility with living matter from another world.

"I'm very interested, Rami. Please let me know what she found, she said.

"You'll know before the news media, I promise." Rami exchanged his lab coat for his tunic and bolted out the door, went directly to Prollett and squeezed into Fraya's cubicle.

"Look at this Rami," she panted. Fraya literally pulled him to the screen.

"We've got something here from the secondary that looks like a human." She replayed the disc and brought the images up again. Rami watched the screen as the still images in the memory flicked on showing the Terres surface, transmitted earlier. They saw a repeat of the vegetation, and then, the upright, two legged animal appeared. His heart started pounding, and Fraya hit a switch that "froze" the image on the screen.

"There it is!" Her mellow voice had a higher than normal pitch. Rami studied the image.

"After all the annums of speculation and arguments as to possible intelligent life elsewhere," he said, "and all those papers published on the statistical probability of life in other solar systems or on other planets in our own solar system, they are all answered now. And Terres is right next door!"

"Look at its features," said Fraya. "Fortunately we got a semi-profile. It's head is bulbous in back, it's forehead is flat, and it has practically no neck. Look at those bushy, protruding eyebrows, and the recessed chin. It's garbed in some sort of animal skins."

Rami looked at the hands. Although the image was fuzzy, he counted four fingers and a thumb on the one he could see. "That object it's holding, it looks like a spear. This creature has weapon intelligence." He paused in thought. "This raises so many new questions; here is a creature that carries a spear, uses animal skins for clothing, and probably conquered the use of fire."

171

"Incredible," Fraya murmured. "Nobody expected this. How advanced do you think they might be?"

"I have no idea." Rami kept studying the image. "Here on Baeta our ancestors looked like that maybe two hundred-thousand annums ago, carrying clubs and spears, and living in caves. On the other hand, there may be people still living in caves in some remote areas on this planet. It's possible Settler-Two just happened to land in a primitive area on Terres, and there are more advanced societies elsewhere. It's impossible to say."

Fraya nodded. "True. One image doesn't tell us much about his state of advancement."

"This is sensational. Now I really want to go there, to see them first hand?" Rami said. "Lots of questions immediately come to mind. Do they have a cell structure and anatomy similar to ours? Do they birth live? Is the birth placental, or cloaca with pouch?"

"We'd better get Arin back here and show him this. He's away on other business, but this should be top priority over anything he's doing."

"Why don't you call him. And while you're doing that, I promised Clodea I'd let her know if there was anything new and exciting in the image. She'll want to see the images too."

Fraya stood up and left the room to contact Arin on the communicator. "I'll be back by the end of the arc," Arin said. "If that image is a humanoid, as you say, get some copies made, and be ready to release them to the media. I doubt if we can beat Centre to a news item again, but its worth a try. They, at Centre, do have their cumbersome chain of command and protocol, so we have a little advantage, but very little this time." Arin had no more idea than Fraya that the image of Arg was stored at Centre in a memory bank, and no one there had seen it yet.

172

When Arin returned, he looked at the monitor in awe. "Shades of Zhu," he exclaimed, looking at the humanoid. "This will be the greatest news event in history. We must get a manned trip to Terres before Centre ... it's a must. But first, lets get some publicity."

As before, Arin called a media conference and introduced Fraya. He explained her position with Restor Enterprises, her former relationship with Centre, and then released the image of the humanoid. Pandemonium broke out and reporters scrambled to get to their communicators. By the next arc, publications had images and glaring headlines; "TERRES HAS PRIMITIVE MAN". The visicom news showed the interview with Fraya, and played the image of the humanoid over and over. Some scenes on the visicom were taken at Centre to get Lockni's reaction. They showed Lockni's reddened face and screaming voice criticizing Fraya and Restor Enterprises. He was furious the image was released to the media by someone other than Centre, and attempted to debunk any suggestions that Fraya should receive credit for the navigation. Transcoms jangled with reporter's questions. Inquiries started rolling in from governments, academic institutions, museums, and zoos all over the planet about the possibility of a trip to capture one of the creatures. Fraya was almost glad she was no longer at Centre, knowing Lockni and the Terres scienomies were spending a great deal of time in media conferences. It was bad enough that many were calling her for interviews, and wanting to see the screen at the Restor building. Arin allowed one additional media conference to take place and it was overwhelming.

"You should see the crowds of the curious," she babbled to Rami. "They want to watch my screen right along with me. Can you imagine more than three people squeezed into this cubicle? Individuals all over the planet are calling with questions or sending advice. Some of the calls are from zealot dominaries screaming that

173

the images are all fake. Some support capturing one of the creatures if a manned landing ever takes place. What do you think about bringing back a creature?" Fraya stopped and took a breath.

"You know I hate to see any animal in a cage," Rami replied, "but as a biologist I'd love to study one."

"Of course," Fraya said, "and if we ever get there, we can study them in their own habitat. We don't need to bring a creature back here."

"I wonder what position Arin will take on this issue."

Arin had his ideas. "We are going to start now, this arc, gathering a cast of specialists, designers, and manufacturing experts to put this venture together. We have some momentum and must take advantage of the hype, and, what was your question? Oh, yes, about bringing back a humanoid. It sounds appealing but that decision is way down on the priority list. Foremost is beating Centre to the first, manned, interplanetary landing, and bringing back some artifacts."

Rami and Fraya enthusiastically agreed, and looked forward to starting on the new venture.

44. Killing the Thing

The fires inside the cave were out, and the cave was cold. The moon glowed brightly in clear skies, leaving a nighttime chill in the air. Zema snuggled her back up against Arg in their bed of animal furs, and pulled his arm around her in a protective fold.

"You have been quiet for days," she said. "Even the children have noticed. What is the matter with parah, they ask. He has not chased us, or scolded as he usually does. You have not relieved yourself in me in as many days. Tell me, what problem occupies your thoughts?"

He paused, and thought out his answer. "Our keep is not a worry, we are safe in our cave and, our larder is full. The ice rivers are melting away from our valleys, and life is good."

"What is it then?" Zema asked. She knew very well what was bothering him. "Is it the thing?"

"Yes, it is the thing. Our elders think it is one of the burning rocks we see in the night sky, that showers sparks, like poking a fire. They can cause the grasses to burn where they hit, and they look like rocks. How then, can this thing that is not a rock be a flaming star?" Arg asked.

"If all flaming stars are like rocks," she replied, "then this thing is not a flaming star."

"I thought it was a living thing, like a huge insect. It made noises, but it never moved. When I bashed it with my club, it seemed to die, but maybe it is still alive, waiting. It is something we don't know, and I think it will bring other things like it in time."

"Tomorrow you should discuss it with the Shaman, away from the elders and their interruptions. He too has been very quiet lately."

"You are right, Zema. I feel better." With that he nuzzled against her and found himself aroused. She pulled at him until he was on top of her naked body, and relief came quickly.

The next day, Arg asked the shaman to walk with him away from the rest of the pack, as Zema suggested. They left the cave and strolled along together in thought, until finally the Shaman spoke.

"We have seen the little light in the sky, and now this strange thing in the field. It is not a flaming star, Arg!"

"No, and I think it may be alive; will awaken, and do us harm. I have looked at it many times and it never seems to move. If alive, it must be some kind of huge insect that will hatch in time, as does the caterpillar to a butterfly. Maybe we should kill it now?" Arg ran his hand over his brows as if to brush the questions away.

"Our way is to kill for food or to defend ourselves. I, like you, do not think it is a flaming rock. Suppose we continue to watch and see if it begins to hatch like an insect. If it appears aggressive, then we can defend ourselves against it, and kill it if we must."

Arg thought about the Shaman's suggestion while they walked, and then rejected it. "No, waiting to see if it gets aggressive is wrong. It doesn't belong here, so we will kill it now. I will send some men to the field tomorrow, and destroy it.

While some of Arg's hunters were beating the "thing" apart with clubs, and gathering some of the pieces, one of the men had stumbled across the billowing wind catchers. Not knowing what it was, he and his companions found it almost impossible to tear, but with sharp rocks and much effort, they cut out a small piece and carried it back to the cave. Everyone felt the material, sniffed, tasted, and pulled on it, wondering what it was. Here was another strange material. It was soft. Not as soft as the fur on the sneaky little carnivora, but it was made of very fine fibers. No woman had ever made, or even seen, finer weaving. Its color was like a bright cloud. The hunter who found it told the group how big it was. "Huge, like the clearing in front of the cave." He walked in a circle to show the size.

Shaman studied the piece of material, picked at an edge and unraveled a small amount of thread. He predicted that this was an omen of more strange things to come, things they may never understand. "This is made by a tribe somewhere strange to us, a tribe in the sky with skills we do not know. It is not the "thing" we need to fear, Arg, it is the tribe that made it. This Skytribe may come with other "objects", and we must be wary."

45. Fraya Queries Millen

Millen was Centre's mission planning specialist, and a good friend to Fraya. Before she left Centre, they frequently took meal breaks together, and exchanged the latest in Centre's gossip and rumors. After the trial was over and Fraya left, Millen wondered if he would ever see her again. She called him to get some advice, and he was both surprised and pleased when he heard her voice.

"Fraya, I'd hoped you'd call sometime. I miss you. What are you doing and how are you? Bring me up to date."

"It's good to hear you voice, Millen. I, too, miss our rapport and meal breaks. I'm doing well, in a new job now. I'm sure you've seen the news on the visicoms touting me as the navigator on Settler-Two. And, how about that picture of the humanoid?"

"Unbelievable. And, oh yes, you should have seen Lockni going ballistic around here. He ripped your banner off the wall, balled it up, and stomped on it.   It was not very pleasant for awhile. Frankly, I'd like to get out. Whatever you are doing, I'm sure it's more interesting and innovative than what I'm doing now. Can you find a place there for me, with an interesting job?"

"Maybe. What I called about is advice, Millen. If you were charged with the responsibility of putting together a bare, minimum team from scratch, for planning a round trip to Terres using the nuclear engine, what kind of specialists would you include on the project?" Fraya tried to act nonchalant, as if it were almost a rhetorical question.

Millen sensed a new opportunity forthcoming. He could hardly control his eagerness, but was congenial and desirous to share some of his knowledge with his friend.

"Well, for planning purposes, you'd need a mission planner, naturally, and in addition to yourself as propulsion and guidance

177

expert, a logistician, a payload specialist, a radiation specialist, and some design engineers and planners. If you are talking about a manned journey, include a biologist or medical person knowledgeable in immune systems. Also you might consider having a Dominary or a counselor in the group, to keep a sanity check on the operations."

"That's similar to the list I had come up with, but I'd left out a few. I appreciate your opinion, Millen. There is a special reason I ask, and eventually I can tell you why, but I can't now. All right?" said Fraya.

"Certainly. You've aroused my curiosity of course, but I can wait until you're ready to tell me what you're up to. After all, we're both trained to query only on a 'need to know' basis," Millen replied. "Obviously, I don't need to know for now."

Fraya thought about telling him more, but hesitated. Millen was a good friend and one she could socialize with at work, share mealtimes, and talk about her frustrations when the need arose. Telling him about the commercial venture now may put him in some unknown danger, and she didn't want that to happen. She was already planning on him to be her mission planner.

"Thank you, Millen, it was just a curiosity I've had. I'll be in touch with you some more."

The commercial venture was officially started. Arin provided Fraya with a large, well decorated office on a balcony overlooking the factory floor, and she felt elegant when in it. However, for the present, her comfort zone lay in the little cubicle where she had hastily assembled the tracking equipment and followed Settler-Two to the landing. It was a sanctuary. In her new office, she was making notes about the flight path, and visualizing what equipment would be needed to get there, the requirements, and alternatives. When duties appeared overwhelming, she went to the cubicle and sat, holding her head in her hands, thinking. The venture, that was so exciting at first, now stretched her capacity to understand all that had to be accomplished in a short time. There were no facilities, no design group, and no organization. This project needed organization. She wasn't even sure she could comprehend all the facets of this project. Certainly not alone - she needed help, much help, and right away. She needed Millen.

She called and asked him to contact her from a private communicator.

"Millen, I'm involved in a forthcoming commercial space venture. Without getting into details, we'll be in competition with Centre, and in my new role as project director I'm already getting close to mental overload. With your talent for organization, and logistics, I could use you on our team. Rami is with us, but he's technical like I am. The project will be built and launched from Ardena, so you'd have to move here and separate yourself from Centre. Before you decide, why don't you come here for an interview, and get more details if you want."

"Of course I'd like to work with you, Fraya, but there are a lot of things to consider. Let me discuss it with Lorol, and get back to you."

"Fair enough, Millen," she replied. "I'll be waiting for your decision."

46. Selecting the Managers

Fraya left her cubicle and went into a conference room to meet with Arin. He was an expert at coordinating large projects, and his guidance and experience could relieve much of her anxiety. He assured her the tasks would get more comfortable very quickly, and he would be there to guide the organization.

"I know you're drenched in details right now, but I have confidence you'll have all the technical requirements sorted out before long. You do need competent managers to design and build this thing to your requirements, and here's what I propose; three senior section leaders, which are, a facilities manager, a chief engineer, and a factory manager. I have recruited a candidate for each position, and they are all here, waiting to meet you. So, whenever you're ready...."

"Now is as good a time as any," she nervously replied.

Arin called them into the conference room next to her office for introductions.

"Presarios, may I present Tribune Fraya Lor, inventor of the micro- guidance system that took the unmanned lander to Terres, and got us the image of the humanoid. She will be director of our project, and will get us a man to Terres and back before Centre does. We are starting with nothing except this factory, that makes farm-equipment. It will be crowded, but we'll build flight hardware and new buildings, all at the same time."

"At first, we'll have offices and temporary work areas on the balcony of this building. Below, we'll start moving some of the tractors and other soil equipment out of the way, and begin shaping parts. There is enough open land adjacent to the facility to put up additional buildings as needed, and there is room for a launch pad complex. For identity separate from Prollett, we'll call this facility Restor Stellar Park.

"Fraya, facilities are a first priority. My selection for a Facilities Manager is one who currently runs the soil-machinery factory right here in this building. Bemon Brockler will move equipment, jigs, and machinery as necessary to make us some temporary working space, and then alter or construct any new buildings needed. He will also oversee the construction of our paved launch pads and associated support buildings." Fraya acknowledged Brockler with a nod.

"Next, we need a design manager. For Chief of Engineering, I lured Canon Johns away from Stratopulse where he created many of their largest boosters and nozzles. He is an old friend who was looking for a new challenge." Fraya recognized Canon, for she had met him at Stratopulse when she was surveying for potential nuper contractors. They exchanged formal greetings, and he said, "Call me Canon."

"Finally," Arin concluded, "my candidate for Factory Manager is someone you've already met because you've worked with him on the nuper at Prollet. Traylor Cabriz will operate the factory, and build the launch and flight equipment that Canon designs." Fraya greeted the manager from Prollet.

She knew Arin would pick very experienced and competent individuals who could manage, but she was concerned about their attitudes toward her as director. She had a brief, private conference with each of them and decided Arin had chosen well. Each seemed easy to talk with and displayed no apparent animosity, arrogance or patronizing attitudes.

"Perfect for the job," she decided. She called a short staff meeting of the three, and along with Arin, laid out the preliminary program for the first commercial trip as she saw it.

"Presarios, we are going to fly a crew to Terres, land, gather artifacts, and return before Centre does. Instead of building one craft to fly to Terres and back, we've decided it will be more efficient to send and keep a supply station in orbit around Terres, for staging. It will be called the Barge, and by necessity will be first in order of priority, to build and launch. The Barge has to be sent on its way as soon as possible because it will use the conventional propellant systems, and take about one and one third annums travel time. The craft that will carry the crew will use the nuper and catch the Barge in about forty

181

arcs. We'll plan to launch the crew shortly after the barge goes into Terres orbit."

Fraya went on, and as she spoke, felt more and more confidant about directing these experienced and knowledgeable leaders.

"Presario Canon, as chief engineer you will have the responsibility for complete design of the launch vehicles, the nuper, and the spacecraft. I suggest you establish sub-projects for each major piece of hardware, and hire an appropriate sub-manager for each project. Draw up outlines and schedules, and be prepared to show them at our senior staff meetings, which I will be holding every three arcs to start with. Your experience with the big boosters at Stratopulse will be invaluable. Our plan is to buy off-the-shelf equipment from Stratopulse, and modify it to suit our needs. Rami Slade, my co-director will handle all life support requirements. You will have to design around his inputs, Canon. I also have a mission planner selected to join us very soon."

"Very good Tribune Lor. By the way, how should we address you?"

"Just call me Fraya, if you like." She turned to the next person.

"Presario Brockler, as facilities manager, you are already aware of a major problem; working space for the designers. Tackle that one first, and then our manufacturing buildings. Later we can begin on the pad and launch facilities. You are also required to participate in the senior staff meetings."

"I know these facilities like the back of my hand," Brockler replied. "We'll need some new buildings, of course, but we can set up temporary portables away from this factory noise until they're built. We'll take care of the people. As you say, production facilities and the launch pad can wait for awhile. By the way, call me Bemon."

"Very well. Presario Cabriz, do you have a preferred call name?"

"Several, but let's settle for Cabby."

"All right Cabby, as factory manager you will fabricate the equipment that Canon designs, in the facilities that Bemon builds. Coordinate closely with Bemon until we start building hardware. Hire a good quality-control manager to run a separate department within your operation, and find a suitable Director of Procurement to set up a materials system. Be at all senior staff meetings." Fraya continued. "I will handle all technical support groups as needed, such as mission planning, logistics, thrust calculations, and the structural analyses that Canon will need. Also, I will design the guidance systems. You haven't met Rami yet, but he will handle life support and biology for the mission. Come see me individually at any time, but be at the first staff meeting three arcs from now."

Before they departed, Arin made strong directives about cooperation. "I know all of you, and your excellent qualifications, and am confidant that you will get this venture off the ground like none others could. There will be design and production problems of course, and facilities won't be available fast enough, and materials will be late or unavailable, but with cooperation, we can mutually overcome those obstacles. I want you to identify potential solutions in your own offices before coming to the senior staff meetings. At the senior staff meetings we will make decisions and mark our progress as professionals. One other thing; most of my enterprises and projects have been successful, partly because my managers spent very little time hunting for someone to blame when there was a problem. I do not tolerate malicious dissension in senior staff meetings. When a production glitch occurs, and they will, I don't want to hear about the other person's late drawings or poor design, or factory inefficiency, or unreal tolerances, or some other department's failures to perform. The first sign of finger pointing in a senior staff meeting means you couldn't settle the issue beforehand, and are tired of working here. You will be relieved of your position. Most problems can be resolved at other than the senior staff meetings, and anyone can come to me or Fraya individually for a personal conference to resolve issues. Incompetence can be dealt with privately. This is going to be the planet's biggest exhibit of cross-department cooperation in history. I know that many of your sub-managers will think belittling subordinates is a management technique. Send them to me; I am very good at explaining belittlement to these types. I am also aware there are those who create problems so they can receive recognition as problem solvers. We need problem solvers, of course, but we also place more value on problem preventers. Are we in agreement on this way of thinking?" All three uttered approval of Arin's approach.

After they all departed, Fraya left the conference room and went into her office. She sat down and marveled at this turn in her life. In less than an annum, she went from terrified confinement in an isolated cell, to this spacious office tastefully decorated in a variety of finely finished woods. Arin wanted her to feel the power of elegant surroundings and it was working. So far, she felt euphoric. She opened a transcom circuit to Millen Cyrriz, and when he answered, briefed him on the project.

"You asked me to find a position for you, Millen. Well, I need you on this project and right away.. Give me an answer Millen ... things are starting to roll here."

"Lorol wants to stay here with the children and let them continue on with their academics, but I've decided I don't want to pass on this chance to work with you and a new project."

"Does that mean you accept?" Fraya asked, elated.

"I'd like to know more about it, Fraya." Millen hesitated, then asked.

"What would I be doing?"

"I'd rather not go into details, Millen, for security reasons. Why don't you come here for an interview and overview, without sacrificing your job or status at Centre. If it doesn't appear to suit you, you can return with no suspicions within your peer group. I'm one-hundred percent sure you'll like the project, though."

"I'll be there, Fraya."

47. Gathering the Work Force

Word got around. Important managers of many large companies were leaving their jobs and disappearing into Ardena, lured to the new project by their former bosses, who were now part of the Restor Stellar project. Rocket boosters were being ordered from Stratopulse, and materials and resources were being stockpiled at the Restor facilities. Millen arrived within a few arcs and Fraya greeted him warmly, showed him around the farm equipment building now undergoing remodeling, and then up to the second level offices.

"If you decide to stay, Millen, this office near mine will be yours."

"Tell me about the project, Fraya. So far, I don't know what it's all about. I need to know more, so I can make a rational decision. Rumors are strong, that you are planning a manned, interplanetary trip. Will this be independent of Centre's efforts?"

"It's true, Millen, we are planning on such a trip, but the goal is to beat Centre in a race to Terres. This will be a capitalist venture, completely independent from anything Centre is doing. I am the Program Director, and I need your help so badly, to keep me organized and sane. There's so much to do, I'm not even sure how to use you yet. I do know I want you coordinating the overall schedules for design and production, but how you do it is up to you. You are also going to handle logistics, and mission planning."

"I'm willing and eager, Fraya, and I accept. I'll bring Loral and the children here in due time, and get them oriented to the new environment."

"I'm grateful, Millen. I hope you can start immediately."

"I will. How about crew requirements?" Millen asked.

"That's part of the mission planning job, but Rami and I want to be in on the decisions for flight crew selections."

"Of course. I understand. Where is Rami now?"

"He left to go home on an emergency. His best friends recently lost a child and he wants to be there for moral support. I expect him back in a few arcs, and then you two can start mission planning together. Until then, come up with some ideas for tracking the design and production items."

With that Millen went into his new office, closed the door, then leaped up with arms outstretched, and shouted 'yes' to himself.

48. Rubel

Several volcanoes on the northern continent of Montes had been popping off a series of eruptions, sometimes causing communication blackouts, but mostly just scattering dust into the atmosphere. One large rogue blasted ash as high as sixty kiloquants into the air, and the prevailing winds carried the suffocating cloud south and eastward, down over the east end of Scorpia, covering the entire valley from Mizzen to Lignus. Rami received a call from Milda.

"We are coping with the ash fallout," she said, "but we have some tragic news from Dorvic and Rachek. You knew little Rubel had a chronic respiratory ailment? She was outside when the ash began falling and ingested a lot of it into her lungs. She choked and ceased breathing. Revival attempts were unsuccessful and Dorvic and Rachek are stricken. They want you to come up."

Rami could hardly believe it. He had never experienced a death of anyone close to him before, and that sudden, hollow feeling characteristic of such a loss wrenched at his insides.

"How devastating," he said. "Is Dory all right?"

"As far as I know, the boy wasn't affected."

"I'll take some time off and come up there immediately."

Rami contacted Fraya and told her of the news, and that he had to leave for Lignus. She wished she could go with him, but the project startup dictated she remain.

"Please express my sympathies, and give my regards to your parents, Rami."

He flew to Mizzen, then drove across the valley and up into the mountains of Lignus. Remaining airborne ash still restricted some visibility, causing him to motor much more slowly than normal, but once he began climbing out of the valley, conditions improved. He made a brief stop to see Milda and Jerod, and learned the final rites were set for the next arc. He excused himself, then quickly left for Rachek and Dorvic's dwelling.

"Rachek, I am so sorry to hear about your loss. We all loved little Rubel so much." Rami was barely able to control his own grief.

He hugged her and at the same time squeezed Dorvic's hand. Touching was comforting at this time of loss.

"Rami." A sobbing little voice emanated upward from the small figure hugging his leg. "Why did Sissie have to die?"

Rami bent down, and hugged the child, not knowing what to say.

"Dory, I don't know why Sissie's life here is gone. You know what I think? Zhu must have needed her very much.... more than we all did. She must be very important to Zhu, and he took her to his place."

He could hardly believe his agnostic mind was forming these words, but they seemed appropriate.

"I hate Zhu for taking Sissie. Why couldn't he take somebody else?" Dory was sobbing openly.

"Nobody knows why he chooses the way he does, Dory. Maybe....she was so important nobody else could do the job he has for her."

Rami knew he should have felt hypocritical but strangely, he actually felt comforted by his own words, and the realization was disturbing. Dory seemed momentarily satisfied.

Rachel, listening, kneeled beside them. "Those are the same things we have been telling him, Rami. It helps to hear it from you also. The two of them were so close."

Next arc, Rami accompanied Jerod and Milda, and Dorvic's family to the final rites service. This was the first time he had been in the Domicasa for many, many annums and he was a little uneasy. The local sect had a new Dominary, Levey Roch, whom Rami hadn't met , but he impressed Rami very much with his message.

"Zhu never promised us sun without rain, nor peace without pain, nor joy without sorrow, nor love without loss. He has only promised us his strength that is renewed each arc by his hand if we reach for it. And if we accept it, he gives us help from above to guide our thoughts, and to help us cope."

Rami was moved by the Dominary's delivery. It seemed so sincere he felt drawn to the man.

"You have lost a flower from the family bouquet. Although no longer with us, the flower you called Rubel is not really lost. She is already blooming anew somewhere in our Creator's arena."

After the service, Rami spoke with the Dominary.

"Dominie Roch, I think you did a fine job of helping those of us who were so close to Rubel, and I thank you. You may know me by reputation; that I am an agnostic, but I certainly hope I'm wrong and that Rubel will continue to live in spirit."

Dominary Roch said he spoke them from his heart and felt the grief along with the others.

"Rami, I have been looking forward to meeting you. I know you are a deep thinker, and the philosophy that your friend Fraya left with Milda and Jerod, comparing Zhu to a farmer sprinkling seeds, made an impression on me. Then, when the fact that life on Terres was actually shown to exist, I become a believer in your theory that DNA has been sprinkled everywhere in the solar system. I hope we can meet again."

"I'm sure we will, Dominie. We're going there, you know. Eventually we'll see, up close, how similar Zhu decided to make things on the two planets."

"I'll be following the project with rapt interest, Rami. I wish you well."

Rami left, but not without thinking the Dominie might be a good candidate for the Terres colony, if the project ever got that far.

Fraya's first staff meeting was short. The three senior section heads brought all their new managers to get acquainted and learn about the project. Fraya introduced Millen, then reiterated Arin's emphasis on secrecy to keep a competitive edge over Centre.

"Remember," she cautioned, "anything we discuss in this room is confidential unless designated for publication. When we develop a hard schedule, it will be top-secret information. Somehow, we have to

189

keep our schedule from Centre so Arin can get the financial advantage he expects by being first."

The new head of security suggested leaking out a false schedule to throw them off. "Tribune Lor, they certainly know that Restor Stellar Park is planning to make a manned landing on Terres, don't they?"

"Call me Fraya," she coached. "Remember we're in Ardena now where communications are less formal than in some other territories." She was getting more at ease in front of her managers as she spoke, and was even enjoying the experience. "I would guess that by now, every technical community on the planet knows, but not the schedule nor the mission. These are the things we have to keep secret."

Next, she introduced Millen and explained his role and authority. Millen went to the front of the conference room and opened a curtain that was concealing a large, scheduling board. He explained that the board would start with only two tics, one at the upper left-hand corner signifying a start, and the second in the lower right-hand corner, identifying the landing time for the first crew back on Baeta.

"Times will be measured in arcs and annums," he said, "and the board will fill up fast. Each piece of hardware will have its own schedule bar, and we'll update the board before each staff meeting. Any questions?"

There were no questions for Millen or Fraya. She let a silent sigh escape her lips, and felt a tremendous burden had just been lifted by Millen's presence. Fraya complimented Millen for his first effort, and with that she adjourned the meeting.

When Rami returned from Lignus, Fraya met him at the stratoport and received a long and robust hug. Having recently come from the somber gathering at Rubel's last rites, and feeling depressed, he needed Fraya's closeness and empathy. At her hostel, intimacy for him became a maze of bereavement and pleasure spun in a vortex of draining emotions. He didn't understand the psychology, but she did. Grief and passion somehow overlap. Her tempo was close behind, and both let out a sound of relief.

Fraya talked while Rami, with hands behind his head on the pillow, relaxed and listened. She explained the facilities plan for the tractor building, and described the three managers Arin had hired. She told him about the preliminary designs that were underway, and that boosters had been ordered from Stratopulse.

"Millen is here, and has begun organizing a schedule board. Right now, I'm overwhelmed. Millen will be an enormous help. Lorol," she went on, "planned to remain in Mizzen, but Millen hoped she would like Solport after she visited a few times." Rami didn't hear her last words. He was fast asleep.

49. Designing the Spacecraft Requirements

Rami, Fraya, Millen, and Canon, met with Arin the next arc to discuss mission requirements, and finalize the spacecraft design details. Fraya proposed the phase-one quick-trip spacecraft have three parts, a command module, a habitat module, and the propulsor on the back end. The three part assembly will be called the "Starflier", and hold a six-man crew. Starflier will rendezvous with the Barge which will be waiting in Terres orbit, and stay coupled until the lander takes four space-pilots to the surface and back.

"How large a cargo can we bring back?" Arin asked.

"On this first flight, with six crew members, we'll be able to bring back two hundred and fifty millidrums," Fraya replied.

191

Arin raised his eyebrows in surprise. "Six crew members? Why six if I may ask? If you reduce the crew to three, then you can bring back twice as much weight, right?"

They were a bit taken aback by Arin's proclamation for a smaller crew, reducing to three, since they had planned to put themselves on this first trip. Rami disagreed.

"Approximately," he said. "We need to keep at least one pilot on the Barge for maneuvering, and had planned to put the five others on the surface to work. Your plan, reducing the number to three, would allow only two on the surface, and they would have an unrealistic work load. That is why I say approximately. Two may not be able to explore and gather five hundred millis of cargo. Also, I had planned to do some bio research while there, to help develop a vaccine for future immunity of colony members."

"Remember," Arin said, "this is not an exploration trip. I'm in hock for billions on this venture so far. I've got many other investors sharing expenses, and they want a return on their investments. I've gotten grants from several governments who want rocks and plants, and I've promised to deliver. If you want to explore, do it on the next phase. Assign yourselves as crew members on the second trip and stay for awhile, but get this first trip going and make us some revenue. Remember, we are competing with Centre for the glory. If they make a round trip first or even shortly thereafter, our cargo value will drop considerably. Shorten the crew to three, one to stay in orbit and two to work on the surface, and get them going. Simplify the craft if you have to. I don't see why you need to include a crew module on this first trip for a three man crew anyway. Let them live in the command module. See if you can lighten the craft by using only a command module with propulsion on the back of it."

"That's too simple an overview, Arin," Fraya said. "Three men cannot live in a cramped command module for forty arcs without going insane. We must have a habitat module. We'll reduce to three crew members, but let us make the design workable."

They would definitely plan on being part of the specialists that traveled to Terres during the second or third trip. After he thought about it for awhile, Rami saw many advantages with the plan of sending three space-pilots on a first trip. From a biology standpoint, the experiments he planned to conduct on Terres with vaccines and gene transfer would have been crude and hurried. Now, with good samples, like a container of teeming stagnant water from Terres or tissue from an animal, he could work with mentorian Polosek in her modern laboratories to do a more comprehensive, thorough analyses. If only they could get a tissue sample from a Terreling, he mused.

Fraya called another staff meeting to explain the new directives from Arin. "Here's the way it's going to be for the first trip, everyone. Besides the command module, we'll have a habitat module, but we'll reduce its weight as much as we can; maybe shorten it. We'll have a crew of three that will bring back about five hundred millis of cargo."

Canon brightened, and said, "all right, we have direction. Now let's get to the specifics."

"The nuper," Fraya said, "will provide a steady push during the interplanetary crossing, so we'll have a slight artificial gravity."

Rami spoke next. "For our forty-arc trip, let's plan on the crew being in near zero gravity, to simplify the module design. Are you in agreement with that, Canon?" Canon nodded.

Millen opened his notebook and read. "First item is environment. We want a 'shirtsleeves' environment for the crew in both modules, naturally."

"No question," Rami replied. "Nobody wants to live in a space suit. Do you know what pressures and mixtures are used for the interior of the space platform?"

"Intimately," Millen said. "We originally started out at low pressure and high oxygen, but that condition caused dehydration in the crews. Also, under high pressure and pure oxygen, there is the possibility of oxygen-poisoning in crew members." Millen hardly paused. "We tried different combinations but the best was normal surface composition and pressure, with fifty percent relative humidity."

"All right," Fraya said, "it's decided. We will have one stratopress at thirty percent oxygen, seventy percent nitrogen, containing fifty percent relative humidity, making an environment that will be easy on the crew. What about replenishment?"

"It shouldn't be a problem," Rami replied. "The nitrogen is not consumed in the breathing process, so one initial charge just recirculates through the filters. The oxygen, dioxy-petron and water vapor levels have to be maintained by the life support systems."

"Any disadvantages?" Canon asked.

"There is one drawback in using normal surface pressure," Millen replied. "That leaves the hull open to severe, explosive decompression in the event of a meteorite-strike causing wall rupture."

"Even a slow leak could diminish the nitrogen charge," Rami added, "so let's plan on taking along spare, make-up nitrogen just in case. Canon, maybe you can thicken the walls to minimize the chance of rupture from a meteorite. Heavier walls will also provide more shielding for the crew from celestial radiation."

"At the expense of payload," Fraya countered. "Instead, let's have a heavy-walled 'radiation cellar' with a pressure lock, that the crew can retreat into. It could also be a shelter in the event of an unanticipated solar flare."

Rami agreed. "Millen, we'll need calculations for prepared food packages for the crew, for a one way trip, and stocking of the Barge for the return. We'll need potable water for metabolism, water for hygiene, and maybe water to make some oxygen."

"Are you planning on a garden to produce oxygen and absorb the dioxy-petron?" Millen asked.

"No," Rami replied. "We don't have good space-gardening techniques yet. We'll plan on carrying liquid oxygen to replenish the atmosphere on the outbound trip, and electrolytically decompose water to make oxygen on the return trip. The dioxy-petron can be filtered out. We'll glean and recycle the excess water-vapor in the air, and use the purifier to extract water from urine and body wastes. We'll periodically discharge solids overboard."

"I'll have a list ready by the next staff meeting," Millen replied, "based on the decision for a three-man crew, and a forty arc 'each way' trip. Also, there are so many different systems of weights and measures in effect around the planet, we need to standardize. Let's use the drum, the same as Centre. A typical one-hundred millidrum person will consume, every arc, two millidrums of oxygen, one and a third of food, and five of water in food and drinks. That's a total of eight point three millidrums total input per arc. He will exhale, sweat, urinate and excrete the same amount."

"Millen," said Rami, "You plan on the supplies for the entire trip, and I will engineer the recycling and disposal."

"Fair enough." Millen felt very contented. "We have a start, and now Canon can get on with the designing."

Canon held up a hand. "How are we getting them back off the surface, once they are floated down by canopy?"

Fraya took a deep breath, let out a sigh, and brushed her forehead. "I don't have that figured out yet, but tentatively, the descent module will land with enough flat-pack solid boosters for the ascent module to get them off the surface and back to the Barge.

"Because of possible contamination from Terres pathogens," Rami said, "we'll have the crew live in a plastic bubble on the surface, and venture out only in isolation suits. After exposure outside the bubble, each crew member will get a wash-down on the exterior of his isolation suit, and then get a disinfecting shower in a small, separate bubble before removing his suit and entering the main bubble. The entire cargo, after being sterilized with a disinfectant, will be contained in a separate isolation area within the ascent module. If we bring back any organic material like plants, we'll have to keep them isolated and quarantined back here, until evaluated. These precautions should eliminate most danger from bacteria or viruses, but the system is far from foolproof."

"Let's include a sterilization oven near the nuper, and give the inorganic cargo, like rocks and sand, a radiation treatment," Fraya suggested.

Arin had joined the meeting and listened to the discussion for awhile.

"I'm enthusiastic about the plans, and from what I've seen, no overwhelming obstacles are apparent so far. Tribune Lockni may attempt to prevent suppliers from shipping materials to us, but I don't think he'll succeed.

"Will we still get an engine?" Fraya asked.

"Absolutely. We have plenty of materials to make at least one engine, and we will have first priority if I have anything to say."

"This sounds more intriguing all the time," Rami replied. "I had no idea so much coordination and finesse were involved in moving a multinational project like this along."

"Leave the finessing to me, Rami," Arin replied. "That's my forte. You managers get the planning and construction done in our time frame."

50. Recruiting and Construction

Whenever Fraya tried to comprehend all the angles she was coordinating, it made her skin ripple. She had a grasp on the technical aspects, but managing people and materiel were beyond her experience and interests. She and Rami were entirely dependent on the competence of the senior managers, and were grateful Arin had selected so wisely. Arin could not remember when, if ever, a facility of this magnitude, and the hardware, were being built at the same time. There were construction crews pouring rockcrete and erecting walls, and the flight hardware people cutting metal and assembling parts, all working side-by-side, and trying to keep from interfering with each other.

Bemon, the facilities manager, had the tractor line compressed and moved to one side of their farm-building. On the other side, he had engineering tables and desks installed. Then he started construction of a large engineering and manufacturing building adjacent to the farm-building. He also had people making modifications to the nuper vertical test stand, to form a launch pad for the Barge pieces. Tracks were being laid to move the pieces from the manufacturing building to the launch pad. Cabby, the factory manager, had materials being cut and assembled as soon as Canon's crew finished the drawings. Canon had recruited dozens of engineers from Stratopulse, where he used to work, and as word got around about the new project, more skilled engineers from many other organizations, including Centre, came to work on the new project.

All these efforts took thousands of people, and they came from all over the planet to work on the project. Before very long Restor Stellar Park was teeming with activity, humming with throngs of individuals, lined up for interviews, and scrambling about to learn the multitude of evolving tasks. The first wave of new employees were chosen for their culinary and domicile skills, to organize the housing demands and food kitchens for the newly arrived workers. Prefabricated housing units were towed in to provide shelters for the flood of laborers, and mobile diners rolled in to feed them. Foundation slabs were poured and buildings started as soon as the rockcrete had barely hardened. Outside the fenced borders of Restor Stellar Park, a disorganized boom-town sprang up, with an abundance of bars and brothels. Security became an immediate problem. Because of the many aspirants who drifted to Solport with very little money, muggings began happening in the boom-town. Inside, a large and aggressive uniformed security force discouraged on-campus crime, but many of the workers wanted the entertainment offered in the boom-town. Arin decided trouble outside the fences of the Park would damage the project's reputation and lead to possible setbacks, so he financed an additional security force just for the boom-town. Then, to discourage his labor force from wandering into the boom-town, he set a corner of the Park aside for off-shift entertainment, and allowed a few bars to operate. Licensed hookers could ply their trade in an area near the bars provided they maintained their licenses with frequent medical examinations, and had no reported conflicts with the security forces. The entertainment corner worked very well to minimize the problems security had to resolve.

After the food and housing administrators achieved some degree of order and proficiency, Arin hired a cadre of select individuals with supervisory skills to manage the construction of his blossoming new city. He was vitalized, in his element as he watched and choreographed the network required to literally fashion a new borough, here-to-fore non-existent. This was to be Arin's greatest project ever, and maybe one of the biggest, non-government projects ever undertaken on the planet. Partly what made it seem so enormous was the rapid influx of laborers coming from all directions, and the multitude of buildings being quickly erected. He had offered exceptional compensation to obtain the needed special skills, and brought in scores of Fenizens from the depressed areas of central Scorpia for labor. The Fenizens, grateful to be out of an area where water was scarce, rebellion was mounting, and killing was commonplace, were proving especially useful in the construction work, and new facilities rose rapidly as a result of their labors.

There were many varied backgrounds among the new workers. Most generally spoke only the language of their home territories, so bi-lingual supervisors had to be recruited. Somehow Arin managed to obtain the needed skills, and the organization seemed to grow in an orderly fashion from what appeared, at times, to be mass confusion.

At her next staff meeting Fraya had an unusually large crowd. Rami and Millen were there, and each of the three directors brought subordinate managers from their various departments to listen and make comments. She began with introductions, and then, gaining ease, sternly reiterated what Arin had emphasized about secrecy in order to be the first to reach Terres.

"Everyone on the planet knows we are planning a manned trip to Terres, Fraya," said one of the managers.

"That's true, but not our schedule," she replied. "Millen will lead us through the over-all plan developed by our senior staff."

Millen had developed a layout for the first mission, but had no details for a time-table. He displayed the large, white, marking board

199

that took up half the room's front wall, and it was covered with event titles, horizontal lines he called planning bars, and triangular tic marks representing points-of-progress.

"At this point, we have no established dates for any of these tic-marks, which are the little triangles. During our next few staff meetings, we will work up the time-table together as a group, and later adjust it as necessary to be realistic but efficient. Once we establish a hard schedule, we'll expect these little triangles to be blacked in at task completion, showing we are on schedule." Millen continued. "I have broken the overall project into two major events, which may seem rather obvious. The first major event is the construction and launch of the Barge, which is the storage and supply craft. The second major event is the mission itself. The Barge will be launched with conventional chemical propulsion systems and will coast to Terres. It will take one and a third annums to get there so the Barge is top priority for all our resources. The activities for the Barge include designing it, obtaining all materials for construction, getting the boosters, making the handling equipment, building it, and launching it into Baetian orbit. While in orbit here, we'll have separate, smaller launches to stock it with appropriate supplies and auxiliary rocket motors for future missions. This will be done in several launch steps. Then the Barge will be kicked out of our orbit for its journey, where it will eventually stay in a permanent orbit around Terres."

Millen sipped water for a dry throat, coughed, and went on. "The manned spacecraft assembly will be called Starflier, and is a combination of the command module on the top, the crew and cargo module in the middle, and the propulsion-module consisting of tanks and nuper power plant on the back end. Because Starflier will have a nuper engine and relatively high speed, we don't need to launch it until we have the Barge in a safe Terres orbit. That gives us a one and one-third annum time-lag to build and launch Starflier after the Barge is on its way."

After much discussion, the staff came up with a schedule that seemed realistic, and Millen summarized it for the group.

"Assuming all materials arrive here on schedule, the Barge will be completed in two annums and launched with a big Super-Dynamo booster. It will take half an annum to stock it while in orbit here. We will send the Barge on its way in just two and a half annums from now." A few sounds of disbelief burbled through the group.

"Starflier design and construction will take place almost concurrently with Barge. Starflier, with crew, will be launched to arrive at Terres shortly after Barge gets there. Starting with this staff meeting as time zero, we are projecting a first landing, with cargo, back here on Baeta at five annums from now."

A hand went up from one of the design managers.

"You say we are in competition with the Centre group. Do we know what their schedule is for a manned landing?" Fraya responded. "No, and I doubt if they have a hard schedule yet; too many unknowns. I do know that while I was still at Centre, they had a schedule for the first, unmanned, orbital test flight of the nuper for about five annums from now. If they still have that same schedule, we'll be landing back here while they are still flight testing in orbit around Baeta."

Another hand went up.

"How much flight testing will we do before we actually launch a crew?"

Fraya answered again. "We don't have the luxury of time or resources for any flight tests, but we'll thoroughly pressure test all the modules and tanks, and cycle all systems here on the surface. We plan to use proven boosters and technology, and stuff our hardware with commercially available equipment and parts, except for the command vessel. We are thinking of using some of the newer heat resistant alloys instead of ablative heat shields, and that will be a new technological challenge. Most of the first production nupers are already spoken for by Centre, but Arin will see that we get one for our use. Everything else will be up to you designers to make it simple, and make it work." Although Rami was still working part-time with Tribune Polosek, most of his time was now spent at Restor Park with Fraya and the senior staff members, grinding on problems and schedules. Rami had never been very mechanical, but was rapidly adapting to understanding designs. Fraya had been so wrapped up in getting the propulsion and guidance systems ready for the Barge that she hadn't given much thought about a flight crew. They needed space-pilots, not only for the manned mission, but also to go into orbit and assemble the Barge and Starflier. She knew Millen and Rami had specified a crew of three in the planning, but they hadn't even begun to recruit. She was surprised and a bit excited to get a friendly call from Corci.

"Hello Paramo, we miss you around here. How are things going with your new project."

"Well, Corci, what a surprise, hearing from you. The project is going well, but there's a lot of chaos with all the construction going on. Are you still making trips to the platform?" Fraya was curious and waiting to hear his motive for calling.

"Yes, I get up about once every quarter-annum. As you can guess, we have a lot of strato-pilots here trying to become space-pilots, and the competition continues to be tough. I am still the best though, and call most of the shots."

"I believe it Corci. Are you going to be the first in line at Centre for the Terres journey?"

"That's the subject I'm calling about, Paramo. The chief space-pilot and I have had a falling out. It was something about that lush he has for a pledgemate, making some moves on me at a party or something. Anyway, he posted the crew list for the first Terres mission, and I'm not on it. Being the best, I'm humiliated and thinking about resigning. Have you picked your crew yet?"

"I don't think we have, but I'll ask Rami. Did you seduce his pledgemate, Corci?"

"Of course not. With unpledged women like you available and falling all over me, why would I chase after somebody's pledgemate. She came on to me."

"Sure, Corci, I believe you. You're almost convincing! Why don't you come over to Ardena and look over our operation. If you behave, I might recommend our planners find a place for you on one of our crews."

"All right Paramo. For a woman with a shapeless torso, sometimes I almost like you."

"Stow it Corci, just get over here."

"I'm practically on my way," he replied.

Fraya didn't want Corci to think she was eager, but she realized his availability could really help them. When she told Rami about it he was elated.

"Corci could solve a lot of our crew unknowns, like recruiting the flyers we need to assemble the Barge and Starflier in orbit here, and pick his best two assistant space-pilots for the trip, men with proven space experience who could handle a half-annum trip without space-nausea or psycho-boredom. Men who had been through the experience of living in close quarters while eating, sleeping, working and tending to hygienic needs in zero gravity." Rami was greatly relieved. He knew he could have found a long list of willing pilots with

203

some space experience, who would lust to be on the mission, but knowing their qualifications for getting along in space with each other was another thing. Corci would know whom he could recruit and work with.

51. Lorol Visits Millen

When Lorol arrived for a visit, Millen tried to encourage her with talk of the great new adventure they were working on. He brought her to Solport to see if she could adapt to the area and climate, but the heat was stifling. Lorol was not a happy person, and now in Ardena, was even more miserable because she couldn't understand the local language. The children, however, picked up words very fast and even during their short stay began to communicate with new-found friends. It seemed probable to Millen the children would adapt readily to the new territory, but his hopes for getting Lorol to stay were waning.

"Why don't you try to learn this language?" he asked. "You could take some tutelage in Mizzen, and be all ready to communicate when you come back again. I can understand your frustration, not even being able to understand the visicom programs, but you can change that. Won't you even try?"

"I tried once, but just couldn't get the hang of it. Besides, Bacamir has everything for me this place has. Even if I want to visit a tropical sea-edge, I can find one in Bacamir."

"You're right." Millen looked at her longingly. "It sounds like I'm not going to change your mind very easily, but I wish you had given this place more of a chance." Her shapely figure with slim waist and long legs stirred an urge in him. She was sitting next to him in shorts and halter, and in spite of his disappointment in her attitude, he moved next to her and began stroking her smooth thigh with his fingertips.

"Couldn't we talk about that later?" he asked.

"Don't do that Millen, it's too hot. I'm going to take a shower now and cool off. The children and I are going to leave next arc," she said.

"So soon? Why?"

She didn't answer, and in frustration, Millen stomped out of the hospice, wandered for a spell, then went to a local pub for some carbosuds.

52. Corci Joins the Project

Corci arrived at Restor Stellar Park quite positive he would take the job unless it was a disorganized mess, and knowing Fraya he didn't expect anything less than exceptional competence. Also, he had been traveling back and forth to the platform for several annums, and it occurred to him he was getting bored with the routine. The prospect of being part of a new project, assembling the Barge in orbit, was exciting. It was as exciting as the original assembly of Centre's Platform many annums ago.

Fraya assigned Corci to work with Canon, who immediately gave him the responsibility to design the cockpit layout for the vehicle to be flown by space-pilots to the Barge, while it was being assembled in orbit. Canon had planned to copy Centre's spherical re-entry ball for his design, but Corci objected.

"I have a better concept, Canon, and one that I'd prefer to fly."

Corci practically insisted they design it with wings, to fly with stratocraft controls so he could make a precision landing back on the surface. This was a different re-entry than used by the Centre space-pilots who always had a rough, clumsy experience returning to the surface. When leaving the platform, they climbed into a ball-shaped structure with a clamshell heat shield. The assembly was dropped into the stratosphere, and when slowed enough, and cooled, the clam shells would open. A billowing streamer freed a canopy that deployed and lowered the ball, with the space-pilots, to the surface with a hard thump. Corci made many attempts to get the system changed, to no avail.

"Make it like a stratocraft, and I can fly it in," he said. "With these newer, high temperature alloys that are now available, we won't even need ablative heat shields. Make me a runway that is six kiloquants long, and I'll make a rolling landing, and coast it up to the hangar door. We can refurbish it and send it back up again and again as necessary.

Arin liked the idea of a reusable unit, and Canon agreed it could be designed as Corci suggested. Fraya decided a skip-cool-skip approach, wherein the spacecraft bounced in and out of the upper stratosphere until slowed and cooled, was feasible with a proper program. They named the reusable spacecraft the "Taxi", and a Taxi design project was started alongside the Barge designers. Construction began almost immediately. Taxi will be used to haul the space-pilots to orbit so they can assemble the loose Barge parts, then return to the surface. Taxi required a runway for the landing.

****

"I can't do it," Bemon exclaimed. "I can't excavate, lay out, and pour a rock-crete runway in time for the first landing. Hardening of the rock-crete won't be complete in time."

"Where else can we land it?" Corci asked.

"That's your problem, Corci. I just build things," Bemon replied.

"Well, how about the municipal stratoport?" Corci asked. It's five kiloquants long, and with favorable winds I could get it on the runway and stopped. Can we get permission to use it at least once?"

Arin said he would influence the locals to allow one landing, "but how will we get it back to Restor Park," he asked?

Cabby said he would have to dismantle it, remove the wings, and transport it by rail. "Almost more trouble than it's worth," he said, "but we have little choice."

"Well, we need a new runway for subsequent Taxi landings, and in the future when we come back from Terres."

"All right, Bemon," Arin said. "I'll get us permission to use the muni for a few landings, and you get on with building the new runway here."

Corci beamed when his design suggestion was accepted. "You see, Paramo, if you had just been nicer to me all along, and made love to me once in awhile, I could have helped your program a long time ago."

"Well Corci, you had your chance once. I still think you took advantage of me but I can't remember anything about it."

"Believe me Paramo, if I had taken advantage of you, you'd remember."

"What a crock, Corci, you don't even believe that yourself. Though sometimes you are kind of sweet, so keep trying. You never know when I might, in a weak instance, give in."

"Now who's dreams are we talking about here, Paramo, yours or mine."

"You'll never know, Corci. Now get to work."

Canon liked having a space-pilot looking over the designs, and found Corci very innovative, bustling about from project to project making suggestions and complaining over cumbersome design details.

The Taxi was intended to haul equipment and modules up to the skeleton Barge so they could be attached. Corci found the hatch couldn't be opened without banging into a circuit breaker panel, so Canon had Corci redesign it. They fixed the hatch so it slid open on tracks, keeping it confined, instead of swinging on hinges.

"After reaching orbit, and docking with the Barge," Corci explained to Canon, "We'll need a two-port gas-tight passageway so the crew members can go either way - into a module, or outside. One of the module designs should include a robotic arm for grabbing and holding a piece while it is being bolted to another or attached to the Barge. All this will take place while the skeleton, the Taxi, and the modules are orbiting the planet in formation. Pretty intricate stuff, so we need good, automated controls on the Barge, and good override capability on the Taxi."

"Corci, all your suggestions have been sound. I'd like you to coordinate the modifications and designs, and make them happen."

"Consider it done, Canon. Your group leaders have been very cooperative so far, and that makes the job easy."

Rami was getting into the spirit of the design and had some ideas of his own to contribute.

"The Barge assembly also requires a habitat module for the crew when they arrive and dock. Inside the habitat, the crew will be able to relax and exercise, reconnoiter, and plan, and the habitat must contain manual controls for maneuvering by a crew if necessary."

Design of the Barge's controlling section, primarily Fraya's responsibility, had her making layouts including several large sun-panels for electrical generation, several banks of batteries, and antennas linked to a master intelligencer unit that controls the guidance.

"Automatic controls will stabilized the craft, but close-in maneuvering will be done manually using my on-board mikrontas and an over-ride system," she said.

Bemon had the new engineering and manufacturing building in work, and now started reviewing requirements for the next major facility, the control building. In spite of the automation put into the design of the space-flight hardware, the actual control of the flight equipment will all be managed from a special building on the surface at Restor Park, called Cubic, for Command, Control, and Communications. Without programs from this control center, none of the flights could navigate.

Bemon, the facilities manager, hired one specialist just to oversee the design and construction of the control center. Most of the equipment was made from off-the-shelf components purchased and thrown together in an expedited manner, but the electrical staff had insisted on putting test circuits and redundancy into the components so they could troubleshoot.

Cubic was so vital to the whole operation, that Fraya begin to worry about security. She expressed her fears to Arin and he responded by assigning a special team to guard and protect the Cubic building. Fraya immediately recognized two of the agents and felt her security was in good hands. The agents were Max and Hunter, who rescued her from Lignus so long ago, and she couldn't help but give them each a hug of recognition. They told her they had been looking after her security from a distance, many times, and considered her their prize assignment.

"Arin won't let just anyone guard you, Fraya. It's a mark of status just to be assigned to look after you."

"Really? I never would have guessed that, but I'm flattered. This cubic building is the most important thing to protect right now, however."

"Leave it to us," Max replied.

Fraya and Millen established a little ritual for the beginning of each work shift. They would stand on the balcony outside her office, look out over the factory, wave to people who looked up, and make notes on the status of the project. An annum had passed since planning and design had begun, and they could see the Super-Dynamo, the largest liquid-propellant launcher on the planet, being final-fitted in the vertical hangar. On top was the skeleton Barge, and its associated equipment. It was an impressive structure, and Fraya hoped it would hold together during the launch. The skeleton Barge was stuffed with docking rings, airlocks, life support supplies, extra rocket engines, power packs, and a large water reservoir. It was ready to leave the vertical hangar, and Cabby supervised the move. As soon as it started down the tracks toward the launch pad, another Super-Dynamo to carry the Taxi to the Barge was lifted to the vertical position.

Fraya was constantly amazed by all the activity going on.

"Look, Rami. Can you comprehend all the separate projects that are in progress? So far, things are going well, and on schedule. Because of their slow bureaucracy, we are annums ahead of Centre. We won't be as thoroughly tested as they, so there are more risks in our program, but we are way ahead."

Fraya assembled the staff for a progress report.

"We plan on putting the Barge into our low orbit soon, assemble it in orbit here, and send it on its way to Terres in one annum from now, to meet the best window for Baeta and Terres proximity. All projections appear that we will boost it out of Baetian orbit on schedule.

210

Arin said a few words of encouragement. "I cannot begin to tell you," he boomed, "how pleased I am with the progress. I knew you could make it on time if you put all your minds to it. I would like to compliment all of you on the effort, and the awesome coordination and cooperation with each other it must have taken. Let's hope we haven't overlooked something important, and that the mission will go without a problem. Notice that you have gotten me calling this project a mission now, but don't be misled. This is a commercial venture, regardless of what you call it. Now let's get the Barge moved to the launch pad, and get it on its way. Then, we'll get started on the manned units." Then he looked to Fraya.

"Don't miss that optimum window for getting the Barge underway. Next meeting, give me your plan for the Space-pilots' phase-one trip, and we'll make sure all design and procurement is underway. Keep up the good work." Arin abruptly departed the meeting.

Fraya told the staff to take some time off and relax, to visit families or whatever, because after they reconvened, there wouldn't be any time-off for quite a while. Rami told Fraya it was time for him to go back to Bacamir for a visit. There were several things he needed to accomplish and he needed a few arcs of time away.

"My life support designs are going well," he said, "and Millen is aware of the status."

53. The Barge Assembly

A loudspeaker boomed the Barge's countdown throughout the launch facility at Restor Stellar Park, into the bunkers and into the Cubic building....." ... four ... three... two ... one ... ignition ... liftoff." The first sight of movement above the searing flame brought a cheer from the crowd. With the Barge at its tip, the big Super-Dynamo boosted by three solid-propellant add-ons strapped around it roared off the launch pad, vibrating the walls of nearby buildings as it slowly lifted. A short time later as it accelerated away from the surface, the solid-propellant powder boosters completed their thrusting burn, disconnected, and peeled off into the stratosphere. The big Dynamo continued to push the massive load at its tip on up to near orbital altitude. When it burned out, the empty hulk disengaged from the Barge, and then the aft-pointing imagers showed the carcass floating behind, gradually moving away. Finally, the Dynamo-remnant tumbled gracefully away from the Barge, and back into the stratosphere. The smaller Mini-Dynamo, embodied in the Barge structure, ignited and with a short burst accelerated the remaining assembly into orbit.

While Fraya and her technomies tracked it from the Cubic building, the Barge looped around the planet for several more orbits, until finally stabilized. Here it would stay until all sub-assemblies were attached. Several smaller launches lifted other components into orbit to couple with the Barge. These sub-units automatically punched into various docking rings on the orbiting structure, and created an enormous and unwieldy appearing contraption ready for "in-orbit" final assembly and the trip across space.

Corci had persuaded two of his favorite companions, Mikel and Glenn to join the space-pilot crew at Restor Stellar Park. Leaving Centre was not an easy decision for them, but the lure of a trip to another planet was more than either could resist. Like Corci, both were experienced space-pilots, and had worked with him on the platform. When it was time for hands-on assembly of Barge components, the three pilots, in the Taxi, flew up to the Barge and docked, exited through the airlock, then scrambled all over the structure checking connections and tightening fasteners. The technomies in the Cubic building checked systems as they were connected, assuring proper operation, then signaled a "go" after each check. Finally, the lead controller declared the Barge "ready" for the trans-Terres firing which would send it out of orbit and on its way to Terres.

The three space-pilots went back into Taxi and secured themselves for the ride back to the surface. Corci undocked Taxi from Barge, backed away, and started the descent. The re-entry plan called for the Taxi to skip in and out of the stratosphere until slowed to entry speed, then land at the municipal stratoport. Controllers at the stratoport restricted all strato-traffic from the area and cleared the Taxi to land. Then Corci took over, and brought the Taxi to a smooth landing as he said he would. Taxi, with drag canopies billowing behind it, coasted right past the terminal and a curious crowd of onlookers, and stopped just short of the runway end.

Media commentators were there to interview the space-pilots. It was common knowledge Restor Enterprises was involved in a commercial space flight to Terres, so questions revolved around the mission they just completed. Corci answered their questions:

"We have been to a spacecraft in orbit here, that we call the Barge. Barge is going to Terres to remain in orbit and act as our space station while we are there. This mission was checkout of the assembly, and preparation for releasing it for the flight to Terres. We found it ready to go."

Barge, with its plumage of extra rocket motors, docking ports, and the big lander assembly, was ready for the interplanetary crossing. The technomies remotely maneuvered the orbit of the completed Barge assembly once again, with a few short bursts, and finally the Barge's Mini-Dynamo fired, this time to full power. The thrust accelerated the Barge out of Baetian orbit and into its looping hyperbolic path toward Terres. When the burning stopped, it was on its way. Fraya personally pushed the button to deploy the solar-panel array, and the antennas, and when everything worked according to plan, another cheer went up from those in the Cubic.

"We're on schedule, and the Barge, with Terreporter, is on its way," Fraya announced at her next staff meeting. "The flight will take 122 arcs to intercept, and then we'll brake it into orbit around Terres. As soon as we are sure everything is working satisfactorily on the Barge, we'll launch our manned assembly, called Starflier, from here.

Starflier will have the command module, habitat module, and nuper, and will take the three space-pilots, propelled by a nuper, to the Barge. Starflier will dock with the Barge in forty arcs. When the pilots are ready, they will leave Starflier at the Barge, and take Terreporter down to the surface. Starflier will stay connected to the Barge until the pilots return from the surface, and then use Starflier to fly back to Baeta. "

Arin stood and faced Fraya. "Why are we waiting so long to launch Starflier?" he asked. "Why not launch it so it arrives shortly after Barge is stabilized in Terres orbit?"

"For crew safety, Arin. The crew is dependent on a working Barge for life support, the descent and ascent modules, and boosters for the return trip. If the Barge is not functional and supportive, the crew will perish."

"I understand that," he replied, "but what can go wrong?"

"The main concern will be the operation of the Mini-Dynamo, to make corrective burns during the trip, and brake Barge into orbit when it gets there. If the Dynamo doesn't work, the Barge will either crash, or coast right on by Terres and become a satellite of the sun. Other possible problems will be the Cubic functions, which are command, control, and communications. All have to be working to make the event a success."

"Regards the Mini-Dynamo, you will be making at least two burns for trajectory correction during the flight, won't you?"

"That's true, Arin."

"Isn't that a true test of the Dynamo before it gets there?"

Again, Fraya agreed.

"Didn't you put at least one redundant system on board for each Cubic function on the Barge, with trouble-shooting and work-around capability?"

"Yes, we did. "

"What are the odds?"

"Of what; failure?"

"Yes."

"Extremely low, with little chance for an anomaly, but still, ...".

"Then we don't have a problem," he interrupted. "I'm betting your designs and programs will function satisfactorily, so let's get on with an earlier launch of the Starflier. I'll give you two corrective burns of the Dynamo, and if it works satisfactorily, get the crew and Starflier under way."

Fraya nodded agreement, then turned back to the audience and finished her presentation. Millen made some new tic marks on the schedule board, with launch of Starflier on Arc-85 of Barge's flight.

"Eighty-five arcs, people," Fraya said. "Not very long from now, so lets get to it. We've got Starflier to design."

Starflier was planned for three sections, the command module, the habitat, and the propulsion unit. Corci, Mikel and Glennick circulated from one design group to another, and displayed so much enthusiasm their attitudes transferred to Rami and others around them.

When they began the layout for the command module, Corci suggested modifying the Taxi and using it.

"Why not Taxi? I'm kind of attached to it, having flown it to orbit and back. It has proven itself, and with modifications we could adapt it to the Terres mission. Think about it. We already have a docking ring on the Barge that fits, tried and proven, and, when we get back, I can fly it in," he said. "I'll make a rolling landing, and coast it up to the hangar door with the cargo. If we want, we can refurbish it and send it back up for the phase two and three trips. Since it will be the brains of the entire mission, let's call the modified Taxi, Cerebel."

Arin liked the idea of a reusable unit, but still wanted the habitat module eliminated for the first trip. "While you're at it, why not design Cerebel large enough to hold all the cargo on a second trip also? Then we wouldn't have to bring it down a little at a time." He was thinking of the possibility of an accident during one of the local trips, as well as the expense involved. Fraya and Rami explained they might be able to accommodate the first cargo load in Cerebel, but barely.

"On subsequent trips, however, there won't be sufficient room in Cerebel to bring all of the cargo from orbit to surface in one trip. The passengers on the phase two and three trips might require several ferry trips from orbit to surface to get them all down. Besides, we can't make any more changes in the design and still meet schedule." Fraya was getting frustrated with Arin's changing directions for them. He grudgingly agreed. Corci had one major complaint with the idea.

"Hold on Arin. Three of us, in spite of being very compatible, can't live in Cerebel for forty arcs without going psycho. Boredom is the worst foe, and Cerebel is hardly big enough to stretch out. By the time we got to the Barge, we'd all be enemies. Why, the twenty arcs at a time on the platform made all of us pretty testy and the platform is large enough to go hide someplace. I want a habitat big enough to move around in, and hold cargo."

Arin didn't argue with Corci.

Millen kept updating the overall plan in the main conference room, while Rami supervised the layout of the crew habitats and life support systems. Crew habitats, they decided, would be designed as modules, so one or more additional units could easily be coupled for more people on phase two and phase three missions. Modules made the design flexible, so, except for that first module Corci requested, decisions didn't have to be made now as to how big and how many. Each additional module could be stocked to support a certain number of people, like adding another unit onto a rail-freighter. As a result of their discussions, they agreed to have one compartment in Cerebel which could be sealed off. It would be configured as a radiation and emergency shelter into which all crew members could fit during a radiation storm, or while a leak was being repaired.

Fraya let Arin know the last possible marktime they could receive the nuper and still keep on schedule. He felt obligated to see that Centre received the nuper units it had ordered on their schedule, but he assured Fraya our project is first priority.

"Lockni tried to block our progress by threatening to put some of our suppliers out of business. Specifically, he told suppliers he will remove them from the approved vendor list if they sell anything to us. I countered, however. Prollet is still under my control, and Prollet has the contract with Centre for nuper engines. If Centre, or Lockni as the case may be, blocks any of our purchasing efforts, he knows I will break the contract and see that Centre gets no nuper engines, at least until we get our spacecraft launched and under way. So far, he's not made any more threats." With configuration details agreed upon, the design teams busied themselves making layouts and drawings.

Rami participated with the design teams, but wanted to leave. He had another task to attend.

"I need to leave for a short while, Fraya," he said.

"Of course, love, we can handle things here for awhile. What's on your agenda?"

"I want to go to Lignus. Its time I visited family and friends. Also, Lethra has disappeared and I want to look for her. I'm sure she's in a shelter, but I would like to see her one more time."

54. Rami and Lethra

Dorvic had left Rami a message saying Lethra had disappeared, taken from her domicile by the social workers and moved to a shelter. The shelter was somewhere in Mizzen, the message went on, but Dorvic didn't know where.

When he arrived in Mizzen, Rami began searching for her, calling and visiting one shelter after another, but no records of Lethra could he find. He knew that a shelter was usually the end for a person, but he hoped to see her one more time before the euthanists did their job. Harassing the social services department resulted in no helpful information, complicated by the fact he didn't even know her formal name. Finally, one agent in the main branch recognized the name "Lethra," and associated it with Rami's. Lethra had left a letter authorizing Rami Slade to have her belongings and documents. The agent contacted Rami and informed him Lethra was deceased, and if he would present himself he could have her things. With that hollow feeling that comes with loss, Rami met with the agent. He was handed one small box containing all the available papers and letters of Lethra's lifetime. The agent gladly turned it over to Rami so she could close the file and be done with it.

Back at his hostel, Rami sifted and sorted through the box, and found a record of Lethra's birth and death, and a few letters from her son, Sakeri. Knowing Lethra couldn't read, he assumed Dorvic or a social agent must have read the letters to her. Some were short notes scrawled in large letters characteristic of Sakeri's few writing skills, while others were longer and more detailed, obviously scribed by someone else while Sakeri dictated. He mainly spoke of his farming and community activities in Central Scorpia before the droughts, and his training with the rebels and their plans to recover their lands. He had taken up the cause of the Fens to combat oppression and regain lands taken by the Highlanders. His last correspondence told of the floods and pestilence, and the migration of his people toward higher and better land, fighting as they went along. Then Rami found an envelope from the Central Scorpian Territorial government. He opened it and read that Sakeri Slade was in an area of the insurgency, was missing and presumed dead. Sakeri SLADE? My name? He had never known Lethra's nor Sakeri's formal name, and now he wondered ... how did they get the name Slade? My name? Maybe it was selected randomly, or maybe they took my last name and attached it to Lethra and Sakeri for recording purposes. Then he remembered the envelope Lethra had given him to open after she was gone. He opened his safe-box, withdrew it, and read the content. It was a hand written birth record of her son, Sakeri.

He read; "Male child, Fenizen - born (specified arc and annum). Female parent, Lethra Saker: Male parent, Jerod Slade:"

He re-read the name, Jerod Slade, then flopped back in a chair and stared at the ceiling, trying to grasp what he had just read, and what it meant. If the child Sakeri was an offspring from Jerod and Lethra, was Jerod, his foster father, a Fen. If Jerod was a Fen, that would explain a few things; for instance why he and Milda never

219

conceived. It could also explain the emotional wall that he couldn't penetrate, around Jerod. Jerod may have lived with mixed emotions; a Fen offspring he couldn't raise, and a resentment that I, his foster son, was a normal.

"I wasn't raised in love," he thought, "I was raised in confusion. Jerod doesn't fit any concept of a Fen that I have ", Rami mused. "He always sounded prejudiced with respect to Fens, didn't look like one, and seemed very intelligent. He couldn't be a Fen, or could he?" Rami's curiosity was aroused.

Rami put the issue of Jerod and Sakeri aside and went to the Institute to see Mentorian Zeiss, his old boss.

55. Rami Visits Mentorian Zeiss

"Rami, it is so good to see you, and from what I see in the news you are deeply involved in the commercial space-trip to Terres."

"I am, and I'm here for advice and your opinion, Mentorian. The Polosek vaccine is not ready yet, so we need to keep the crew pathogen isolated."

"What are your plans, Rami?"

"We are going to have three space-pilots on the trip, and two will descend to the surface. We plan to have a plastic bubble for a transition chamber right outside the landing module. They'll be in isolation suits when they go outside the bubble, and before re-entering, they'll get a disinfecting shower over their suits in a smaller bubble next to the big one. The cargo of soils, rocks, and flora will be kept in a separate, sealed locker outside the bubble until it can be given a disinfecting shower. Then the cargo locker will remain sealed until back on the surface here, on Baeta. We will quarantine all the cargo, the suits, and the space-pilots, while Tribune Polosek takes samples

220

and makes cultures. The cultures may help with vaccines for immunity in future crews, as well as make vaccines to protect the crew that just returned. Then we'll sterilize everything."

"Good approach, Rami, but quarantining the crew won't be necessary. The forty arc trip back will essentially be a period of quarantine. Before they depart Terres orbit to return home, have them stow the cargo locker in a compartment near the nuper. Forty arcs of radiation during the return trip will kill all the viruses and bacteria in the cargo. Unfortunately it will also kill any live flora you intended to bring back, but you could gather some seeds and keep them in separate isolation until back here on Baeta."

"Thank you Mentorian. I think we can do all that, and we'll plan on it."

"Even though you don't work here any more, can you bring some of the samples back here for me," Zeiss asked?

"I can't promise, since this is a commercial venture and the cargo will be for sale, but if I can influence Arin in some way, you'll get a sample. It's too bad we are in competition with Centre for the Terres missions or you could bid for some samples. As a matter of fact, now that I think of it, Arin probably won't care who bids, and will sell to the highest bidder, even Centre. He's capitalist all the way."

"Interesting thought, Rami. The availability of samples is a long way off, so there is no hurry to make a bidding decision, but it is a possibility."

Rami switched the subject back to a vaccine. "Polosek's naked DNA approach to a general vaccine is very promising. If only we could get a sampling of Terreling tissue or blood, it would help the process along."

"Yes it would, Rami, but I don't know how you'd do that. It would be very difficult to get a tissue or blood sample without capturing or killing a specimen. Is that on the agenda?"

"No, at least not on the first trip. We don't even know if our crewmen will see any of them, let alone get close."

"If possible, Rami, have them try to find some feces. It will contain most of the viruses necessary for Polosek's naked DNA experiments. How they'll distinguish Terreling feces from animal feces is up to you."

"Will it make a difference?"

"Probably not. Most of the viruses will be common, but try to get something."

"Thank you again, Mentorian. I'll keep you informed of our progress."

"I hope so Rami. I, like you, can hardly wait to see some of the Terres life up close."

"So until we meet again, good-bye, Mentorian."

"Good-bye, Rami."

56. Launch Schedules

With the Barge launched on schedule, and the Taxi being modified to become the Cerebel command module, Canon and his design teams were optimistic about what the factory team could accomplish. Cerebel was in many ways the most complicated hardware in the factory line. As the brains of the Starflier assembly, it had to contain all the intelligencers and control mechanisms for the entire three modules of the Starflier assembly, yet, when back from Terres had to disconnect and separately descend out of orbit, and land like a stratoliner.

Corci was constantly fussing around Cerebel, going over its details and construction, and Mikel and Glennick were never too far away. They had decided among themselves that Mikel would be the interfacing specialist for the Starflier parts, and Glennick would operate the power plant. Cerebel would join up with the nuper by backing into a docking ring. On contact, locks would automatically engage and seal the two together. Mikel wanted these rings and seals tested again and again to make sure they operated smoothly, and that the connections sealed properly. He also insisted on a manual backup method for engaging and locking the modules together. He convinced Fraya and Rami to allow a special section of the factory be set aside for testing the docking procedure. The rings and inserts were suspended from overhead cables, while he hung from a sling himself. He pushed the components together and manually engaged the locks several times, until he was satisfied he could do it in orbit if the automatic systems malfunctioned. In the event the locks did not engage, Mikel, in a pressure suit, would go outside and make the connections manually.

The electrical circuits were tested as thoroughly as the docking rings. All controls were operated by signals through wires from the Cerebel to the propulsion-module. Once the modules were mechanically locked together in orbit, the electrical connectors between modules were designed to be manually engaged. These connectors, large, circular plugs, would be manually pushed into mating receptacles at the interfacing bulkheads.

Glennick had very little experience with nuclear reactors, but power management was his responsibility. When the nuper was fired up in a remote test stand, he was in the control room watching it perform. He learned how to activate the reactor, and it seemed simple enough. So simple in fact, he figured there must be something significant about it he didn't understand. He went through the steps in mental organization.

Merely withdraw the moderating rods at a slow rate, and allow the reactor to stabilize at each step, until it reaches operating temperature. Seems uncomplicated. When at temperature, Corci will activate the throttles to send liquid through the reactor and achieve propulsion. My job will be to activate the reactor after we are connected to the propulsion-module, and keep it at the correct operating temperature while it provides propulsion for our journey.

"Fraya?" Glennick asked. "Why do I feel so apprehensive about this elementary operation? I've handled mechanisms that seem much more complicated than this. I've been blown out of strato-crafts, made emergency landings, and once had a leaking pressure suit outside the platform, and survived. What is it I don't know that I should, that has me apprehensive?"

"Well, we have never tested the nuper in a vacuum, Glennick. Given time, we could build a vacuum chamber large enough to hold it, but there is no way we can simulate zero gravity.   At Centre, we were going to send one up into orbit just for testing purposes. We don't have that luxury here. You will be testing it on the ride to Terres."

"Oh, is that it? Now I feel so much better," he joked. "What can go wrong, and how can I fix it if it does?"

"The major hazard may be sticking rods. When you start the reactor, your controls pull the moderating rods out from between the nuclear fuel rods. This allows the chain reaction in the fuel rods to begin. The moderating rods may get stuck while the controls are pulling them out, and therefore you will never reach operating temperature. Or, you may get them out too far, and want to adjust the temperature by inserting one of them back in. If it sticks, you may overheat and melt the propulsion-module off the back end of the Starflier. Need I tell you the consequences of that?"

"Not necessary Tribune. If that happens, we'll coast around the sun forever as an artificial satellite, to be found eons from now by stellar explorers who will wonder which star cluster we came from. How can I fix one if it sticks?"

"Sorry, we haven't figured that one out. If you attempt to go behind the radiation shield, you will become fatally ionized. All you can do is cycle the controls to full position both ways, and try for a slamming shutdown."

"Why don't we add a remote hammer to the ends of the moderating rods, to slam them back if sticking occurs?"

"Like solenoids? That would mean some more complicated mechanisms. Actually, the emergency shutdown mechanisms are like solenoid hammers. I will say, however, that the chances are very remote you will get an overheat that you can't control. These Prollet people have lots of experience with nuclear reactors. By the way, as you bring the power up, you will find the temperature constantly overshoots for awhile. You will have to be very attentive to the controls, changing as necessary until everything is stabilized to an even temperature for the thrust you need."

"That I can handle. You've made me feel a little better about the propulsion-module, Fraya."

"I'm glad of that. How are the new radiation shield installations coming along?"

"We have enough of the foil material from Kirken to shield all areas. It's installed in the interfacing bulkhead between the propulsion-module and Cerebel, and in the nuper compartment on the forward side." "Very well, what about the fuel tanks?" she asked. "We're nearing completion of the large fuel tanks. When the tanks are done and installed in the propulsion-module, we can move the nuper from the test bay into the factory, and install it in the module. That should take place shortly."

"Good. Now why don't you go and play for awhile in the Prollet stratocraft. You'll feel better." A grinning Glennick leapt up. "All right, I'm on my way."

57. The Schedules

As time went by, the controllers who were tracking the Barge had to make two short burns to correct its trajectory, and the Dynamo worked smoothly. Barge was now one quarter of the way to Terres, and functioning normally. Fraya watched the events on the remote visicom in the staff conference room, and relayed compliments to the lead of propulsion-and-guidance. She remembered that 'propulsion-and-guidance' was once her job at Centre. How long ago it seemed.

The Starflier construction was proceeding with only minor complications, and activities were frenzied in the compound. The plan called for the propulsion-module to be launched first, before the Cerebel, and kept in orbit until the units could be joined together. Glennick supervised moving the nuper from the test bay to the factory, and its installation into the propulsion-module. Grapplers that hooked into lifting rings handled the nuper remotely on overhead rail carriers. Glennick didn't want to chance any one getting a burn from stray radiation, so as a safety measure, all personnel were evacuated from the factory. Although the reactor core had its fuel rods in place, they were not actively fissioning because the moderating rods located between the fuel rods prevented the chain reaction.

The nuper engine mounts in the module had very tight tolerances, and the nuper had to be wiggled, using remote handling equipment, in and out of its mounting harness several times before it settled into the correct grooves. Once accomplished, temporary lead plates were robotically lowered around the nuper so the factory workers could resume their tasks.

Corci was not happy with something on the Cerebel and stopped by Fraya's office to complain.

"Hello Paramo. Take your clothes off. I came over to make love to you right here and now, on top of your desk." He grinned.

"Corci," she paused. "Besides being obnoxious, sometimes you act like a foolish juvenile just going into puberty."

Corci's eyes widened in surprise. He stammered a bit, and feigning deep distress said, "You just hurt me, you know, unless that was a compliment."

"I intended to, Corci, and no, it wasn't a compliment. You've always been obnoxious, but you've never been crude. Don't start now," Fraya scolded.

"Okay. What I came in here for was to make a change in Cerebel," he said.

"That thing is about to be mated to the Annex. What is the problem?"

"When the Cerebel and Annex connect to the propulsion-module, all controlling is done by con-wire circuitry. I have no problem with that, except some of the electrical cables are not shielded. They could cross talk at the wrong times, giving stray, false signals, and cause a controlling malfunction. You know, electromagnetic interference."

"I thought all the cables were shielded. Let's find out." She buzzed her intercom and signaled the head of the electrical staff to come into her office.

"Amprason, have you checked all the con-wire cables to see if they are shielded?"

"Not personally, but they are supposed to be," he said.

Corci spoke up. "Well they're not. I can show you at least one that isn't, and before I climb aboard that thing I want them all checked."

"Go check them Amps," said Fraya. "Corci, go with him, and show him the cable you saw. Then, go find yourself a girlie."

"Won't do any good, Paramo. The anticipation of these flights puts my brain in full gear, but my other batteries go dead."

"What batteries?" Amprason asked. "Do we have some dead batteries too?"

"No Amps, just a figure of speech," Corci replied, and Fraya grinned, knowingly.

Fraya and Rami called a senior staff meeting so Millen could bring all the mark triangles up to term. Arin was there to hear the progress. Fraya discussed the Barge's launch and status, saying the trajectory was excellent and they anticipated no problems with achieving Terres orbit in the scheduled one annum. Millen adjusted a triangle on the big board.

Canon discussed the designs of the Starflier components one by one. "Design changes," he said, "were being made on the spot in the factory to accommodate fit and function, while the construction of the units was taking place. All structural and electrical designs are completed for the phase one trip."

"What is the status of life support?" Arin asked.

Rami stood and lit some projections on the screen. He detailed the consumables required for the Starflier, and how they would be managed. He went through the list of materials stored on the Barge and what they were for. He explained the life support atmosphere in the modules, and the biological isolation they would maintain once the crew reached the Terres surface. Arin seemed satisfied.

"Bemon, you have provided facilities to keep ahead of all the Barge and Starflier construction, and have done well," Fraya said. "What are the plans for the runway we'll need when Cerebel returns for a touchdown?"

"We have a site selected near here that required removing some old building structures, filling in lowlands, and stabilizing the base. All that has been done, and construction has been started. A contract has been let for rockcrete paving, which will begin shortly, and completed about the time Starflier reaches the Barge at Terres." While Bemon spoke, Millen moved triangles around on the status and schedule board.

Arin asked if the rock-crete would be sufficiently hardened for a landing by the return of the Cerebel.

"It will be ninety-nine per cent hardened, and will easily withstand the loads imposed by the Cerebel with its cargo," Bemon replied.

"Ampers, what about the instrument landing system. Do you have that designed?" Fraya asked.

"Designed, and all components are ordered. It will be installed while the rockcrete pouring takes place," Amp replied.

"And now we come to you, Cabby, the builder. The Starflier components are nearly completed. When will you assemble them for launch?" Fraya asked.

"For the propulsion-module, we have all tanks and structures done, and the nuper is tested and installed. The complete propulsion-module assembly, including a Mini-Dynamo as a core, will be carried to orbit on a Super-Dynamo in thirty arcs. It will be launched on schedule. No complications to report at this time.

229

Millen then summarized.

"Remember we declared the start of this project as time 'zero'. After moving these marks around, it appears the Cerebel will return here and touch down in slightly under five annums from program start, beating our original projection. We have reliable information that the Centre launch isn't firmly scheduled yet, and will probably not take place for an annum after we land on Terres. If all goes well, we'll soundly beat Lockni and his Centre teams. The global news media are following our progress closely, and many have guessed at our timetable, even though the schedule is still classified. Once Cerebel is rolled out for launch, we'll no longer be able to contain the schedule, nor will we need to. As a matter of fact, we are so far ahead of Centre right now, I suggest we declassify our schedule, and let the news be known. It might be good publicity."

"That's a good idea," Arin concurred, "let's do it. Also, I have a few more comments I'd like to make to this assembly of fine people.

"This has been quite a challenge for us all, over the last three annums. I can hardly believe we accomplished what we did in such a short time. I have collateralized every asset I have all over the planet, and actually I have never had more fun. The most interesting part of this, for me, has been obtaining the materials and components from other marketeers who were also supplying the same items to our competitor, which is Centre. Not only that, I had to supply nupers to Centre, while building one for us, an unusual situation, but as it turned out, a very beneficial position.

"There was some pressure put on our suppliers, from our competitor, namely Lockni, to hold up materials and components and delay our program. I countered with my own moves, including a threat in one case to build a competitive factory for certain components.

"I mention all this now only as an item of interest to you, the people who are making me a winner in this game. Without you, my little games would be meaningless. There are, as you know, many paper investors out there who do not create or build anything. Their assets are shares of paper that artificially fluctuate in value. They contribute nothing to the planet's inventory of goods. Not me. I found out early in life that I like to build things, win or lose, and invested toward that end. This project has been the biggest financial game in this planet's history, and you people are what made it work. When the history of this project is finally written, I hope the name of each and every one of you will be in it. Keep up the pace, and let's get on to Terres and get something in return for our efforts."

The entire staff broke into applause. Arin was a master at motivation, and his eloquence and timing were extremely polished. Rami was drawn to Arin's technique of leadership, and marveled at how much he had learned about marketeering since he left the Institute in Bacamir. Biology was fascinating, but this commercial venture was consuming. He still wished he could spend more time to support the environmentalists' efforts and get the dioxy-petron buildup reversed. That point of no return for the planet's warming was still a threat, and was out there in their future somewhere.

58. Assembly of Starflier

The Cerebel was the cockpit; the command module; the brains of the Starflier; and was large enough to accommodate the three man crew for short periods. On the back of Cerebel was an adapter for connecting a crew habitat, and on the back of the habitat was an adapter for the propulsion module. Arin didn't think a full sized crew habitat was warranted for the first trip with just three space-pilots, so

Fraya had Canon design a shortened version, called an Annex. The Annex was designed to hold most of the housekeeping and life support systems for the forty-arc journey, and also the cargo on the return trip.

Prior to mating the Cerbel-Annex with the big booster, Mikel had the adapters hung from cables in the factory so he could move them together and back. He tested the interfacing locks and electrical connectors until he was convinced the connects and disconnects were smooth and would be easily accomplished in space. When the Annex connections proved to work smoothly, he declared the Cerebel-Annex assembly ready for stocking, and launch.

The propulsion module was already orbiting, awaiting to become part of Starflier. After the propulsion module was launched, Bemon's crew had started refurbishing the pad for the next launch as soon as the pad had cooled. The third Super-Dynamo with its Cerebel-Annex assembly was loaded onto its carriage for the move to the launch pad, and while waiting for the pad to be readied, the Annex was stocked with equipment and supplies for the trip. Launch was scheduled to occur within forty-eight arcs and there were still many things to accomplish.

Launch time had arrived. Even though most everyone had witnessed the previous launches of the Barge and the propulsion module, infectious excitement rippled through the factory in anticipation of Cerebel-Annex going into orbit. After only a few minor delays, the final countdown sounded over the speakers, and the Dynamo headed upward with a crackling, thunderous resonance. The launch was flawless.

59. The Landing Site

Millen called a meeting with Rami, Fraya, and the space-pilots to finalize some details of the first Terres mission.

"You have all seen the detailed images of Terres that Alpha-Surveyor sent back," Millen said.

"Any strong feelings about whether we should head for the area where Settler-Two landed, or pick a new site."

Corci spoke first.

"Let's face it, the images from Alpha-surveyor aren't that detailed. Settler-Two, for lowest risk, was originally heading for a site, which appeared to be desert-like, on the south side of the Middleterran Sea. It missed its mark and settled northeast of the sea, and nobody has been sorry. The navigation error was not your fault, Fraya. Lockni didn't have it lined up quite right. But look what we saw! All those life forms we might not have seen in the desert area." He went on. "Now, if we want to, we can descend in the area first chosen for Settler-Two, and bring back a cargo of sand for Arin. Or we can descend near Settler-Two and try to get some life forms along with the rocks and other items."

"Or," Millen added, "we can settle at an entirely different spot."

Rami waved for a turn to speak. "We made a commitment to Arin to bring back a wide variety of materials; and I want some organic animal matter and some swamp water for analyses and experiments. I say let's go with the known, and settle near Settler-Two. We know there are open, flat fields around there that can provide a relatively safe landing area, and we know there are humanoids somewhere near there. All the elements we're after exist near that lander."

They agreed on the landing site, and then the group met with Arin and the three senior managers to tell them what they decided.

"Here's what we plan so far," Fraya began, addressing the group, with projections on a screen.

"We should have the Barge in a stabilized orbit before Starflier arrives. Starflier will travel to Terres in forty arcs using the nuper

233

engine for sustained thrust, and when reaching the orbiting Barge, will dock with it, and stay while the landing crew descends in Terreporter. She projected another image showing an illustration of the Terreporter on the surface, including the plastic bubbles beside it.

"Terreporter, as you know, is already on the Barge. It contains the descent module which doubles as the surface living quarters; and an ascent module. Mikel will stay on board the Barge-Starflier combination, while Corci and Glennick board the Terreporter. When the proper landing program is calculated and transmitted to Terreporter from our Cubic, and everything checks out, the Terreporter will undock and land near the site of the now-defunct Settler-Two lander.

Corci and Glennick will deploy the isolation bubbles and set up camp for the ten Terres rotations they will be on the surface. To protect them, and the people back on Baeta against biological contamination, the two will never leave the shelter without isolation suits. When they return to the bubble, they will first spray each other with bleach from a pump-sprayer, then rinse. After drying, they'll go into the smaller decon bubble where they can remove and store their suits, and then go into the main bubble for rest.

"After they have collected the planned cargo; rocks, soil, seeds, and plants, they will return to the Barge in the ascent module. Starflier will leave the Barge, and bring the payload and the three crewmen back to Baetian orbit.

"While they are gone, we'll build a staging craft to leave in orbit here, a mini barge so to speak, and Starflier will connect to the staging craft. Cargo will be transferred to Cerebel, which will disconnect from Annex, and then Corci will bring the crew and payload back to our runway."

"When will the landing back here take place," Arin asked?

"Cerebel will be back here in 172 arcs, from now," Millen replied.

"Seems like a long time, but it's actually better than I expected. Any conflicts we have yet to resolve?" Arin asked.

"We have yet to develop the process for authenticating all samples brought back," Millen said.

"I'll handle that. I have the authenticating system all worked out," Arin replied.

"A group is all set to serialize and document all samples before they go out for bid. Many have already been spoken for; and paid for by the way."

Rami explained the contamination measures.

"The primary cargo locker will be stored near the nuper. All samples in that locker, the rocks, soil, and plants we don't need to keep alive, will be sterilized by radiation from the nuper. Seeds and live flora will be stored separately, and handled by experienced biologists in Polosek's labs. The storage locker for them can be given a shot of oxidizing gas before the return trip begins, and then quarantined when we get back. It may be some time before the items can come out of quarantine to be released for sale."

"All right ... the cargo sounds satisfactory. How much are we bringing back?" Arin asked.

"Five hundred, as you requested," Rami replied.

Arin switched subjects.

"What's the schedule for the runway completion?" he asked.

Millen looked at the big schedule board, and confirmed the runway would be completed in time for Cerebel to land, 172 arcs from now.

"I asked about completion, not the landing date. I already know the landing date." Arin replied.

"Bemon, you'll have to answer that one," Millen said. "I'll put a completion mark where you tell me."

Bemon stood. "The pouring will be completed in seventy-five arcs." Millen put a mark on the board.

"Then we'll allow twenty-five arcs for hardening, and another twenty-five to complete the installation of the instrument landing electronics. That will give us fifty arcs for the space-pilots to practice landing on the new runway with our test bed stratocraft."

Millen put more marks on the board.

Corci had convinced Arin to obtain a conventional high performance stratocraft that had, with a moderate power setting, a high speed descent rate similar to the Cerebel's anticipated approach to the runway. All three space-pilots frequently used the craft to practice and maintain their skills in the stratos, and also to just play once in awhile. Corci had practiced with it on the muni stratoport before bringing Taxi down from the Barge, and the trial sessions were very helpful. Now, they would modify the craft again, with all the instrumentation of Cerebel, so they could practice on the new runway.

"Sounds like things are on schedule," Arin replied. "Let's keep it that way."

Millen looked up at the big schedule board and nodded with pleasure to himself. In just three annums since the project started, they had designed, built, and launched the Barge, stocked it, and kicked it into trans-Terres trajectory. It was now traveling across the solar system on schedule, and Millen filled in another marking point. The next schedule bar on the big board covered construction and launch of the Starflier with its crew, which, if no complications arose, would be back with cargo within two annums. Fraya wasn't sure how long it would take to get the Barge into the right orbit when it got there, nor how long to rendezvous Starflier with the Barge, but contingency times were put into the schedule, just in case it took longer than planned.

Fraya convened a special meeting with the space-pilots to plan the surface activities on Terres. Millen and Rami were both there.

"We'll plan on our landing crew to be on the surface for four arcs," said Millen.

"Now arcs and rotations of Terres don't coincide, so lets decide on more meaningful terms and times. Here's what I propose. Four Baetian arcs equal ten rotations or cycles on Terres. Lets call each rotation a daytum. Once the Terreporter and crew separate from the Barge and descend toward the surface, the best return time will be four arcs later, or ten daytums. They will work only during light periods, or daytums, and will rest in the hospice for safety during the dark periods."

"Sounds acceptable," Rami said. "Are you comfortable with that, Corci?"

"I'm happy with that. We get ten daytums on the surface?"

"That's it. It's not much time, and you'll have a big workload. On the first daytum, you'll erect the isolation bubbles next to Terreporter. You'll sanitize and shower outside each time before entering the decon bubble, then stow your suits and enter into the main bubble. For the next eight daytums, you will gather the cargo. On the tenth daytum, you'll leave the surface, and join up with the Barge."

Rami desperately wanted some samples of human tissue from Terres, but figured the chances of an encounter with a Terreling were almost nil. However, as a contingency, he had a plan for trying to get a sample short of killing one of the humanoids. He furnished the space-pilots with a pistol-grip launcher of light metal, capable of firing a gas propelled projectile.

237

"The projectile will collapse on contact emitting a tranquilizing mist. The mist will instantly spread over an area of several square quants, and is powerful enough to immobilize an animal the size of a human with one ingested breath. The excess tranquilizing mist becomes inert from exposure to oxygen in the air within a short time. The affected animal remains tranquilized for approximately twenty milliarcs, and remains docile for another ten milliarcs after that. Take several of these projectiles with you, and attempt to down an animal, or, if the chance arises, a Terreling. I also suggest you take along some of these small, hand-thrown grenades to make noise and drive away any aggressive animals or Terrelings." Rami handed some of the gadgets to the space-pilots.

"I also recommend you each carry a small firearm for personal protection, as a last resort while on the surface."

To many, the fifty arcs since the propulsion-module was launched passed quickly. The mission plan had been rehearsed again and again, and now the Cerebel-Annex assembly, fitted to its big Super-Dynamo launcher and strap-on solid boosters had been moved to the pad. With all supplies stowed aboard, Corci, Mikel, and Glennick were ready to go, to make history as the first known humans to reach another planet. Corci was especially thankful as he reflected on the stroke of fate that had him bumped from Centre's roster for the Terres flight. If that hadn't happened, he would still be in Bacamir training for an eventual second or third flight in a Centre craft.

60. Starflier Gets Underway

Fraya, Rami, Millen and Arin were all at the pad when the three space-pilots, garbed in their pressure suits, finally arrived. Good wishes were exchanged, and the group watched as a lift took the three up the gantry. One at a time, the pilots disappeared into Cerebel, and then technicians closed and secured the hatch. Fraya led her group into the Cubic building to watch the launch with her senior staff members.

The light petrol used for the Dynamo's fuel had previously been loaded into its appropriate tank. When the Cerebel's hatches were closed and the lift backed away, liquid oxygen was loaded into the Dynamo's other tank, and the fueling boom disconnected and removed. The three pilots, fastened in their seats, checked switches, lights, and instrument readouts while listening to the countdown:

"Fifteen, fourteen, thirteen ... fuel pressure rising ... ten ... internal power on ... eight, seven, umbilical dropped ... four, three, ignition ... and liftoff." They felt the vibration in the Cubic building. Arin watched with an obvious display of pride as the Dynamo and its Powder motors flamed a huge trail with a mighty roar. Cerebel looked majestic way up there, in gleaming silver, with swept back wings. Fraya had watched many launches, both at Centre and the two here, but this one was the most thrilling for her yet. She picked up a transcom and spoke softly into it.

"Have a good trip, boys."

The assembly was just starting though the vibrations of dynamic transition and Corci's voice sounded a bit shaky.

"We'll do our best," he replied. Activity snapped throughout the Cubic. Instrument readouts were called out with a "check" quipping back and forth over the communications system.

"Manual maneuvers complete", called Corci.

"Set for Powder staging." The solid boosters flamed out and disengaged.

"Who put the brakes on," yelled Mikel.

"Throttling up now," reported Corci. At this point they were now burning only the Dynamo engine, which had been at partial thrust until staging, to save propellant. Corci now applied full power and Mikel hollered "that's better", as he felt the thrust kick him in the back.

Cerebel achieved orbit and circled the globe several times hunting for the orbiting Propulsion-module, eventually matching its path and position. Steering thrusters hissed and popped as Corci made the rendezvous and prepared for docking. Now flying closely together, he turned Cerebel slowly around and aimed for the docking ring. Frontal-pointing thrusters pushed Cerebel backwards and a probe on the Annex nudged into the ring on the module. Automatic sensors felt the ring, and a loud clang reverberated through the structure as the capture latches engaged. Green lights indicated capture, and Mikel and Glennick left their seats in Cerebel to check things out. They floated back into the Annex, checked the pressurization and the gas analyzer, and all seemed okay. Then they continued further back to the connecting bulkhead between the Annex and the Propulsion-module, opened a hatch, and went into a small, inter compartment chamber.

"Checking intercom," Mikel spoke.

"Loud and clear, how's our progress," Corci replied from the flight deck.

"We're in the chamber, and we'll engage the con-wire connectors now," said Glennick. "These connectors sure are huge, but handle easily."

They had to push large, circular electrical plugs from the Annex side, into corresponding receptacles in the Propulsion-module side, to make solid electrical connections from Cerebel all the way back. Pushing in zero gravity is difficult, but Canon's designers incorporated foot restraints near each connector so Glennick could anchor his feet.

When the job was completed, they floated forward to Cerebel, and belted into their seats once again.

Corci reported to Cubic.

"All locks engaged, and all connections secured. We're checking all circuits now to make sure everything works, and waiting for your cross-check. Pressure is holding at one stratopress in all compartments. Looks like we are no longer a separate Cerebel-Annex, and a Propulsion-module. We are Starflier."

"Congratulations, Starflier," Fraya replied. "We were wondering if you were just sight-seeing or working up there."

"That's cute, Paramo. Don't get smart with me, or I won't chase after you any more when I get back."

"Just get there and back, and worry about the chasing later," she chuckled.

When they reported that everything checked out, they got the go-ahead from Cubic to power up the nuper. Glennick began retracting moderating rods, and watched the temperature start to rise. It rose very quickly and as it neared propulsion temperatures, he backed the rods down a little, to minimize overshoot. Temperatures finally stabilized within the green arc on the gages, and Corci waited for the launch time for the trans-Terres-kickout, the acceleration process to get out of Baetian orbit and on the way to Terres. At a precise pre-calculated countdown, he throttled up with a prayer that the valve system problems were all corrected, and was relieved when the Starflier shuddered and leaped to life. The little Dynamo, along with the nuper, kicked them out of orbit and maintained a steady acceleration until they were on their way. He then throttled back to a programmed light thrust from the nuper as planned, to carry them on the fast track to Terres.

"Lookout Barge, here we come," shouted Mikel.

They got out of their pressure suits, and settled down for the forty arc, nearly weightless ride.

"This is different than the platform," said Glennick. "That sustained thrust gives us a little feeling like gravity. Not much, but it's there."

With all the hardware launched, and personnel given some time off, the factory seemed as quiet as a tomb. It wouldn't be empty long, however. Rami and Fraya knew they had a little over one annum before the Cerebel returned with crew and cargo. They had a runway to complete, and "staging" craft to build and launch. Time would go by quickly, and they already had two more Dynamo's and some Powder solids about to be delivered.

Stratopulse was happy about the commercial venture because it was giving them a lot of business. Prollett was also doing well. It had delivered a nuper to the commercial venture and two to Centre, who planned to use one for flight testing in orbit around the planet, and another for their own manned landing mission to Terres. Kirken had not made any progress on their nuper or electric pulser, but had perfected the lightweight radiation shield. They were selling foil shielding to both Centre and the Restor project, and very happy about that.

Rami, Fraya, and Millen were relaxing in the conference room.

" Well, it seems like we have nothing to do, doesn't it," Rami said.

"Yes, for the moment and it feels pretty good." Fraya leaned back and rested her head. "How are you holding up Millen?"

"Actually, pretty good. I have enough currency to bring my kids over here once every thirty arcs or so, and we have a good time while they're here. I've met a very nice lady who likes to do outdoor things.

We even go dancing once in a while. She says she met you two once or twice."

"Oh really? What's her name?" Fraya asked.

"Maggie," Millen replied.

"Yes, we met her briefly. Seems nice."

Fraya didn't feel like explaining the involvement with security forces.

"Have we come up with a total number for Phase II crew, yet?"

"Not yet. Let's get phase I successfully over with first."

"All right, Millen. Let's take some time off for rest and recreation."

Millen closed the sliders over the schedule board, and headed for the stratoport. It was his turn for the children and they were arriving on a stratoliner from Mizzen. He was anxious to see them, and missed them so much, but knew he would have to force himself to make time for them.   He was work-driven, and as he had done before he left Centre, found it easy to use work as an excuse to neglect them. This time, he resolved, would be different. He would plan quality time with his children and he would put work aside and try to keep it out of his thoughts. Now, he wondered, what kind of activities would the children like to do? He would ask his friend Maggie for suggestions, but better yet, he'd wait and ask the children.

61. Starflier meets the Barge

Starflier maintained its steady, slow acceleration and accomplished the rapid journey between the two planets without any major problems. The forty arcs it took to make the trip seemed to go by so quickly hardly anyone at Restor could believe it. The pilots in Starflier were in good health and good spirits, and found little time during the flight to be bored. Corci had chosen his two assistants wisely. They each spent some time every arc on exercise machines, and frequently cross-checked the navigational tracking with Cubic to make sure they were on course. The nuper-engine maintained a constant power output for the entire journey, and fortunately needed little adjustment. It was monitored by Glennik, but the others were also interested in its operation.

The pilots watched Baeta recede behind them and disappear into the blackness of space. Terres eventually came into view as a bright dot that kept getting larger and larger, fascinating them as its roundness took shape. It began to appear as a large oval as some of its darkness masked part of the surface.

The crew began to get a little concerned when the view of Terres became so large it no longer looked like a sphere, but filled their windows from side to side. Cubic hadn't given them a program for slowing into orbit, and their track appeared to head them right for the center of the looming Terres. Although the bluish planet was spectacular from their altitude, an impact seemed frighteningly imminent. Corci began to pressure Fraya for a program to enter orbit.

"Fraya, the ball in the window is getting very large. Do you have a program for us?"

"Do you think I forgot you, Corci? That's impossible. You're too obnoxious to forget."

She kept reassuring them all was well, and they were on track.

Finally, they got the word from Cubic that it was nearly intercept time. Cubic relayed their instructions and the intelligencers were updated, ready to perform. Starflier was ready for the slowing maneuver.

"Per the plan, we're swinging the Starflier around now for retro-braking, Cubic. Give us a count and we'll hit the button," Corci said.

Interplanetary communications are awkward because of the long, round-trip delay for each message. Signals still required over five milliarcs to reach Baeta. The count Corci requested was not really an action command, but rather an initiation of the program now loaded into the intelligencers. At a precise time, braking thrust slowed the Starflier into a large, elliptical orbit around Terres. It took more than an arc and several burns to circularize, and change to a low orbit near the Barge.

Orbital mechanics dictated they had to orbit farther away from Terres than Barge, to let it catch up with the Starflier. When both spacecraft were on the same radial line, or imaginary spoke from the center of Terres, the Starflier dropped to a lower altitude matching that of the Barge, and moved closer for a rendezvous. The Barge, with all its gadgetry sticking out in various directions made an ungainly looking arrangement of struts, trusses, tanks, modules, antennas, and sun-absorbing panels. While they were closing, the crew donned their pressure suits in case of a collision-rupture or other impact causing loss of pressure.

Corci was still distrustful of the valve system on the nuper, but it worked smoothly during the Starflier maneuvering. His skilled judgment and hands brought it up close to the Barge, and when the two craft were aligned, he nudged the Starflier forward. The nose of Cerebel slid into a docking ring on the Barge. A loud 'clank' took place and the centering springs compressed, but the locks did not snap into place. Starflier hesitated, then retreated as the springs pushed it back out of the docking ring.

"No capture on the first try, Cubic," Corci transmitted. "I'll bump it again."

The capture latches had not engaged. Cursing the mechanical failure, Corci made another try, and again the locks did not engage.

"Negative on the second try. Mikel is getting ready to go outside."

Mikel got out a breathing pack and was preparing to go out for manual engagement when, on the third try, the reassuring sound of snapping locks pinged through the structure. A relieved Mikel grinned when the indicator light appeared on the panel, confirming the locks had engaged.

"Lock is green," he called out giving Glennik the go-ahead to cool down the reactor. Corci passed on the "Capture" news to Cubic.

Coupled together, the Starflier and Barge now orbited Terres as one unit, into and out of the light period once every fifteen milliarcs. All three pilots stared at the surface below while the reactor temperature was cooling. In so many ways it looked like home, but the cloud patterns were not as heavy, and the polar caps were larger. Some of the land masses were visible and the whole planet had a bluish color, from the oceans and atmosphere.

"What a beautiful sight," Mikel said. "I know I'm not going down this trip, but I feel privileged to be this close."

Glennik finally called out, "temperatures in the green. Let's go to work."

The forward probe in Cerebel was designed to form a passageway to the Barge from a hatch underneath the cockpit. The crew checked their pressure suits, and opened the equalizing valve. When the hissing ended, and pressures were equal in the Barge and Cerebel, they opened the hatch and shined a hand-light into the crew module on the Barge. Peering in, everything appeared to be just the way they stowed it before it left Baeta, giving them a comforted feeling. Mikel floated into the Barge and switched on power for internal lighting. He circled inside the entire module checking things out, then signaled the others to come aboard. The three of them checked over the

246

equipment and supplies, and when satisfied that nothing had degraded during the one and a third annum journey, they readied for their next task, getting Terreporter set to take Corci and Glennik to the surface and back.

Terreporter was attached to the Barge on a different docking ring, and had a separate hatchway. Once again the crew opened another valve and let the pressure equalize between the vessels. Glennik opened the hatches and glided into Terreporter, looked around and thought about living in this cubicle for the next ten lights.

"Mighty small, Corci. I'm glad we'll have the bubble to live in."

When everything appeared ready to go, Corci joined Glennik in Terreporter and switched on its electrical power. Mikel returned to the Starflier, where his job was to handle communications and wait for Corci and Glennik to return from the surface. They tested the com systems between the two craft, and all worked fine. Then Corci tried calling Cubic from the Terreporter, and waited. Transmissions cannot be sent or received when the spacecraft are behind Terres relative to Baeta. Each orbit takes thirty milliarcs, and they are blocked out for about one third of the time. So each communication had to be timed to occur while they were orbiting on the Baeta side of Terres.

"Cubic, this is Terreporter here, give us a check on the com system, over."

Fifteen milliarcs later, Corci heard the reply.

"Corci, it's loud and clear. The boards are all looking green at this time. Undock when you are ready, then let us know when you are clear. We'll give you a program for retro-fire at the right orbit and position over the surface. Remember, that globe you are looking at is turning pretty fast. Light on the surface only lasts about a quarter-arc. We'll give you an entry time so you will land on Terres on the next rotation, in early light. That will give you and Glennik a full light period to set up camp - over."

"Got all that," Corci replied. "Sure is cloudy down there, but not much different from looking at our planet from orbit. Beautiful sight though, from what we can see. Lot more ice on the poles. Is Fraya on deck? If so, Fraya, I hope you have this funny box programmed for the right spot. I can land it but your intelligencer has to get me close." Then he said, "we are undocked from the Barge now, moved away, and ready for retro-fire. Over."

The delayed reply arrived. "I'm here, Corci," Fraya's voice came over the com. "Don't worry about the program. We've checked, and double checked it. Besides, if we're wrong, no great loss, you're expendable." She chuckled.

"Now initiate program Zimbol, and start the sequence when the clock registers 00127. You'll be in descent before I hear back, so have a good time, work hard, and leave the Terres girlies alone. Over."

"How can you say I'm expendable, Paramo. You know you'd miss me. Program is initiated, and time set at 00100, awaiting for 127. Over."

"I really would miss you, Corci. Now do a good job and make us a profit," Fraya replied, but due to the delay Corci couldn't hear it at the time. Mikel recorded the message to play it later, when Corci was on the surface.

62. The First Landing on Terres

In the early light, the Terreporter with all its booster flat packs underneath and canopies above, came to rest in a field, but in spite of careful programming, nowhere near Settler-Two. Corci made a visual approach and guided it to the middle of a field that looked dry. He touched down as gently as possible, then they waited with trepidation, hoping the landing site was not soft or marshy. The canopies on Terreporter remained attached until the actual touchdown, and then collapsed over one side, covering one of the visiports. Looking out the other, they were relieved to see solid, grass covered soil. Terreporter felt stable. After they secured the landing thruster, Corci blew the explosive bolts on the canopy hooks. The fabric assemblies fell to one side and opened the view from the second visiport.

"Mikel, we're down and stable. So far so good; log us on the surface at 00155, for the history books."

"Glad to hear you're safe so far, and the ride down was successful. Much different than riding off the platform back home?"

"Not a whole lot, same re-entry friction and forces, but the equipment is all different."

"What's it look like, I'm sure the history books will want to record your impression."

"The Terres landscape is magnificent, with lots of green trees, and blue stratosphere. The only word that comes to mind is, "beautiful," and it really is. I hope that the life on the two planets will exist in harmony. Now, we've got to go to work. Keep the vigil for us, Mikel."

Glennik went through a pressure equalizing sequence and a breathing test. He allowed Terres air to enter the Terreporter through a filter, until the pressure inside equaled the outside pressure. Then he opened his face plate and took the first breath of Terres gas. It was tasteless and odorless, as they expected. Glennik breathed the mixture for thirty milliarcs to determine if there were any unforeseen surprises, like something toxic, but nothing happened. They really didn't expect any problems knowing humanoids breathed this same gas. Corci opened his face plate, and adjusted to the breathing. Then they both changed out of their pressure suits into light isolation suits, stepped out onto the ladder, and descended five quants down to the surface. Corci went first while Glennik recorded the event on a hand-held imager from the cabin. When both were outside, they placed an imager nearby the Terreporter so those in Cubic could watch their activity. They also set up a positioning antenna for Cubic to home in on, so they could find their location relative to Settler-Two.

Their first task was to erect the bubbles, which would be their main living quarters and decon room for the next few lights. With the bubbles erected and housekeeping chores done by mid light, they relaxed and surveyed their situation. Gravity was about the same as their home planet, so they felt no noticeable difference. Breathing was easy through the filters in their suits. The outside temperature was far cooler than Baeta, but they were comfortable in the thermal garments they wore underneath the isolation suits.

They were in a grassy field, surrounded by broad leaf trees in full foliage. No water was evident, but they figured they could find some nearby. For the remainder of the light, they walked around the field checking the hand-held homing devices they carried, and marveling at the wonders of plant life on Terres. They also found a myriad of insects scurrying about in the grasses and fallen leaves. Both carried imagers with changeable discs and they imaged everything of interest, while describing what they were imaging in a voice recorder. Corci spotted a small rodent and tweaked it with a stick. It scurried off and buried itself under a pile of leaves. When the light ended they watched the sun sink over the horizon and felt the darkness envelope them. It was different from annurdark on Baeta, because of the large, glowing moon above. It looked huge and bright, and reflected the sun's light down onto the surface to make it appear only semi-dark. They told Mikel they could still see the stars in spite of the brightness of the moon, a fact that Centre had not had a chance to determine while Settler-Two was still operational.

The communication link with the Starflier worked clearly, and there was no transmission delay since it was so close. To save battery power, they described their activities to Mikel at predetermined intervals. The remainder of the time they left the transmitters switched off. Cubic had pin-pointed their location and relayed to Mikel they were ten kiloquants due west of Settler-Two. Fraya apologized and said she now knew where the error had crept in. She said to tell Corci it could be corrected from now on.

Corci and Glennik worked swiftly for the next few daytums, and loaded rocks, flora and water until they were near the prospective capacity. They never saw a large life form, but did catch a small, slow moving rodent, which they anesthetized and froze. They also collected many insects, and decided to bring back a sample of fresh as well as stagnant water for analysis. Water on Terres had to be potable if future colonists were to survive, and they hoped they wouldn't have to sterilize every drop before consuming it. They were disappointed at not seeing a larger life form. Part of the mission was to find artifacts of Terrelings if possible, and of course the blood sample or feces was still a desirable goal.

Corci asked Mikel to get them coordinates for Settler-Two, and permission to go find it. If it were truly only ten kiloquants away, they could walk there and back in one daytum. Eight daytums had elapsed since they arrived. Their departure time was set for the tenth, and they had the cargo area nearly full. Mikel received a message from Cubic authorizing the exploration trip to Settler-Two, but they wanted the Terreporter programmed for automatic departure if Corci and Glennik failed to return. The cargo in the Terreporter was the payload for the mission. If something happened to Corci and Glennik, the Terreporter

251

would automatically initiate a blastoff and go into orbit. Mikel would have to undock the Cerebel, chase down and capture the Terreporter, and tow it back to the Barge. Then he would transfer the cargo to the Starflier, and return to Baeta by himself.

"You got that Corci? Set the timers and programmers for automatic departure whether you are there or not. I'll go crazy if I'm all by myself for forty arcs, so don't miss the ride. Okay?"

"We have no desire to stay here for any unplanned time. There may be some cute Terrelings here, but I didn't see any in the Settler-Two image. We'll be leaving at first light and we'll continue to be in contact."

Corci and Glennik each loaded a backpack with food and water, imagers and discs, fireworks, blood samplers, and the tranquilizing projectiles. They also included a small bubble to erect near Settler-Two, so they could eat, drink, and relieve themselves as necessary. Each also carried a small firearm in a holster. Their homing devices had distancing measuring capability, and they had precise coordinates to the Settler-Two. All they had to do was find a passable route and keep on track.

At sunrise on daytum nine, they contacted Mikel. "We're departing now, heading east. We expect to average a kiloquant every ten milliarcs, so we'll be there before mid light, and back before sunset. We'll check in at each ten milliarcs on the mark."

They wound around groves of trees and several bodies of fresh water, skirting a large swampy area. Swarms of insects buzzed over one of the water bodies, and occasionally a splash from a ring of ripples indicated aquatic life existed in the water, leaping up to feed on the insects. The terrain was relatively flat in a wide valley, but they had to cross many low hills on the valley floor. A quarter-arc into their journey, they spooked a herd of antlerquads with curly horns, and

252

managed to snap some images of them. They reported to Mikel that progress was slower than expected, and that they were about two thirds of the way to the destination at the quarter-light point.

They reached the Settler-Two site about mid light, and had to hunt for it. The coordinates had gotten them to within a quarter of a kiloquant, but to actually find it required walking in a circle around the coordinates. When they finally found it, they looked over the Settler-Two, took some images, and reported that it appeared damaged, as if hit several times with something. Corci called Mikel and told him of their findings.

"The imagers on Settler-Two are both knocked over, and wires are splayed out in all directions. Some pieces of the sheet metal have been ripped off. I think the Terrelings may have had a hand in this damage,"

"Are you recording it on the imager?" Mikel asked.

"Yes we are," Corci replied. "Relay our findings on to Cubic."

Thirty milliarcs later, Mikel heard back from Cubic that the message was received and recorded. He also heard a 'thank you' from the Centre people who were monitoring Mikel's transmissions right along with Cubic. The Centre Scienomies were anxious about the fate of Settler-Two, and had hoped it would be found and examined by the landing party. Arin, Corci knew, would sell the images to Centre to help cover the expenses of the trip.

Next to the Settler-Two, Corci and Glennik set up the small bubble they had brought along so they could relax in isolation. They entered the bubble, sealed it up, then got of their suits, and rested. They tended their personal needs, ate and drank, and prepared for the return trip. Back into their suits, the adventurous Glennik circled the field once more, before they left, and on the far side found an old encampment of some sort, obviously left by the humanoids. By a fire pit there were some bones and some stone tools, which had been left, and nearby were several piles of feces. Glennik gathered all the bones and tools he could in collecting bags, and got several samples of the dried feces. Elated, they left the small bubble standing next to the remains of Settler-Two, and headed back toward the Terreporter.

Searching the encampment and gathering the artifacts took more time than they had planned, the artifacts were heavy, and they were tired. They began the trek back to Terreporter in the early dusk, and before they got very far the sun was already approaching the western horizon in the direction they were walking. This became a serious concern for them, because they had spent all the other darks in the bubble next to the Terreporter and didn't have any idea what they might encounter by staying out. If they got stuck and couldn't get back during the light, they would have to spend the dark in a field in their suits. They had no extra contingency bubble.

They got about half way back to the Terreporter before it became too dark to safely walk. There was no alternative for them but to chance the elements, and spend the dark away from the Terreporter. The two of them surveyed several clumps of trees, and picked out some with a large pile of soft leaves beneath them, and stretched out. For safety sake, they agreed to alternately stay awake to listen for intruders, so each slept in thirty milliarc shifts, while the other sat ready with his firearm and some noise-maker grenades. They continued to maintain contact with Mikel during the dark at the prearranged intervals, in spite of his complaints about broken sleep. However, he kept reassuring them as best he could all through the dark. The people at Cubic were especially upset and regretted having agreed to let the two pilots go on the exploration trip to find Settler-Two.

During the dark, they opened portions of their suits as necessary to relieve themselves, but breathed only through the filters in their hoods. Each drank water from a tube in the hood which he inserted into a water carrier, and they ate nothing. When dawn finally arrived, the two tired, sleepy and hungry pilots donned their packs and began stumbling along the last five kiloquants back to the Terreporter. The sun had barely risen to full circle when they passed in the shadow of a steep ridge. To their horror, large stones began raining down around them from an unknown source. Corci and Glennik darted for the protection of an overhanging outcrop. Corci made it but Glennik wasn't quite so fortunate. A big stone hit him a direct, hard blow on his head, and knocked him unconscious. The isolation garments they wore were thin, finely woven coveralls with hoods and clear face-plates, but no protective padding. He fell toward the overhang, but his body was still exposed. While Corci pulled on him, trying to get him under protection, another stone hit his midriff. Finally he got him out of the line of fire, and Corci just sat there dumbfounded. This was daytum ten, the ascent module was about to blast off without them, and they were under siege by some force he had yet to see.

63. Terreporter Departs

Stones continued to fall sporadically, but the aggressors obviously backed off when the prey did not flush into the open. Fifteen milliarcs passed, and the stoning stopped altogether. Corci got out some grenades, stood up and threw one upward toward the edge of the ridge. It hit the wall of stone above him and exploded, making a loud bang. Immediately a few more stones thundered down, and then all activity and noise stopped. He had the eerie feeling they were being stalked. Another fifteen milliarcs later, he heard yelling and

255

looked up to see five or six humanoids clad in skins and furs charging toward him, brandishing spears and clubs. Corci stood again and began throwing some of the grenades at them. Most stopped, startled by the noise. One of the more aggressive kept coming toward them with his spear upraised, and Corci didn't hesitate. He held his firearm in one hand ready to fire, and with his other hand raised the dart-launcher and shot the aggressor in the chest with the tranquilizing projectile. The man stumbled and fell just a few quants from them. The others turned and ran away, and Corci threw two more grenades to frighten them.

After the others disappeared, he waited a short time with his firearm in his hand, anticipating another aggressive charge. Nothing happened for another five milliarcs, so he went over and checked the downed man. The man was alive, but the projectile had hit him very hard in the chest. His breathing was labored and blood oozed from his mouth. Corci assessed their dilemma. Terreporter's clock was ticking away for a blastoff very shortly and Glennik was still unconscious. Here was a magnificent Terreling specimen at his feet, and time was running short. He made a quick decision to capture the details of the Terreling on disc, so he got out his imager and began clicking. He stripped the animal-hide coverings from the body, and imaged every part of the creature, from feet to genitals, to chest, to neck, to head, and even opened the man's mouth for a final shot. Blood was a very desirable item, so Corci took the time to swab some blood from the creature's mouth, and stow the swabs in a plastic container. Then he took the man's necklace and wrist band and stuck it in his pack. Now he had to get Glennik back to the Terreporter. First he took time to quickly relay their predicament to Mikel.

"How far are you from the Terreporter, Corci?" Mikel asked.

"A little less than three kiloquants." He replied.

"The program is set for automatic ignition in one hundred and fifty milliarcs, Corci. Do you think you can make it?"

"I can't think otherwise, Mikel. Now I'll close off and get going. I'll skip next call and talk to you later."

"Okay. Remember, I don't like to travel alone. If you have to leave Glennik, do it."

"I'll make that decision later," Corci replied. "Out."

Corci pulled Glennik's pack off him, grabbed a few of the artifacts and the feces out of it, and stuffed them into his own pack. With Glennik crossways over his shoulders, on top of his own pack, he started trudging along. He was extremely tired, but found he could make a quarter kiloquant before he had to stop and rest. By the time thirty milliarcs had elapsed, he had traveled slightly more than one kiloquant. At this rate, he thought, we'll make it provided I don't get totally exhausted, or we don't encounter another hostile attack. He came to a lake and remembered it was a long way around. How he wished he knew if the other direction was shorter, and seriously considered trying it.

"No!" he thought. "Go with the known."

He struggled around the lake, and, with rest stops, made it to the other side in thirty milliarcs. Trudging along, carrying Glennik, the times between rests were becoming shorter and shorter. He seriously began to doubt if he could carry him all the way. When he came within sight of the Terreporter, another fifty milliarcs had elapsed. He was within one kilo and could see the ascent module in the distance, atop the large array of flat-pack boosters. Carrying Glennik for 110 milliarcs had taken almost all his energy, and he could barely lift him after each stop. The bubbles next to Terreporter were collapsed and he immediately thought of the aggressive tribe.

Maybe they had been around, found it, and probed it with their spears. What else had they destroyed? Are they still here, watching me from cover? Time would tell.

"Mikel, I'm within sight of it but not there yet. Countdown is less than forty milliarcs, and I'm totally exhausted."

"Keep going, Corci, drag Glennik if you have to. If you get to the ten milliarc point and don't have him inside, leave him. No sense both of you staying on Terres. Shut up now and don't answer. Move it!"

Corci mustered adrenaline he didn't know he had, and dragged Glennik to the ladder. It seemed like a long way up and he carried Glennik, one agonizing rung at a time. He got to the entrance hatch with five milliarcs to go, lifted him up and over the lip of the entrance, and rolled his torso into the hatch. An intelligencer was sounding the last ticks, and Corci heard an artificial voice counting "......nine, eight, seven...." He tried to scramble over Glennik's limp form, but couldn't get through the hatch with his pack on. He pulled off his pack and threw it into the cabin, dove in and started pulling on Glennik to get his legs inside. He heard "two, one, ignition".....just as he slammed the hatch and spun the lock. The Terreporter lifted off with a bang, and the sudden acceleration from the solid-propellant rocket engines threw him to the floor on top of Glennik, where he stayed, glued from the thrust, until the solids burned out. Corci floated upward, and quickly grabbed a rail to guide him into his seat before the liquid-propellant engine came to life. He made it to his seat and took over control just as the engine came up to full thrust. The craft rocketed up and into orbit. He thumbed the switch on the com-console and said, "stand by, Mikel, we're both aboard and going to chase you down for docking."

The Terreporter met up with the Barge and docked. Before they opened the hatch between the two, Corci showered a disinfectant on Glennik and placed his suit in a plastic bag, and then repeated the procedure on himself. He bundled the plastic bags and disinfectant into another container and sealed them for future disposal. Then, and only then was the hatch opened for a happy reunion with Mikel. Glennik was still unconscious.

"Mikel, take over for awhile and do what you can for Glennik. Then get the reactor heated up and ready for Terres departure. Right now, I'm going to eat something, and then sleep for a while."

Mikel tried to make Glennik comfortable, and then transferred all the cargo into the Starflier for the journey home. That completed, he backed the Starflier away, leaving the Barge in Terres orbit for future use. While Corci slept, Mikel got the programs from Cubic, and inserted them into the intelligencers. Then he fired up the reactor like he had seen Glennik do, and got the nuper stabilized. When it was in the green, he awakened Corci for the ignition and departure away from the Terres orbit. Mikel controlled the reactor while Corci throttled up, and headed the Starflier for home.

Glennik's head wound had left an indentation from the rock strike, and his abdomen was badly bruised from the second strike. Those injuries were undoubtedly compounded by the acceleration forces during ascent to Barge, with Corci pinned on top of him. He never regained consciousness, and died within a few arcs during the trip home. Corci and Mikel encapsulated his body in a sheath and sadly ejected it into the stellar void. Corci quoted some appropriate passages he knew, and recorded it as the first ceremonial burial in space.

The Starflier, pushed by the nuper, arrived back at Baeta thirty arcs later. The staging craft was waiting in orbit, and Starflier made a rendezvous and subsequent docking. Mikel and Corci transferred the five hundred milldrums of cargo from the Annex into Cerebel, closed

259

and sealed all hatches, and readied for descent. The Annex and nuper were left attached to the staging craft, hopefully to be used for a future mission. Cerebel disconnected, backed away, and descended through the stratosphere. The news media were quartered all around the park, awaiting the arrival of Cerebel, and Arin welcomed the publicity. Corci brought the gleaming, silvery craft to a smooth touchdown on the new runway at Restor Stellar Park, and was greeted by a cheering throng of people from all over the planet.

A memorial was established for Glennik, and he was mourned in many languages. Corci and Mikel were among the most ardent of mourners, and both had to make several public eulogies, which they did willingly. After the final rites service, thoughts of Glennik had to be put aside. The profession of space-pilot is high risk, and those in the profession know that some will die. They have to be mentally disciplined to accept it, for dwelling on a loss could only interfere with tasks before them.

64. The Mission Ends

The first mission was over, and except for the loss of Glennik, results were proving to be more fruitful than Arin had planned and hoped. It was giving him global prestige for accomplishing the largest commercial endeavor in the history of the planet, fame for engineering the first Baetian footsteps on another planet, and fortune for the return of actual items from another planet. The pictures of the humanoid that Corci brought back were printed in every major publication. Arin gave some pictures of the smashed Settler-Two to the Centre organization, expecting a "thank you" from Hirl Lockni, but none came. Lockni had been outclassed, outmaneuvered, and beaten in the race to Terres, and Fraya was a global celebrity.

Arin had an organization of specialists to set up sterilization and certification procedures for the rock samples and other cargo the crew had brought back. One thing he feared was fakes or counterfeits cropping up and diluting the market. Some counterfeiting would go on, he knew, but he wanted all possible precautions taken. The rocks were all identified by spectrographic and holographic analyses, sliced, and the slices were encapsulated in clear plastic. A serialized certification tag was imbedded in the plastic with each rock specimen. Arin knew most scienomies would chop their samples into little pieces for further examination, and he also knew some collectors would keep theirs for display, while others invested for a profit. He didn't really care what the purchaser did with the specimen, as long as the price was paid. Before the sale and distribution of the artifacts began, he gathered all the managers in the conference room for a briefing.

"You have done well," Arin told the staff. "The publicity has been enormous, the cargo is excellent, and we will satisfy most all of our investors with this one trip. The five hundred millidrums of rocks and artifacts will bring in billions. Glennik's death was a great loss, but the surprise encounter with aggressive Terrelings was something we hadn't expected. Those images Corci took of the Terreling are priceless, and the blood sample is more than we'd hoped for. Rami tells me we can develop an enhanced immune system with that blood sample, something we need before setting up a rotating colony. I'd say we were so successful with the first trip that we can skip right over phase-two and proceed for preparation and launching of the colony on Terres."

The surprised group, some not sure they heard him right, wondered about Arin's bold proposal, and Fraya was stunned. She had no idea he was thinking of skipping over phase two. Fortunately, most of their designs and plans had compatibility among all three phases in mind when they were made, but crew requirements were not even considered at this early stage. When she thought about it, the proposal made sense, as Arin's proposals usually did. Baetians will have a lot to learn about surviving on Terres, but making a phase-two trip wouldn't help that much. Now that they had some plant samples, and the blood from a Terreling, their immune systems could be fortified to better cope with the environment. A colony would have to learn the necessary skills and diplomacy to interact with the Terrelings by living there.

Clodea Polosek had moved part of her operation to Mizzen and was working with Mentorian Zeiss at his Institute laboratories. Since Rami saw her last, she had accomplished some excellent work toward isolating specific enzymes capable of stripping the protein coatings from some of the viruses. She had three goals; first, to find a broad-spectrum enzyme that would attack and strip many different viruses; second, to see if the naked viruses would become harmless antigens capable of generating specific antibodies; and third, to see if the antigens and antibodies would be compatible with the human immune system. With the help of Zeiss, she made some enzyme soups, and mixed them with lethal viruses. She had her enzymes but didn't know what range of activity she could expect. When she injected some of the naked viruses into lab rodents, antibodies were indeed produced against the viruses as she had hoped. Now she had to find out if the antibodies would work in a human being.

Rami traveled to Mizzen with the samples of the Terres water, flora, and blood, and met with Mentorian Zeiss. The antigen contract between Centre and the Institute was still in effect, but Arin didn't want to be obligated to Centre. He told Rami to take what he needed for vaccine research, and Zeiss could charge his efforts to the Centre contract. Besides, he believed the research would benefit Restor Enterprises.

Clodea began experimenting with the blood swabs that Corci had taken from the Terreling humanoid. She wasn't surprised to find some antibodies in the Terreling samples similar to those which exists in the Baetian human system. Encouraged, she immediately went to the next step; that of isolating some viruses in the Terreling blood, and stripping the protein covering from them using her enzymes. Next, she injected the naked viruses into rodents to see if she could grow Terres antibodies. If successful, Rami and all crew members could receive antibody injections before they left, and have an immune system at least equivalent to the Terreling who generously, though unknowingly, donated the sample of blood. Rami was excited about being a part of this research. Not only could such a breakthrough in immunology be an asset to interplanetary travel, but it could actually be used to rid Baeta of some dread diseases now resistant to the immune system processes. Naked viruses in an animal's bloodstream send signals to make the appropriate antibodies. He hoped the Terres antibodies would be compatible in a Baetian blood system.

"How soon will you have the new vaccine ready to test on humans, Clodea?"

"In less than twenty arcs, but I can't begin until the government approvals are received," she replied.

"What if you bring the vaccine to Ardena, and experiment on me? The Bacamirian government couldn't interfere with that, could they?" Rami asked.

"No, but the Ardenian government has similar restrictions on new vaccines."

"Well come anyway. I'll volunteer to be your human specimen and we'll keep it a secret. Will you do that?"   "There is danger, of

263

course. The risk is that the naked DNA might be infectious in a human and you might come down with the Terreling disease. We'll have to keep you in an isolation chamber for a few arcs." She thought for a moment.

"The risk is very low, so I'll do it. I'll use you."

Before Rami left for Solport, he had a lengthy discussion with Zeiss about the environment.

"I wish I could help more with the efforts and campaign to change the planet warming, Mentorian. I feel guilty about not doing more."

"Don't whip yourself, Rami. We know planet temperatures are climbing, and polar ice is melting, but we are fighting for an attitude change that will be slow in coming. Unfortunately, many of the planet's residents welcome the coolness of dark for half of each annum, and refuse to recognize a greenhouse disaster is in the making. Those in Central Scorpia, however, know there is a problem. They are living it. The planet is overusing its fresh water supply, and shortages will lead to more unrest and fighting. And the analysts are in denial about the cause."

"We know the cause of the problem," Rami said, "and so do most of the thinking bureaucrats. Rising dioxy-petron in the stratosphere is the root cause, trapping heat and causing severe climate changes."

"I know, Rami."

"Are we at the point of no return yet, Mentorian?"

"I don't know. I don't even know what the point is, and unfortunately I don't think anyone does. We won't know until we're past it. Factions are now arguing over where river-water should be diverted for irrigation. Wells are falling below the water tables. When the reservoirs and wells start running low, and we have a shortage of

264

drinking water and water for irrigation, we'll be past the <u>point of no</u> <u>return</u>."

65. The Planning Starts Again

The Queen of Bacamir sent a congratulatory note to Arin, and expressed a desire for some multinational cooperation on future space programs. Arin later heard that Lockni's tantrums had earned him a visit to a shelter for a mental evaluation.

Rami returned to Solport to await for Clodea and the additional testing she planned to do on him. Fraya was relaxing in her hostel away from the demands of the media and the project, and awaiting for Rami. When he arrived, they embraced, and he saw that she had been crying. "What is it, Fraya, are you all right?"

"I'm ecstatic," she blubbered. "I just got a call from Khanwali and he is alive and well. In fact he is back in charge of the council."

"Where has he been, did he say?"

"Yes. He said that Lockni had stacked the council with individuals who were weak, and let him take over. Then, when the media showed me as principal designer and programmer in the unmanned lander, and hinted that Lockni was at fault for losing Settler-One, the Queen ordered an internal investigation. Lockni was declared incompetent, and Khanwali was rescued from the shelter where he had been hidden. Fortunately he escaped euthanasia or any harm. He profusely apologized for not recognizing the coup that was taking place and for the way I was treated. He said I was welcome to come back to Centre any time I wanted, to work or visit. He also hoped, that if I stay with Restor, perhaps some joint, cooperative Terres venture could be managed sometime in the future.

"What did you tell him, Fraya."

"I acted like a fool. I was so overwhelmed I couldn't talk coherently. I said things like I thought you were dead, and thank Zhu you're all right. I just cried, thanked him for the call, and said I would talk to him later."

"Would you ever consider going back to Centre?"

"No Rami. Even with Lockni gone, Centre has no appeal for me. I can do any research I want right here, and I want to be near you." Fraya reclined on a sofa with her arms behind her head.

"It won't be hard to put thoughts of Lockni behind me. He is a multinational fool, now in a dreaded shelter, and there was a lot of satisfaction in beating him to Terres."

"I know, Fraya, and you are the real brains behind the venture."

"Not really. Khanwali was the visionary. He promoted the idea to get recognition and funding, and sold the council on the Terres program. Without those first flights and the unmanned landing, the commercial venture wouldn't have happened. Arin was an opportunist who saw the profit, and figured out how to fund and build the hardware. We were in the right place at the right time, and Arin dragged us along, ready and willing."

"I guess it would be impossible to pinpoint any one player that made this a success. Certainly Khanwali had the vision, but you had the brains to make the guidance system, and you promoted the nuper, making the manned trip possible. Both were extraordinary accomplishments."

"Thank you Rami, but we all did it. And finding Khanwali still alive was an unbelievable ending to our adventure."

"Ending? Fraya, have you forgotten? Our goal was to fly there ourselves, and we haven't done that yet. Arin has given us the go-ahead, you know, for the rotating colony."

"Yes!" Fraya jumped up. "He has. The commercial venture is not ending, it's just beginning. Let's call Millen and set up a meeting at the factory. We're starting the next project right away." She paused. "A flight to Terres ... our dream. I wonder how the Terrelings will react to us landing in their midst?"

"Peacefully, I hope," Rami answered. "Although I don't really think a tribe of intruders falling from the sky will be readily welcomed. We'll have to establish a relationship with patience and diplomacy, and show that we're not aggressive. Do you think they will call us the Skytribe?"

"I like that name," Fraya said. "Let's go and find out."

About The Author

Dewey's numerous activities, besides writing, include flight instructing, camping, and fishing. In the past, he sailed in the merchant marine, and operated a US Army M-boat in the Philippine Islands during the Korean war. As a graduate chemical engineer from Utah, he spent a career in materials science, helping design jet aircraft, hydrofoils, missiles, and the International Space Station.

Writing fiction was his foremost desire, but by necessity, always had to be subordinate to the technical writing demanded by his profession. Now retired, his writing is unbridled, and seasoned by his many work experiences and hobbies.

Dewey believes global warming is a serious problem, is man-made, and will eventually lead to chaos when drinkable water becomes scarce. In this first novel he put characters in a setting on Venus, a planet he theorizes may have been wet but succumbed to overheating from global warming. The over-heated atmosphere led to evaporation of all waters and thick cloud cover, with constant virga unable to cool the surface.

With no universally accepted theory linking Neanderthal and Cro Mangnon, Erlwein's writings have us coming from Venus and intermating with Neanderthal. The result is modern, artistic and creative homo sapiens.

He and his wife Marilyn raised four children in the northwest Puget Sound area. The main family activities were enjoying the outdoors.